For the Love of Ireland

JUDY LESLIE

Ireland

To some, Ireland is no more than an island of rock and dirt
shaped by the hand of God.

To the Irish, it is a poem, a myth, a clan, a country.

To the British, Ireland is a possession
they don't want to release.

She is a place of happiness and love,
also sadness and sorrow.

Ireland is like Venus to many men,
turning their hearts and
creating warriors out of peasants.

She is an idea many would lay down their life for.

PART 1

Ireland

1879

Chapter 1

LIGHTNING FLASHED, SPLITTING the heavens as rain emptied down upon the ocean. Footsteps scurried outside of Margaret's stateroom door as passengers and crew raced down the hall seeking shelter. Margaret sat in her chair and clutched a blanket around her shoulders with one hand and her rosary in the other. Moving her fingers from one mother of pearl bead to the next, she repeated the familiar words, *"Ave Maria gratia plena..."* It was a nervous habit to distract her mind; something solid she could touch. She prayed that God would calm the waters just enough to deliver the *S.S. Gallia* safely to its destination in Liverpool.

There was a loud crash in the passageway. She heard footsteps stop in front of her cabin, followed by a pounding on her door. Margaret rose from her chair, grabbing furniture to steady her balance while she made her way across the room. Grasping her blanket tightly around her, she asked, "Who is it?"

"Please, let me in," a desperate sounding voice replied.

"Who are you?" She hoped he wasn't in any danger, but even if he was, she wasn't about to let a stranger into her room.

"Please, I'm..."

"There he is," another voice yelled.

Several footsteps ran past her door.

Margaret listened. Outside the rain pelted the side of the ship and things creaked and rattled as the boat tossed on the waves. However, there was no sound of the stranger, nor the other man pursuing him; they had apparently moved on. A whoosh of spray smacked the tiny window of her cabin, sending shivers down Margaret's back. She clung to the handrail bolted to the wall for support.

Why did the stranger knock on her door? She quickly reminded herself that his business was not her concern and there was no need to worry. Besides, he was most likely tucked away safely inside wherever he was. Now, if only this wretched storm would calm down, she could get some rest.

The ship swayed. Margaret grabbed the back of the chair and carefully made her way around it. Thank goodness, she wasn't prone to seasickness, or surely she would be ill. Her rosary was no longer sitting on the table. Letting out a sigh, she settled into the chair. Perhaps enough prayers were said for the night.

The ship was over halfway to its destination in England, and other than this storm, Margaret found the voyage boring and uneventful. She had kept to herself the previous days, preferring solitude over listening to the mindless gossip of other women passengers. Whenever she turned a discussion to politics, it was met by obvious smirks. She was well aware that women like her were rare. Fortunately, her husband was not offended by her political interest. In fact, he adored her because of it.

Much to her surprise, this trip had been his idea. "You've always wanted to see Ireland. Besides, Mrs. Parnell has offered you a place to stay," Alex had said. "Go and write about your experience; then come back home to me."

Normally, he complained when she was away from him more than a week, and this trip would require her to be gone at least two months, if not more. She didn't need anyone to chaperone her, she was quite capable of taking care of herself. After all, she was a journalist. Still, she couldn't help but think it rather odd that he would be so willing to let her make the trip alone. Then again, Alex had taken a sudden interest in Irish politics. Perhaps he was hoping she would have something new to tell him about the political situation in Ireland when she returned to Chicago.

Margaret had brought her portable writing box, plenty of paper, ink, pens, and a journal in which to capture her observations and thoughts along the way. At the present moment she was grateful these were latched inside the cabinet and not strewn across the floor with her shoes, hats, and books that tumbled from one side of the cabin to the other with each roll of the ship. Margaret retrieved her copy of *An Illustrated History of Ireland* she had wedged in the side of the chair and attempted to read.

For what seemed like hours, the vessel bounced and swayed as it made its way across the frothy sea from New York to Liverpool. Then sometime after midnight, the swaying finally stopped.

Margaret put down her book and, unable to locate her rosary, clutched her dreams of Ireland instead.

Margaret noted the morning call for breakfast brought fewer passengers than normal to the dining room. A long table covered in linen and dotted with tired, well-dressed travelers awaited her. Margaret introduced herself to a round-faced woman with graying hair and sat down, placing her satchel on the floor next to her. She never went anywhere without it.

"It is a pleasure to meet you, Mrs. Sullivan. I'm Mrs. Boylston. Will your husband be joining you?"

"No, I'm afraid not." Margaret placed her napkin in her lap and glanced at the other guests seated at her table. She took a sip of her freshly poured tea.

"May I ask what brings you to England?" The woman sitting next to Mrs. Boylston blotted crumbs from her lips. She looked to be in her late thirties. A proper British woman, no doubt, Margaret thought. However, she was just guessing.

"I'm traveling to Ireland. I plan to write a book about Ireland's problems," Margaret said confidently while spreading jam on her scone.

"My dear, I don't want to appear rude, but do you seriously think anyone will read a book about Ireland written by a woman?" The lady grinned.

"I don't see why not," Margaret replied. She took a bite of the dry pastry.

"Well, I wish you luck with your publication." Mrs. Boylston looked down and sipped her tea.

"I have heard there is a notorious Irish rebel on board," a young woman with blond hair commented. From the sound of her accent, Margaret thought the lady might be German.

"Apparently, they will let anyone travel for the price of a ticket," a balding man further down the table replied.

"I hope he doesn't stir up any trouble on the ship," the British woman across from him added. "It would make our trip most unpleasant if he did."

"What leads you to think he would?" Margaret asked. "A ruckus on board would be of no benefit to the Irish."

A woman put her hand up to cover her mouth and whispered to the woman next to her. "She's an American. They'll mingle with anyone."

"If he tried anything, I'm sure someone would toss him over-board," replied the balding man, pulling out his pocket watch to check the time.

"I believe a man did go overboard last night," said the German woman.

"How unfortunate, I hope he didn't leave behind a wife and family," Mrs. Boylston added, before shoving a piece of scone into her mouth.

The blond-haired German woman leaned forward so everyone could hear her gossip. "I heard a couple of the ship's stewards talking about it this morning. They were wondering if there might have been some foul play involved."

Margaret contemplated the idea that he might have been the same man who knocked on her door last night. If a crime had been committed, what was the reason behind it? She was curious. Just the same, she reminded herself that the purpose of her trip was to write about Ireland, not about some stranger who ended up in the ocean. Still, she couldn't help but wonder about the circumstances surrounding his disappearance.

"It was most likely an accident," the British woman added. "Only a fool would be out in a storm like that, if you ask me."

"Well, let's hope it was that Paddy rebel who washed overboard," the balding man replied. "We could do with a few less Irish, I say."

"I have heard quite enough." Margaret stood up and slapped down her napkin on the table. "I happen to be Irish, and I find your comments rude and uncalled for." Margaret was tired of this conversation and didn't care whom she offended. She snatched up her satchel and headed outside.

The sun was shining brightly. A beautiful day with no trace of last evening's storm. On the promenade deck, Margaret spied a family with young children gazing at the endless horizon at the point where the ocean and the sky melted together in shades of the lightest blue. A little girl with blond curls clutched a china doll while a boy ate a biscuit, dropping crumbs that the wind instantly whisked away.

Margaret was reminded of the fact that, after countless attempts by her husband to impregnate her, she had been unable to produce a child. She shrugged. It was just as well God hadn't given her any. At the present, she couldn't imagine giving up her career. Still, it would be nice to have someone to spoil and lavish with love. Her life was a void in that area.

Margaret watched the siblings interact. In an effort to get closer to the railing, the little boy pushed his sister aside and her doll fell onto the deck, rolling out into the pathway of a man who unsuspectingly kicked it while walking by. The child cried out. Margaret rushed over to the area where the doll had landed and retrieved it before anyone else could do it harm. She dusted it off and handed it to the child's mother as the little girl peeked out from around her mother's skirt. "Your doll is safe now."

"Alice, be polite and tell the nice woman thank you," the child's mother urged the girl.

Alice only giggled shyly, while hiding her face in the folds of her mother's dress.

She waved goodbye to Alice as the child peeked out from behind her mother again, and then Margaret continued her stroll along the promenade. People milled about near the railings, some pointing at squawking seagulls flying overhead. A couple of young women holding parasols paraded by, dragging yards of satin and lace behind them.

"Do you think he will propose marriage?" the women asked her companion.

Margaret smiled. Dreams of love and romance were a young girl's fantasy.

"I am sure he will," the other young woman replied. "Unfortunately, Father would prefer I marry someone with more money."

"Didn't you tell me Robert had plans to go into business out west with his brother? He isn't expecting a dowry, is he?"

"He has assured me he doesn't. However, any money Father could provide would help him tremendously."

"And if your father won't, will you still marry him?"

Yes, Margaret thought, marriage was much like a business deal, based on mutual aspirations, nothing more. A woman needed to adjust her expectations before the wedding vows. If not, she certainly would have to adjust them afterwards or be doomed to a life of disappointment. Besides, romantic love only existed in poems and silly novels, not between a husband and a wife in a real marriage. Heavens no. Nevertheless, one could never tell infatuated young women these things. They were blinded by their own ignorance.

Margaret continued her stroll, inhaling the cool salt air and catching snippets of conversation along the way. Spotting a place in a secluded area, she sat down in a deck chair, retrieved her book from her satchel, and began to read. After a few pages, the sound of an angry voice interrupted her.

"You, sir! I am speaking to you," a man with an English accent yelled as he came up behind a gentleman in a black jacket. They both stopped in front of Margaret's chair, apparently unaware of her presence.

"Please, keep your voice down," the other man replied in a deep Irish brogue.

"I recognize your face." The Englishman reached out and grabbed the other man's shoulder. "You're Davitt aren't you?"

Margaret now stared at the Irishman. Could it be? Had they been referring to Mr. Michael Davitt at breakfast this morning? She was aware that he had recently finished a lecture tour in America, but had no idea he would be returning home on this ship. If it was Davitt, she certainly couldn't let this opportunity to speak with him slip away.

The Irishman slowly turned around. "Remove your hand, sir."

"I heard about you. You were convicted of treason." The Englishman brandished his walking stick in the air as though he would strike the other man with it.

"Sir, I do not wish to quarrel with you," the Irishman replied.

"You're a traitor to the Queen and should hang from the gallows." The Englishman, with his beak of a nose, leaned back with his chest puffed out like a well-dressed pigeon. Then he leaned forward and gave the Irishman a slight shove.

Margaret watched as the Irishman reached inside his unbuttoned coat with his left hand. She jumped to her feet.

"Excuse me," she interjected. "I find your rudeness appalling." She waved her finger at the Englishman as if he were a naughty schoolboy. "If you have a problem with Mr. Davitt's freedom, then I suggest you take it up with the Queen's court."

The man pinched up his face, adjusted his hat, and walked off muttering to himself.

Shocked at her own behavior, Margaret blushed with embarrassment. She had overstepped her bounds as a woman and insulted Mr. Davitt. "Please, forgive me for my actions. I meant no disrespect to you." He must abhor me, she thought. "I'm sure you didn't require my assistance with the gentleman, and I am a fool for interfering."

Mr. Davitt laughed. "I admire your courage." He pulled his hand from under his jacket, and Margaret could see a revolver tucked in his waistband. She winced at the thought of what might have happened if she had not spoken up. It brought back memories of the night two years before when her husband had killed a man while she sat helpless in a carriage nearby. If Alex hadn't lost his temper, or if she had intervened, perhaps that man would be alive today.

"I'm Mrs. Sullivan, journalist with the *Chicago Tribune*." Margaret extended her hand, and then quickly withdrew it when she realized his right sleeve was flat against his coat.

"Forgive me." She suddenly remembered reading he had lost one arm.

"Madam, do not fret about it. I assure you many people make the same mistake." He gave her a nod. "Pleased to meet you. As you apparently know, I'm Michael Davitt."

"I understand you have been on a lecture tour in America." She noticed that his brown hair curled in waves around his head, his dark eyes sparkled in the light, and a thick mustache adorned his upper lip.

A seagull squawked at her from overhead, diverting her attention. Margaret shaded her eyes and glanced up. When she looked back at Mr. Davitt, he was pulling on the hairs of his mustache near the corner of his mouth, hiding what she perceived to be a grin.

"Perhaps I could schedule an appointment with you?" Margaret asked. "For an interview, that is."

His eyebrows went up and he smiled. "Of course. In fact, it would be my honor, Mrs. Sullivan, if you and your husband would join me later for a drink." He gave her a slight bow.

"Thank you for your kind invitation. However, Mr. Sullivan is not accompanying me on this voyage."

"That surprises me. I wouldn't think a woman of your standing would be traveling alone."

Margaret looked out to the ocean, trying not to be drawn in by his eyes. "Actually, I enjoy the solitude. I am working on a book."

"What is your book about, if I may ask?"

"Ireland."

"Have you been there before?" When she turned back to him, his eyes told her she had his full attention.

"I was born in Ireland. Unfortunately, my father died a few years later and my mother decided to come to America. We lived with my older brother in Detroit, Michigan. That is where I grew up; however, I now live in Chicago." Margaret didn't know why she was telling him this. Her personal life wasn't his concern. "I've heard much about Ireland, and I have always wanted to see it for myself."

"Are you interested in Irish politics?" His smile widened.

"Of course. I intend to write about Ireland's struggles for self-government." She looked at him sidelong now and smiled.

"Ah, a subject close to my heart." He reached out and gently touched her arm.

She stopped smiling. She had not expected him to touch her. He was being too familiar for someone she just met. But then again, it could be just a friendly gesture, she told herself, and she should treat it as such. Margaret gave him a weak smile. "I must go now," she said.

"It was a pleasure, Mrs. Sullivan." He nodded. "I will look forward to speaking with you later."

Margaret tried to hide her grin as she gathered up her satchel and made her way back to her cabin. An interview with the famous Irish hero Michael Davitt would make an excellent addition to the book she intended to write.

Chapter 2

NORMALLY, EATING ALONE didn't bother Margaret, but tonight she was hungry for male companionship. If only she had someone to discuss something noteworthy with, like the news of the world or the balance of power abroad, her evening wouldn't be so boring. She missed her co-workers at the newspaper. Perhaps Mr. Davitt could entertain her. Margaret glanced around the dining room; however, he was not seated amongst the other guests. Before yesterday she hadn't even noticed Mr. Davitt amongst the other passengers. Now that she had met him, she was eager to learn more about his life.

Finished with her meal, she wandered the promenade in hopes of finding this mysterious one-armed Irishman. Unfortunately, though she made several trips around the perimeter of the ship, he was nowhere to be found. Finally, she asked a ship steward if he knew the whereabouts of Mr. Davitt.

"I believe he went to the bar, madam."

"Thank you. Could you please tell me where the men's bar is?"

"Women are not allowed in there, madam."

Margaret rummaged through her satchel. "Could you give him my card? Tell him I will be waiting in the lobby."

Margaret found a table in a corner facing the entrance so that she could watch for him. She neatly arranged her papers and wrote down several questions in pencil.

1. *What was it like spending eight years in prison?*
2. *What are you planning to do with your life now that you are out on parole?*
3. *Do you have any political ambitions?*

Pleased with her queries, she moved the paper to the side and looked around. Well-dressed couples drifted by, heading to the evening's concert. She waited.

A steward approached her. "May I get you something to drink, madam?"

"A glass of wine; claret, perhaps." She needed something to sip on to calm her nerves. He would be here any minute, she assured herself. She counted the crossbeams in the ceiling, twenty-one. The number of tables arranged around the perimeter of the room, twelve. She studied the clothes of lingering passengers trying to guess their economic status.

By the time the minutes turned into an hour, her second glass of wine was empty and she knew he wasn't coming. Margaret gathered up her papers. His name was scribbled several times in calligraphy on a sheet. She wadded up the paper and shoved it in her satchel.

Outside, the salty breeze caressed her face. Margaret carefully stepped down the stairs, holding onto the handrail for support. The lower deck was nearly empty except for some of the ship's crew. Huge sails flapped in the wind above her as men adjusted them. She wondered if someday steamships would cross the ocean without the assistance of sails.

Wandering over to the bow of the ship, she watched shadows of the waves in the ocean as moonlight danced on its surface.

"Mrs. Sullivan," a deep voice called out. Mr. Davitt came striding toward her. "I apologize for the delay."

Margaret was both glad to see him and angry at the same time. How dare he make her wait for him? Then again, they had not set an official time to meet. It was she who had made assumptions.

"Do you still desire an interview?" he asked.

What should she say? She had waited too long, and now the effects of the wine were compromising her thinking. "Perhaps another time would be better," she replied.

Above, the wind caught a sail and the boat lunged to the side. Margaret stumbled, losing her balance. Mr. Davitt spun around and caught her with his left arm.

Steadying herself again, she said, "I really should get back to my room." How embarrassing. She must appear like a schoolgirl and unprofessional to the man.

Mr. Davitt held out his arm for her to take. "Here, let me accompany you."

Margaret's eyebrows went up as she stared at him. Was this for her support or was he being forward?

"You can ask me your questions while we walk."

The lilt of his voice was charming and she did want his story. Margaret hesitated as she tried to read his intent. They were outside and away from the eyes of others; still, she wanted to trust him. But should she? If his behavior became questionable she could leave immediately. Margaret took a deep breath and exhaled; she chose to follow her instinct.

Mr. Davitt continued, "It appears that your legs have forgotten the rhythm of the sea. If you don't object, I will guide you until they remember again. Of course, I don't wish to make you uncomfortable in any way. If it helps, think of me as a brother. I recall you mentioned earlier you had a brother."

"Why, yes I do." Margaret had not seen her brother in years and reminded herself that she needed to write him a letter.

She turned her thoughts back to Mr. Davitt who was standing before her with his arm poised, ready for her decision. Margaret timidly placed her fingertips on his arm; now she couldn't remember what she was going to ask him. She stood there for a moment, then finally she asked, "What is Ireland like, really like?"

"Excellent question." He stopped and held her gaze. "You ask this because you want to know what to expect, I presume?"

"I've heard many stories." She remembered new immigrants sharing tales of hardship and people they left behind.

"I must caution you, do not let others color your vision with the blood of their ancestors. There are many ways to see Ireland." Mr. Davitt stopped, and Margaret quickly let go of his arm.

Putting his hand on the polished wood railing, Mr. Davitt stared out across the night sky. Stars glistened above.

"To some, Ireland is no more than an island of rock and dirt shaped by the hand of God. To the Irish, it is a poem, a myth, a clan, a country." He hesitated. "To the British, Ireland is a possession they don't want to release." He tilted his head sideways and toward her. "She is a place of happiness and love, also sadness and sorrow." He looked back at the sea. "Ireland is like Venus to many men, turning their hearts and creating warriors out of peasants. She is an idea many would lay down their life for."

Margaret gazed at the silver glimmer of moonlight on the dark water. She felt as though he had cast a net out into the ocean and pulled in something mythical to share with her.

"I am surprised. You describe Ireland not as the bitter son of a peasant, but instead as a man of considerable depth and affection."

Speaking more to himself than her, Mr. Davitt turned and leaned his back against the railing. "Yes, it is true." He paused. "My family was very poor." He took a deep breath. "However, my father valued education and instilled in me a desire to learn. As you can see, I was not destined to work as a laborer in a factory. Thanks to a wealthy benefactor, I had the opportunity to attend school in England. Once I finished school, I studied on my own, reading everything I could find on philosophy, history, political ideas, and government." He looked at Margaret and smiled. "So you see, Mrs. Sullivan, the son of a peasant can ponder the same ideas as do a poet and a lord."

"And a revolutionist?" In the moonlight she could have mistaken him for a saint, but she knew he was just a man and a criminal at that. "You were arrested for smuggling weapons to Irish rebels, as I recall."

"I will not deny what I have done. When I was a child, I watched my home burn to the ground under the torch of a greedy landlord who would rather see our family perish than allow us more time to come up with the rent. The shame in my father's eyes as we walked down the road homeless still haunts me. We had no place to go and lived huddled together in doorways. Father desperately tried to find work in Dublin and Mother begged in the streets while I watched her from an alley nearby. After a while, someone took pity on us and let us sleep in their barn. We barely survived."

Margaret heard the tightness in his voice as he spoke, obviously this affected him deeply.

Why would a landlord burn your home?" Margaret asked.

"Unlike in America, where anyone can buy land and build a house of their own, all the land in Ireland is controlled by aristocrats and governed by the British. The Irish people do not own their homes and their landlords can treat them however they choose."

Margaret now detected a touch of anger in his voice.

"After my education, I joined the Irish Republican Brotherhood. At nineteen years old, I thought violence the only answer. I quickly moved up the ranks and soon was an officer organizing attacks against the British. As a cover, I took a job as a traveling salesman and smuggled weapons into Ireland. Unfortunately, I was reported to the authorities by a spy and arrested and then sentenced to fourteen years in prison. I was released on probation after eight years." He looked at her as though he might be wondering what she thought of him. "Now you know my story."

"I'm sorry to hear you suffered such an unfortunate childhood, and I can only imagine your time in prison must have been a dreadful experience," Margaret replied.

"Don't be sorry for me. I paid a price for caring for the people of Ireland, and my imprisonment only deepened my love and concern for them." He smiled at her.

Margaret admired him. His commitment came from deep within his soul. She had never felt that strongly about anything or anyone before. For a brief moment she was ashamed of her shallowness. Then she reminded herself that it was necessary to maintain a fair distance from other people's struggles. How else could she write about them in a non-biased way?

The next day, Margaret set her portable writing desk on the little table by the chair and wrote down what she remembered about her conversation with Michael Davitt. Though she tried, it was difficult to remain indifferent toward him. She found him interesting and she liked him immensely. He was mysterious, and yet for a reason she couldn't quite comprehend, she felt comfortable around him. She was curious about his future. What was he going to do when he returned to Ireland? He seemed so passionate about his country. He must have a plan.

Margaret sat back in her chair and thought about her trip. She was going home to a place she had never seen. She had no memory of Ireland; all images of her birthplace came through stories from her older brother, the nuns at school, and priests. Stories of mythical heroes and martyrs from Ireland's past captivated her imagination and eventually threads of patriotism and folklore wove their way into the fabric of her being. She could no longer separate reality from the fantasy. She only knew the stories others laced around her. Now at the age of thirty, she was making the voyage across the ocean to confirm the stories were not myths.

Other than her writing materials, she hadn't been sure what else to pack for this trip. The latest women's fashions had never held her interest. Though Alex insisted that she be well dressed at all times, believing her appearance was somehow a reflection of him. She wondered if perhaps at Avondale the Parnells dressed for diner; she hadn't considered that possibility when she accepted the invitation to stay there. Her wardrobe would have to suffice. Thank goodness she remembered to pack an extra pair of sturdy shoes for walking.

"Enough." She put her pen down. It was now late in the day. "I'm going to get some air. I can't stay in this cabin another moment." Margaret grabbed her coat, put on her hat and gloves and left.

Several men, deep in conversation, leaned on the railing as Margaret approached. One man looked up at her and then went back to his discussion with the other gentlemen.

"I say we do something," said a dark-haired man with bushy eyebrows. "We can't let him get away with this sort of thing or none of us will be safe."

"You think the other fellow was an informer, do ya?" a man with his cap pulled down asked.

Margaret's ears were now tuned to their conversation.

"Keep your voice down," one of the men said, eyeing Margaret as she approached.

"If he was an informer, then he deserved to get tossed to the whales."

"Davitt told us not to get involved."

"Yeah, tell it to the some of the other blokes. They're the ones causing trouble."

The men nodded at her as she walked by. Margaret wanted to stop and ask them questions about their conversation, but it was not her privilege to do so. Something obviously had happened to fire up their talk of revenge.

Around the corner, Margaret saw Michael Davitt striding toward her.

He stopped in front of her and tipped his hat. "It is good to see you again, Mrs. Sullivan."

"I heard some gentlemen talking around the corner. Irishmen. They appeared concerned about something. I heard them refer to a spy. Would you happen to know more about this?" she asked.

"You shouldn't concern yourself with their conversation. You know how men are. After a few drinks they are prone to exaggeration," Mr. Davitt replied. "Now, if you will excuse me, I was just heading off to join some of my comrades. Perhaps we can meet again later? That is, of course, if you don't think it is too forward of me to make the suggestion?"

"No, that would be fine." Margaret was pleasantly surprised by his invitation.

"At sunset, on the back deck?"

"Yes, I will see you then, Mr. Davitt." She watched, determined to find out more about this mysterious handsome stranger, as he disappeared into a crowd of men ahead.

Margaret could hear music coming from the stern, an old Irish tune played on a fiddle. She leaned against the railing and watched the remaining light of the day as it reflected off waves trailing behind the ship. Up above, the great mast poles were empty of sails. Now, only the steam from the engines propelled them across the sea. Deck lights appeared as people below gathered to hear the music. The sound of the fiddle brought back memories of when she was a child. She used to sit at the top of the stairs at their house in Detroit and listen to her brother's friends while they played their musical instruments in the parlor below.

While she descended the stairs, Margaret spotted Mr. Davitt talking with a man. When she got closer, she noticed the stranger's reddish-blond hair ran down the side of his face into wooly mutton chops. He wore a big smile that she suspected came easily to him.

Recognizing her, Mr. Davitt motioned Margaret to join him. She made her way past several informally dressed men and women standing about enjoying the impromptu concert. She assumed they were from the third class steerage cabins below deck.

"Good to see you again, Mrs. Sullivan." He smiled as he spoke.

"Can I get you a drink, mum?" asked the red-haired man. "I was just running off to fetch Michael here something to quench his thirst." He extended his hand. "Name's O'Doul. Thomas, O'Doul."

"Pleased to meet, you, Mr. O'Doul. My name is Margaret Sullivan. And yes, a drink would be welcomed."

"What does the lady have a fancy for?"

"Whatever you are drinking will be fine."

"You sure now? We got a taste for the brew."

"Then I will have one also, thank you."

"Yes, mum. A brew it is." O'Doul left to fetch their drinks.

Mr. Davitt brushed the hair back from his eyes. "You surprise me, Mrs. Sullivan. I thought you would have preferred a lady's drink, or perhaps wine."

"I am not as pretentious as you may have assumed." Margaret tilted her head to one side. "I grew up drinking beer with my brother."

"That is refreshing to hear. I was afraid you would find the entertainment unsophisticated."

"Well, Mr. Davitt, you would have been wrong." Margaret grinned. "I have many interests besides intellectual pursuits." She enjoyed flirting with him.

A sudden gust of wind tugged on Margaret's hat, and it fell to her shoulders. Margaret fumbled with it. She had forgotten to use a hat pin.

"It's mahogany," Mr. Davitt commented.

"I beg your pardon?" Margaret asked, while placing the hat firmly on the front of her head and retying the ribbon.

"I was referring to your hair. Your green eyes and dark red hair are very becoming."

Margaret blushed and turned her head to avoid his eyes. Perhaps he was flirting with her, as well.

Mr. O'Doul appeared with three beers. He handed her one. "Here you go, Maggie." O'Doul winked at her and nudged Michael Davitt with his elbow.

Margaret was about to correct him, but when she looked into his cheerful face she changed her mind. At the present moment she preferred not to be Mrs. Sullivan.

"A toast to Michael here." O'Doul raised his glass.

"Here's to a long life and a merry one,

A quick death and an easy one,

A pretty girl and an honest one,

A cold beer and another one."

Margaret took a sip, and then wiped the foam from her lips with the tip of her gloved finger while Mr. Davitt chuckled.

"Michael here tells me you are going to write a book about Ireland."

"Why, yes, I want people in America to have a better understanding of the current situation so they can lend their support to make sure freedom is achieved."

"Sounds like the words of a rebel, if you ask me." O'Doul laughed.

"Oh, I'm not a rebel, I assure you."

"Then why are you talking to our boy Michael?"

"I..." Margaret didn't know what to say.

O'Doul reached over and touched Margaret's arm. "That's okay, Maggie. We all love him."

Margaret could tell by the expression on Mr. Davitt's face that he was amused by the conversation.

"Perhaps she doesn't hold a membership card because she is a lady," Mr. Davitt replied.

"Not having a membership card hasn't stopped some of the women I know from doing their part to further the cause."

"I'm sure she will do whatever she can when the time comes." Mr. Davitt winked at Margaret.

They weren't expecting her to do anything illegal, were they? Margaret took a gulp of her beer. What had she gotten herself into?

Mr. Davitt leaned over to her ear. "I was referring to your writing."

"Oh, of course." Margaret took another gulp of beer. She liked being included, rather than an observer. It felt nice, for a change.

Two men, one with a drum and another with a whistle, now joined the fiddle player. Irish voices rang out in the crowd, singing songs from their homeland. The music was lively, and Margaret swayed to the beat while Michael Davitt tapped his foot. A few women in the crowd hoisted their skirts to their knees and began dancing. Even O'Doul hopped around doing a jig like a bug on a hot surface. Bursts of laughter bubbled up inside Margaret, and then both Mr. Davitt and O'Doul took turns entertaining her with their footwork.

The beer flowed, and as the evening wore on, Margaret found herself joining in as Michael Davitt and O'Doul serenaded her with ballads. She couldn't remember the last time she felt this free or happy. She loosened the ribbon under her chin, letting it slide across her neck as the hat fell to her shoulders. Her curls fluttered in the breeze. Mr. Davitt twirled her around and they laughed together. She found herself filled with lightness and contentment, with joy. Certainly, this was how life was intended to be.

After a fast-paced tune, the music turned soft. The romantic sounds of longing coming from the strings of the fiddle and on the breath of the whistle brought forth strange feelings within her. If she allowed herself to be absorbed into these whispering urges, would she ever be able to exit again? The very question made her uncomfortable.

She looked up at the stars twinkling like a thousand eyes in the darkness, watching her. She must resist the temptation to think she was free to enjoy the company of another man, especially one as charming as Michael Davitt. She chastised herself and guilt settled around her. She shouldn't be here.

Mr. Davitt leaned in. "Are you all right?" he asked.

"I think I had better go," Margaret replied.

"It has been a long time since I've heard those wonderful ballads," Mr. Davitt commented. "All those years in prison, I truly missed listening to music."

Somehow, she understood what it meant to be isolated in the world.

"You mentioned you were interested in Ireland's history. Here, let me show you something." He motioned for her to follow him up the stairs. They walked down the hall to a room. He unlocked the door. She stood there like a schoolgirl. He stepped inside, leaving the door wide open behind him.

"I have a book I thought you might enjoy." Tossing books here and there, he searched through a pile stacked on the floor of his room.

Margaret walked down the hall, but as soon as she left, the dilemma seemed absurd to her. He wasn't trying to seduce her. Why had she run away? When she turned around, he was standing behind her with a book in his hand.

"I think you will enjoy reading this."

After pulling off her gloves, she thumbed through the pages. It was *The General History of Ireland* by Geoffrey Keating.

"Thank you, but I should be going now," she said.

"I have made you uncomfortable by bringing you here." He frowned. "Forgive me; I am not used to entertaining a lady. God knows how long it's been… I am at a loss as to how to behave." He moved toward her with his head dropped like a child who had done something wrong. "You must think I'm without social graces."

"No, you've been a perfect gentleman." Margaret impulsively reached over and touched his cheek. Its warmth surprised her.

He looked up at her with an unspoken request in his eyes. His mustache brushed lightly over the surface of her skin as he kissed the back of her hand. Shivers traveled down her body, and she closed her eyelids. For a brief moment, she allowed herself to experience the yearning. When she opened her eyes, he was smiling at her as though a secret had passed between them.

"Well, Mrs. Sullivan, I think it is best that I walk you to your cabin now before I make a further fool of myself." He gestured down the walkway.

"Margaret. Please call me Margaret."

He leaned closer to her and asked, "Would you mind if I call you Maggie instead?"

Margaret had never thought of herself as a Maggie. She had gone by many names as she stepped in and out of various aliases, but nothing as common and familiar. That name belonged to a peasant girl, not to her.

"Let's start with Margaret."

"As you wish." He nodded to her. "Since we are putting aside formality, please call me Michael."

"Michael, it is."

Chapter 3

BORED WITH BEING cooped up in her room, Margaret opened her cabin door and stepped outside. Light fog hung in the air and dampness penetrated her clothes. She shivered. In the distance a distorted glow of sunlight struggled to overpower the mist. Margaret clutched her coat tightly and scurried down the passageway. There would be no fire in the ship's library to warm her, only new books to explore.

From the entrance, she saw Michael reading in an overstuffed chair. It was just a chance meeting, she told herself, trying to squelch her sudden nervousness. Margaret walked to the rows of books on the closest shelf and began examining their titles. She reread the same gold-embossed lettering over and over. Finally, she pulled out a book and walked to a chair next to a small mahogany table. She sat down, opened it, and pretended to read. After a few moments, the inscription took on meaning. It was a book of poems by Thomas Moore.

"I hope I'm not disturbing you." Michael leaned over, speaking in her ear, "I was just admiring your choice. He is an Irish poet as you no doubt already know." In his deep baritone voice, he read from the page she had opened in her lap:

"Come o'er the sea,
Maiden with me,
Mine through sunshine, storm, and snows
Seasons may roll,
But the true soul
Burns the same, where'er it goes.
Let fate frown on, so we love and part not;
'Tis life where thou art, 'tis death where thou are not.
Then come o'er the sea,
Maiden with me,
Come wherever the wild wind blows;
Seasons may roll,
But the true soul
Burns the same, where'er it goes."

Margaret's hand quivered.

"I'm sorry," he said. "I should have picked a different poem."

"No, it is a lovely poem, and you read it beautifully." Flooded with goose bumps, she closed the book and swallowed. "I think I need a little air."

"Would you mind if I joined you?"

Torn between running away and allowing him to accompany her, and somehow knowing that either choice would lead to regret, she gave in to her growing desire to be with him. Her mind told her it was wrong, but her instincts told her to let go and trust her feelings.

As they strolled together through the lobby, Margaret noticed a shiny object on an empty table. Recognizing what it was, she rushed over and picked it up.

"What do you have there?" Michael asked.

"It's a button." Margaret held it up for him to see. It was silver with an ornate carving of a bird surrounded by leaves. "I collect buttons."

"Do you pick up every stray button you find or only special ones?" He looked at her inquisitively.

"Some of the buttons I have are from people I care deeply about, like the ones I have from my mother and brother and dear friends. Others are more like tokens from places I've been. A few I just like for their design."

"You surprise me. I would not have guessed that about you."

Margaret put the button into her pocket for safe keeping. It was her first one from this trip. A good sign, she thought.

"Could I interest you in something to eat?" Michael asked. "Cr tea, perhaps?"

Heads turned when they entered the dining room.

"Do you get this response everywhere you go?" Margaret glanced around at the darting eyes and could not help but notice the conspicuous whispers of other afternoon diners.

"I was going to ask you the same thing." Michael stroked the side of his mustache, trying to hide his grin. "Perhaps you are not aware that you are admired."

Margaret tried to stifle a laugh. These people had no reason to admire her. Then the thought occurred to her that he might not be speaking about them.

He pulled out a chair for her, and when she sat down, he placed his hand on her shoulder for a brief moment and then took a chair across from her. She straightened up. Placing her hands in her lap, she tried pressing on her lower abdomen, hoping to suppress the tickling sensation she was feeling.

"I presume you desire something?" Michael asked.

Margaret glanced down. Then she brought her fingers to her mouth and blushed. "Tea. I would like some tea."

He leaned toward her. "Is that all? I thought you might fancy something sweet."

Eventually she chose the currant spice cake. When it arrived she poked out the currants with her fork.

"I thought you requested cake with currants," Michael remarked.

"I did. I like to eat them separately." She tried scooping up a current with her fork, but ended up chasing it around the plate. Finally, she picked up one with her finger and popped it into her mouth. Then she slid her fork into a generous portion of frosted cake.

Michael looked at her with an odd expression, leaned over, and wiped some frosting that had fallen on her chin with his napkin.

She was amused at his action. "Oh, dear. Now I am the one without social graces," Margaret said, blotting her face with a napkin. She cut off another piece of cake and pushed her fork into it.

Michael smiled. Margaret felt guilty as she looked down at the cake. She hadn't offered him a piece. "Would you like a taste?"

"Most certainly." He wet his lips. Their eyes met, and she shoved the plate toward him. He picked up a currant and tossed it into his mouth. "Ah such sweetness," he said.

Margaret cocked her head sideways. She found his flirting endearing.

"Is there anything you haven't asked me that you wish to know?" Michael asked.

Margaret wanted to know everything about him: where his home was, what he liked to eat, if he always wore a mustache.

"Perhaps you would like to know what happened to my arm. Most people do."

Margaret had been too afraid to ask. She hadn't wanted to appear impolite.

"At the age of nine, I went to work at a cotton mill, and two years later my arm was crushed by a machine and had to be amputated."

"I'm so sorry." She didn't look upon him as a disfigured man. In her eyes, his soul out-shined any scar he might carry under his shirt.

"Is there anything else you would care to know about me?" he said.

Margaret remembered only a year and a half had gone by since his release. "What was it like in prison?" she asked.

He looked down at the table. After a moment, he said, "Do you really want to know?"

"Yes, of course I do." Margaret couldn't imagine what it must have been like.

"How can I describe to you an aching heart or the most unbearable hunger that cries out for the warm touch from a loved one? Or my soul's constant longing for the time when I would be free from prison rules, the threat of a warden, and the oppressor of my country?" He looked up at her. "Someday, I'll write about my time in prison, but not just yet."

His honesty left her vulnerable. It was as if a strange fate had drawn them together.

"Tell me. What sort of books do you like to read? Who are your favorite authors?" Michael asked.

She assumed he was trying to change the subject, but without giving it much thought, Margaret replied, "I enjoy Irish and British authors, in addition to our American ones, such as Mark Twain. I have even read *Madame Bovary* in French." Margaret realized with a sudden flushing of her cheeks that she had admitted more than she intended to.

Michael's eyebrows arched. Then she saw the corners of his mouth go up. Margaret quickly tried to explain herself. "One must read about these things in order to understand them. I'm not suggesting that I approved of that sort of scandalous behavior. However, I am not naïve to the desires of the flesh and the ways of the world." She hoped she hadn't offended him. Most men would have found her vulgar and left her sitting there alone. However, Michael did not.

"Living in America, I suspect you must encounter a variety of individuals of questionable moral fiber," he said. "Forgive me, I didn't mean to sound insulting."

Oh dear, she indeed must have given him the wrong impression, she thought. "I don't fraternize with them, mind you," Margaret stated. "Perhaps you wrongly assume that I visit dance halls and saloons."

"It never crossed my mind." Michael looked amused.

"I will have you know that I studied at the Society of the Sacred Heart and was taught by French nuns. I even lived for many years in a convent. I hope you don't think poorly of me for speaking my mind."

"Please, you don't have to defend yourself. I quite enjoy you."

Margaret felt relieved. She was afraid she had frightened him off. Now, what had they been previously discussing? "So, what type of books do you enjoy reading?" she asked.

"I am afraid I am more inclined to read classical literature, Shakespeare, and poetry, than some of these newer authors. However, I do enjoy Dickens. I have also read a great deal about subjects most people would consider drab and boring."

As he spoke, she imagined what it must be like to be with a man who was interested in literature instead of dime novels. Her husband's reading tastes were very narrow and almost always included a crime of some sort. Michael's intellect intrigued her. He was a man she could spend hours in conversation with, discussing a variety of topics. He spoke several languages, she had read in a news article somewhere, just as she did. If his life had been different, he could have been a scholar. However, he had chosen a different path.

"I am still puzzled about your involvement with the rebels." Margaret picked up a currant. "Do you still intend to organize attacks against the British?"

"If I was, my dear, I would not be telling you." He grinned. "To answer your question, however…" He leaned back in his chair. "Much to the disappointment of my fellow Irishmen, I would have to say no. I do not plan to stage any armed attacks on the British in the future."

"I thought you were committed to changing things. Are you now advocating doing nothing?" Margaret placed a piece of cake in her mouth. She had resorted to using her fingers.

"No, but we need to take a different approach. In the past, every time an uprising occurred, the Irish lost their lives. Too many have died already, and now, with so many immigrating, we do not have the men or the weapons to form a decent army."

"So what do you suggest they do?"

"While in prison, I had a lot of time to think. I asked my friends to bring me books containing ideas regarding nonviolent resistance and arbitration. I studied the subject until I came up with a plan. Now I hope to incite enough interest to test my idea."

"I hope you share the results with me so that I can write about it."

"Ah, that's right. You are a journalist. But you are a woman. Isn't that an impediment to getting published?" Michael asked.

"I write under a male alias. Actually, I use several different names or no byline at all," Margaret replied.

"If I'm not mistaken, you said you worked for the *Chicago Tribune*.'

"They are well aware that I am a woman, and they are quite happy to have me write for them, I assure you."

Michael stood abruptly. Margaret looked to see who had attracted his attention. A man dressed in a brown suit was leaning against a pillar some distance away. He was staring in their direction. "Excuse me, Margaret, but I must leave you." Michael glanced around before quickly walking away.

The man who had been watching them was now in pursuit of Michael. Margaret sat there for a moment. Should she follow or mind her own business? She stared off in their direction, then back at the table. A pile of crumbs, the remainder of the cake sat before her on a dish. She tried pushing them into a pile to make a decent pinch, but when she lifted the crumbs to her mouth they fell away, leaving her with only a small taste. She wiped the bits from her face, got up from the table, and went to the outer deck. Whatever Michael was up to, it was something that didn't include her.

Strolling amongst the maze of people on the promenade deck, she glanced at some of their faces and wondered about their lives. A man with a long handlebar mustache diverted his attention when she walked past, but she caught him staring at her when she looked back over her shoulder. A pale woman in a blue taffeta dress looked out to the ocean as if she had some tragedy in her life. A wealthy-looking distinguished older gentleman puffed on a cigar. Two spinsters walked by arm in arm. They all carried their own secrets, Margaret thought.

As she strolled along the deck, Margaret found herself glancing around in hopes of spotting Michael. What was his secret? The longer she pondered what he might be hiding, the more curious she grew as to why he abandoned her so abruptly. She determined to find out the reason why. Unsure of what to say to him if she did find him, she went through various scenarios in her mind. Perhaps she could tell him there was an important question that she needed answered. Yes, that would suffice.

Margaret peeked in at the door to the men's bar. The bartender was wiping down an empty wooden table. He turned to look at her. Michael wasn't there, and so she left.

Margaret went to Michael's cabin and knocked, but there was no answer. A man down the hall opened his door, stuck out his head, and stared at her. Margaret smiled at the snoop and then moved on.

There was only one other place she hadn't looked. Opening the door, she stepped inside and descended the stairs into the belly of the boat, to the hot and stuffy third-class section. Before her was a maze of corridors that looked to have been created by temporary wood partitions. Most of the doors lining the hallway were closed, but those that were open led to rooms with crates of cargo stacked in them.

"What are you doing here?" a gruff Irish voice asked from behind her. Margaret turned around to find a dirty-looking man with sweat dripping down his face. His blond hair was stuck to his forehead and the arms of his shirt were dark with perspiration.

"I… I'm looking for Mr. Michael Davitt," she said. "Have you seen him?"

"Davitt?" He took a handkerchief from his pocket and wiped his face. "What you want him for?"

"It is a private matter," Margaret replied.

"Lady, I think you better go back upstairs. This is no place for women like you." He opened a cabin door and stepped inside.

Margaret was backtracking her way through the corridor toward the stairs when she saw the man in the brown suit emerging from a cabin ahead of her. He took off in a hurry, leaving the door ajar. When she got to the room he had exited, she pushed the door open further and peeked inside. Michael was kneeling over a man. Margaret saw blood on the floor.

Michael turned and looked up at her. "Margaret?"

"Is he all right?" she asked hesitantly.

"It's O'Doul. Someone got to him." Michael blotted O'Doul's bloody head with a handkerchief.

She immediately went to him. "What can I do?" There was a deep gash in O'Doul's head and his shirt and vest were soaked with blood.

"Nothing, I'm afraid," Michael's sad voice replied.

"Is that Maggie?" O'Doul whispered, then swallowed hard.

"Yes, I'm right here." Margaret knelt and put her face next to his.

"You take care of our Michael, now. He is our only hope." O'Doul whispered. They were his last words. His breathing became shallow and then suddenly stopped.

Margaret bit her lip. She made the sign of the cross, and then kissed his cheek.

Michael sat there for a moment. He held out his upturned palm and Margaret slipped her hand in his. While Michael said a prayer in the dusty light of the little cabin, Margaret sensed O'Doul's spirit leave his body. It surprised her that she felt such a profound sadness for this man she hardly knew.

Michael finished with his prayer and looked over at Margaret.

"Why would someone want to harm O'Doul?" Margaret asked. She couldn't imagine him doing anything that would have brought about such a consequence. Who would do such an evil thing?

Michael just shook his head.

<h1 style="text-align:center">Chapter 4</h1>

TWO DAYS HAD gone by since Margaret last spoke with Michael. Thoughts of O'Doul's death occupied her mind. Had he been killed by someone who merely hated all Irish? She didn't understand the disrespect the British held for them. Back in Chicago, no one would have stood for the needless murder of an Irishman, for the Irish held positions in all levels of society. Her husband was a highly respected attorney and there were many Irish politicians. An investigation would have been ordered immediately and suspects rounded up. But here at sea, different rules seemed to apply. Margaret wondered if the murder had even been reported. Did the captain know? She knew her years as a journalist gave her a heightened sense of curiosity and that she should refrain from getting involved. Just the same, she wanted to know what had happened.

Margaret checked her timepiece. It was four o'clock and many women would be having their afternoon tea in the dining room, which made this a good time to go to the men's bar. Margaret picked out one of her nicer dresses that she had saved for Avondale. She secured her corset, slipped on her dress, and buttoned it up the front. A dab of perfume was placed behind each ear. She decided not to wear a net over the bottom of her curls; instead she would let them hang freely in ringlets down her back. She chose a small hat, rather than hide behind a large one, and peered at herself in the mirror. Pleased with how she looked, Margaret then stepped outside and locked her door.

As she made her way along the deck toward the men's bar, she asked herself why she took such great pleasure in Michael's company. Perhaps her zeal for him came from the lack of love she felt for her own husband? Her marriage was a duty; a corset holding in her feelings to create a shapely façade for Alex's pleasure. Still, she reminded herself, she was married to the man, however much she regretted it. Margaret dismissed any thoughts of guilt. Certainly God wouldn't punish her for allowing herself a little pleasure. She wasn't committing adultery, after all. She was only engaging in a flirtation, and besides, Alex would never know of her indiscretion.

Outside, surrounded by a group of men, Margaret spotted Michael drinking a beer. As she approached, she heard the sound of Irish voices broken up with an occasional burst of laughter. Two men jousted in a mock boxing match as others spurred them on. There didn't appear to be any talk of revenge amongst these men, only playful interaction. One man raised his glass.

"To Michael Davitt. God bless him. May he free us all," he shouted.

The men cheered and gulped beer.

When Michael saw her, he said something to a thin man in a vest next to him and then handed the man his drink. Using his sleeve to wipe the beer from his mustache, he walked over to join her.

"Good day, Margaret. It is a pleasure to see you again." He leaned over and kissed her gently on the cheek. When he pulled back, Margaret detected a glint of mischief in his eyes.

"Forgive me for taking such liberties with you. As I told you before, the social behavior of the upper class has never been one of my finer points." There was a grin on his face.

She blurted out without thinking, "Nor mine. I am an American, after all, and not governed by British social rules." The boldness of the words surprised her. Oh, she thought, I've said too much.

"A modern woman." He winked at her. "An admirable trait, I assure you."

Margaret was a woman of high morals, or at least she liked to think of herself as possessing them, and she hoped he didn't think of her as decadent. "I'm not spoiling your social time, am I?" Margaret asked, looking over at the men at the bar.

"No. I was hoping to spend some time with you today." He reached into his vest pocket. "I didn't know if you wanted this or not. I took it off of O'Doul's jacket." He looked at the ground, avoiding her eyes. "You don't have to keep it."

"Thank you. Yes, I will keep it." Margaret gazed at the little button, then put it in her pocket.

"I'm glad." Michael smiled. He looked out at the water then back at Margaret.

"What happened? Is anyone investigating the crime?"

"I doubt it. Actually I would prefer it if no one from the outside poked their nose into his death."

"Don't you want justice done? The man who did this horrible act should be caught and punished."

"I would prefer we spoke of something else."

He obviously wasn't going to answer her question. Though she tried to understand, his reaction still annoyed her.

"Have you seen the view from the top deck?" Michael grabbed her hand.

A jolt rushed through her and it was not one of fear. Quite the opposite.

When they reached the upper level, Margaret looked out at the ocean spreading for miles before them. The wind whipped her curls and her skirt fluttered around her as though she had wings.

Michael pulled her to a sheltered spot out of the wind. He stood next to her looking out at the water.

They were only a day from Liverpool. An assortment of ships dotted the blue-gray surface of the ocean, all heading west toward America. In the distance, plumes of smoke could be seen rising from the double stacks of another steamship. A schooner and a rig under full sail headed west.

Reaching inside his coat, Michael brought out a plain, curved meerschaum pipe and put it in his mouth. From his pocket, he retrieved a pouch and carefully packed the pipe with tobacco, then struck a match along the wall and lit it. He took a draw and then exhaled. It had a spicy and smoky earth scent. "We are almost to port," Michael said.

"Yes." Margaret felt a little sad. She didn't want to think about it just yet.

"My dear, you have made my voyage home very pleasant, and I wanted to thank you for spending time with me."

She smiled to herself.

"I must say, you are one of the most interesting women I have ever met. Besides being beautiful, you are intelligent, independent, and Irish. All qualities I admire in a woman."

Warmth rushed through her. He shouldn't be saying these things to her, she thought, but she cherished every word.

Michael took a slow draw on his pipe, staring out to sea, then blew out the smoke. When it traveled beyond their little shelter, it dissipated in the wind, leaving behind a trace of its scent.

"I hope you never betray yourself for others." Michael turned his eyes toward Margaret. "There are many people who would like to destroy your spirit. I've seen it done to others. Don't let them."

The reality of Margaret's life cut into her. If he only knew how difficult that was, she thought. An unexpected tear pushed to the surface and trickled down her cheek.

He bit down on the pipe that hung from the corner of his mouth, and reached up with his thumb and brushed the wetness away. The warmth of his touch disarmed her. Her lips trembled. He took a draw on his pipe. "Oh, dear, sweet Margaret…" From the side of his mouth he blew the smoke into the air. They stood in silence, looking into each other's eyes without saying what was in their minds until Margaret had to turn away. Two seagulls hung in the air above them for a moment then parted, flying off in different directions.

When they arrived at Margaret's cabin door, Michael turned to her. "I am sorry, but…I must leave you now." He reached over and picked up her hand.

Margaret was confused. She leaned back against the door. "I was hoping we could share a meal tonight." Her dress suddenly felt heavy on her shoulders.

"I've made other plans." He watched her as he spoke.

Why was he dismissing her so abruptly? "What plans?" She jerked her hand away. It was too soon. She wasn't ready for their time together to end.

"I have some unfinished business I need to take care of." His eyes had lost their softness and now looked like dark stones.

"I don't understand." Her mind raced looking for answers.

"It is just as well that you don't."

"This isn't about O'Doul, is it?" Margaret asked.

"Please, Margaret."

"You know who killed him?"

"I do not want to discuss this with you."

She was hurt. Why wasn't he telling her? "Is this because I am a journalist? Are you afraid I will print something?"

"I think this would be better handled by people other than the authorities, and thus not for public knowledge."

"You can trust me," she said. She wished he could see that her concern was genuine and not because of her profession. "Are you mixed up in something illegal?" Perhaps he was afraid of being incarcerated again and that was the reason he wouldn't tell her.

"Of course not."

"Is this connected to the gentleman who fell overboard?" Margaret asked.

His eyebrows arched. "What do you know about Sean?"

Michael knew the man's name. Were they friends?

"The night of the storm, someone pounded on my door begging for help. Was he the man who fell overboard? Was that the man you call Sean?" An unsettling feeling rose in her stomach.

"Margaret, it is important to me that you let go of your concern. Can you do that? Promise me that you will?" His face appeared unusually serious to her.

"If you insist. I promise," Margaret replied. How could he expect her to promise not to be curious, which seemed another word for concern at the moment? Now she was more than concerned; she was worried.

"Thank you." He smiled. "If it will ease your mind, I will tell you this much: I am not going to shoot anyone, and I am not in any danger. Tonight I will be speaking to some individuals about changes I would like to see in the Irish Republican Brotherhood. It is my last opportunity to do so before we arrive in Liverpool."

Margaret was hurt that their time together had now come to an end. She selfishly wanted him to stay with her and not rush off to these rebels. Thank goodness he wasn't in any danger. However, there was still the matter of O'Doul and the man named Sean's death which Michael had failed to address. He was frustrating her in more ways than she wished to count. Good riddance, she thought. Take your mysteries and be gone with you.

"Now I must go. It has been a pleasure spending time with you. I hope you enjoy your travel through Ireland."

Margaret didn't respond. Instead, she turned her back to him and placed her hand on the door handle. His feather-like whiskers brushed across her ear and his soft lips kissed her cheek. "Goodbye," he whispered in her ear. She opened the cabin door, but when she turned around to say goodbye in return, he was gone. She stood there for a moment staring down the empty walkway. Her lips trembled. Then she stepped inside her room.

Not knowing what else to do, Margaret opened the cabin wardrobe and began pulling out her dresses and throwing them in a pile on her bed. Frantically, she packed everything except what she needed for the night and the next morning into her traveling trunk.

What was Michael mixed up in and why would he not tell her? There were too many unanswered questions. A thought struck her. She may never see him again. She collapsed into the chair. He had his own life and she hers. They were merely companions on this voyage; not much more than fellow passengers. She should have never participated in this flirtation. After all, she reminded herself, she was a married woman.

She tried distracting herself with thoughts of visiting Ireland for the first time. It had held such importance earlier. Certainly seeing the country of her birth would again, once she was on shore.

After dinner in her room and a cup of tea, Margaret got ready for bed. While pulling the brush through her hair, it flipped out of her hand and slid across the floor. When she got down to retrieve it, Margaret spotted her rosary under the table. How could she have forgotten it was missing? It poked her palm when she grabbed it. The brass crucifix was unique and longer than most, and its rod-like pointy end was sharp.

The crucifix had been a gift from a dying spinster she met while living at the convent in Chicago. Supposedly the cross had been in this woman's family for generations and been touched by Joan of

Arc. Margaret had heard this sort of story about old relics before and doubted there was any truth to it. Just the same, she kept the cross and had it fastened to her rosary beads to use in her daily prayers.

Margaret turned out the light and climbed into bed clutching her rosary. *"Ave Maria gratia plena..."* She needed something solid to hold onto as she prayed for protection, protection from the feelings she now had for Michael.

Chapter 5

AFTER DISEMBARKING FROM a ferry in Dublin, Margaret paid a boy to move her luggage to a cab. She regretted bringing so much, but this was her first adventure abroad. While her carriage traveled down the cobblestone streets of this large, old Irish city, Margaret gazed out the window studying the sites. Men in dark suits hurried along the sidewalks, much like back home in Chicago, and an occasional carriage rolled by carrying ladies holding parasols. Street urchins begged on one street and newspaper boys called out on another. Along the way, Margaret noted a bakery that looked appealing and a place she might want to go for breakfast in the morning. Soon the cab stopped in front of the Morrison Hotel. From outside the place appeared merely adequate. Inside though, the subtle touches of the hotel indicated that it catered to the wealthy. A grand marble entrance was filled with an assortment of stiff-looking staff waiting to assist. Margaret checked in and had her luggage delivered to her room, then she went outside and searched for a place to eat.

A casual restaurant a few doors down from the hotel caught her eye. A gentleman opened the door for Margaret and she stepped inside. It wasn't a fancy place, just wooden tables with oiled cloths. Upon entering, Margaret noticed a chubby man with a long waxed mustache in a white apron behind the bar. He was talking to a customer about a horse race. From their conversation she gathered a wager was about to be made. The room got quiet while Margaret made her way to a table and sat down, but after the patrons had their gander the chatter resumed.

"I would like fish and potatoes and a beer, please," Margaret told the waiter.

"Wouldn't you like lemonade or a lady's drink?" he asked.

"A beer would be fine, thank you." She knew it would relax her and she wanted a good night's sleep as she was not able to have one last night. Around midnight, she had been pestered with thoughts about honor, fidelity, and temptation swirling around in her head, exhausting her and yet not letting her enter the world of sleep that she so craved. She couldn't remember when she had been so unsettled about her life and her marriage to Alex. There was nothing she could do about it, and yet her mind continued to frustrate her, toying with the possibility she could. A stranger had turned her world upside down and now she was trying to right it again. Feelings were not allowed in her life, for feelings would only lead to misery. Nonetheless, rounding them up and putting them back in her secret place was not easy.

"Suit yourself," the waiter replied.

Margaret glanced around at the other occupants of the eating establishment. From across the room, a balding man with a small mustache winked at her, but she ignored him. She didn't know if ladies frequented this place alone or not, nor did she particularly care. She was here to eat, just like the rest of them.

While waiting for her food to arrive, she took out her map and jotted down places she wanted to visit. She had given herself two months to tour the southern half of the island, taking the train first to Galway then moving out to visit nearby villages. Next she would travel down to Cork. She would include the Ring of Kerry to see areas where the peasants lived. Her plan was to understand the hardships of the common people. Then she would take the train heading back toward Dublin but get off at a small town along the way and rent a carriage for the rest of her trip. She planned to travel through small villages whenever possible.

Two men entered the restaurant wearing top hats, a dark-haired man and a gray-haired one. They sat at the table next to Margaret.

"I heard Davitt just got back from America," said the dark-haired man as he raised two fingers, signaling the waiter to bring them each a beer.

Could she not escape from Michael Davitt? Margaret took a sip of the beer the waiter had set before her. Would she hear his name on the lips of everyone in Ireland?

"Yes, and I understand a couple of Irishmen didn't make it due to what I gather was some foul play on the ship." The man with gray hair put his napkin on his lap.

"Was Davitt involved?" the dark-haired man asked.

Margaret's ears pricked up. Maybe she could learn more about what took place on the ship—what Michael had refused to tell her.

"I would not know. Nevertheless, the fellow needs to keep out of trouble, or he'll end up back in prison."

"I suspect any questionable activity will have to be done by someone else."

"There are certainly plenty of IRB members for that."

"Is he still a member?"

"I am not certain if he is or not. I heard there is talk of expelling him for his new passive ideas. Of course, not everyone would like to see that happen. They still need someone to look up to so the fight for freedom does not dwindle away."

"Leave it to the rebels not to agree. They can fight it out amongst themselves just as long as the British leave the rest of us alone."

Margaret was confused. Michael had assured her that he no longer supported violence. Yet he still carried a gun. Could she trust that he was telling her the truth? Margaret took a sip of her beer. Then she reminded herself that what Mr. Davitt did was none of her concern. Well, perhaps if she only viewed him as the subject of one of her articles it would be all right to think about him. He was something of an Irish hero, after all.

When she finished her beer and her meal, Margaret went back to the hotel to rest. It had been a long day.

After returning from breakfast, Margaret picked out a comfortable chair in the hotel lobby to wait in. She chose one near the front desk so she could watch the comings and goings of guests. Her luggage sat next to her, along with several hat boxes and, of course, her satchel. She expected Mrs. Parnell to arrive any minute. Several British gentlemen drifted by. An elderly woman entered but Margaret could tell from her appearance that she wasn't the woman Margaret was waiting for. Though the stranger was elegantly dressed and wore a large hat with a long feather, the similarity ended there for there was only one Mrs. Delia Parnell.

Margaret remembered the first time she met Mrs. Parnell at an Irish social gathering in New York City. Several people had migrated to one side of the room, and Margaret, always looking for a story, investigated what had drawn everyone's interest. In the middle of the crowd stood an older, well-dressed American woman.

"I was staying in Dublin at the time," Mrs. Parnell told the audience gathered around her, "providing a place of refuge for Irish rebels hiding from the law. The poor dears needed somewhere safe to go. However, that particular evening, I had been warned that the British authorities suspected what I was up to, and would soon be at my door." Delia held her hand to the side of her mouth for a brief moment as if being coy.

"I instructed the young man I was harboring to slip into one of my gowns and let me know when he was dressed. I then buttoned him up and arranged his hair under one of my older hats. Of course he had no facial hair or my plan would have been ruined. I put him to work chopping vegetables on the table. When the authorities arrived they looked around, but after searching the different rooms for hiding places, they left. The fools never suspected that the person in the dress was the rebel they were looking for. I then sent the rebel out the door in my costume, and the next I heard of him, he was safe in America."

Everyone laughed at the story, including Margaret. After that, Mrs. Parnell was at the top of the guest list for Irish socials.

Margaret glanced up to find the woman she had been thinking about walking across the lobby toward her with a male servant trailing behind.

"I'm so glad you could make it, my dear." Mrs. Parnell squeezed Margaret's hand. "I take it your voyage was enjoyable?"

"Yes, thank you." Margaret was ready for her new adventure.

"Please, call me Delia." Mrs. Parnell requested. Then she instructed her servant to manage the transportation of Margaret's luggage. "You can't always trust the hotel staff to manage things properly. I know it is a first class establishment, but even such places have their indiscretions."

They took a cab to the Harcourt Street station where they caught the train for Rathdrum. Margaret watched through her window as brick buildings and whitewashed houses rushed by. Around every corner was land painted a lush green. Hills rose up in the distance and then the train went over a bridge, and before she knew it, the engine was slowing down. It stopped at a platform next to the tracks. They got out and her luggage was retrieved. Nearby loomed a large building that she presumed was the train station, though it appeared quiet and without any patrons.

"Welcome to Rathdrum," Delia said. "And this, my dear," Delia gestured to the hills, "is the county of Wicklow, the most beautiful county in all of Ireland, if you ask me."

They walked to a carriage waiting for them and Margaret looked at her surroundings while the servant secured her luggage for the ride to Avondale. Margaret could see that Delia, with her raven black hair now laced with gray, though her hat hid most of it, was still a strikingly beautiful woman. Margaret settled in the seat across from Delia, and in the subdued light of the carriage, Margaret noticed how Delia's blue eyes danced as she spoke of her children with pride, especially her bluestocking daughters, Fanny and Anna who were living with her in New Jersey.

"It is a pity neither of them married." Delia let out a sigh. "Anna at least will not, though I still have hope for Fanny. However, if she does marry a certain gentleman, she will be poor, I'm afraid."

Delia continued, "If only my late husband had left them a decent amount of money instead of giving everything to Charles and his brother, the girls would have a proper dowry. Of course, as you will bear witness, Charles lets me stay at Avondale whenever I want. He wouldn't dare refuse me. Nonetheless, I prefer to spend most of my time in America these days at my parents' old house. Apparently, so do Fanny and Anna.

"God knows, I did my best to find husbands for both girls, making sure they attended coming-out balls in Paris. However, without considerable wealth, society would not accept them, I'm afraid. Of course, being educated and having minds of their own might have contributed to the problem. Society men don't like their women to have opinions beyond those required to run the house." Delia reached over and touched Margaret's knee. "You don't have that problem in your marriage, do you, my dear?"

"I am rather fortunate, I suppose," Margaret replied. At least she didn't have to worry about a dowry; however, choosing a compatible husband, well, that was another matter. It was hard to believe that only three years ago she was living at the convent with other intellectual women discussing history, science, and politics. Back then, the idea of marriage seemed stifling and unappealing. Her career was just beginning, but as a single woman, she was unable to access many of the people she wanted to interview. Having a well-connected husband socially certainly provided her with the opportunities she had been denied.

The night Alex proposed to her, they had been walking back to the convent. She thought he was joking. Then he said it again.

"Be my wife and sit next to me on my throne." Alex got down on his knee and opened a small gray box, revealing a ring with a tiny diamond stone.

Alex appeared suitable enough. He was a smart and ambitious lawyer; and furthermore, he seemed truly smitten with her. She had known then and there that getting married would solve many of her problems, but she had hesitated.

"I promise, if you marry me, I will always love you and provide you with a life you could not have imagined," Alex had said.

She was amused by his romantic talk and his confidence back then, but it was his support of her writing career that ultimately convinced her to marry him. She had been quite lucky in that respect. Most women she knew were destined to live in the shadow of their husbands, whereas she was able to move about and enjoy her own success. However, her freedom did have its price.

"We all make concessions, don't we?" Margaret replied.

For a brief moment Margaret's thoughts drifted to Michael. Now, *he* was truly a prize. Any woman would be lucky to be married to a gentleman with such integrity and compassion, not to mention his charm.

Ah, if only she could create a whole new life to step into whenever she wanted instead of just taking someone else's name to make her byline palatable to her readers. If she could assume an entirely different persona, she could drift from one scenario to another without the watchful eyes of others passing judgment upon her. Unfortunately, such things were not possible for her, and she was stuck with the life she had chosen.

As they traveled up the hill, Margaret saw tiny whitewashed homes along the edges of a patchwork of green spreading out into a valley below. A forest protruded from the wrinkles in the hills, providing an uneven border across the land. There was even a thread of a river wandering out into the open only to vanish again behind a hill.

"Oh, look there." Delia pointed out the open carriage window. Margaret watched as a deer disappeared deep into a clump of aspens on the side of the road. Through an opening in the forest, a flock of birds flew off into the sky. Margaret smiled. She was glad she had decided to accept Delia's invitation.

"You must see some of the old castles while you are touring the countryside, though most are in a deplorable state," Delia continued, and then spoke of dinner parties at Avondale and the many cricket games played on the grounds when Charles was young, but Margaret only half listened. She was looking forward to having a bath, and then sitting in a comfortable chair by the fire wiggling her toes.

Eventually the carriage passed through turreted gates and traveled down a winding avenue lined with beech trees. The horses stopped in front of a two-story Georgian structure with granite pillars on both sides of the entrance. When she stepped out of the carriage, Delia was warmly greeted by Mr. and Mrs. Gaffney who managed the house and the grounds. Other staff included a housekeeper, a cook, and the cook's assistant.

"We have only a small staff, but then there is hardly anyone here anymore. Charles isn't married, and he spends most of his time in London."

When the door closed behind her, Margaret could see the entry was quite large with high ceilings that went up to the second floor.

It was painted brick-red with white molding. Above was a balcony from which one could peer down upon guests or perhaps have musicians perform for a ball taking place below. Like branches on a tree, a rack of elk antlers protruded from one wall.

"Those are the largest ones in the world. Charles's grandfather found them here on the property in the bog. They are extremely old, as I recall. These are from his many hunting adventures." Delia gestured to the animal skulls on the wall. "Not my cup of tea, though."

Several Irish flags hung down from poles mounted high above on one of the walls. Margaret admired an old dark green flag decorated with a golden bare-busted angel on the front of a harp. A newer plain yellow, white, and green flag hung next to it.

"Let me give you a tour. This is the sitting room where we do our visiting. It has a marvelous view of the countryside."

Margaret glanced around. The room was furnished with antique tables and chairs. Several well-placed sofas were arranged for conversation near the fireplace. The room curved out in a semi-circle with three windows through which she could see the lawn and the hills and valley below.

"The famous Italian painter Bossi did the art around the mantel. You can see where he signed it if you look." Delia pointed to a scribble in the corner of one of the embellished white tiles. "The library is in the next room. We have quite a collection of books from around the world and in many languages. I feel reading is most important in developing the mind. Don't you agree?"

The dining room reminded Margaret of a cameo with its Georgian design. It was painted a pale aqua blue with white plaster branches and oval frames decorating religious paintings on the walls. She had no idea that Delia ate in rooms like this. How could she not dress for dinner in here?

Charles arrived in the early evening. He only politely acknowledged Margaret, then excused himself and disappeared.

"Forgive him, dear," Delia told Margaret. "He is no doubt tired after spending the last few days arguing in Parliament."

It was just as well, Margaret thought, for she had her mind on other things and didn't want to force herself to play the role of interested guest with Delia's son.

After a warm relaxing bath, Margaret put on one of her finer dresses. She went to the dining room where she joined Delia for a hearty dinner of fowl, various greens, turnips, and berry pie with clotted cream. Charles had chosen to eat alone in his room. Delia decided to retire early and left Margaret to entertain herself.

Intrigued by the library when on her tour, Margaret entered to pick out a book to read. Everywhere she looked there were books: on tables, the floor, and the shelves that covered the walls. Stepping over the piles, she bent down, browsing their titles. There was no rhyme or reason to their order. It was as though someone had read them and tossed them aside rather than put them back in any kind of logical order. Picking through them, she found books written in French, German, and Italian. Hidden amongst a pile in the corner she found a book of poems by Thomas Moore. Happy with her find, she retired to her room.

The sweet, smoky aroma of the burning sod from her fireplace greeted Margaret when she opened the door. Several oil lamps flickered, casting shadows on the wall. Her dresses had been pressed and now hung neatly in the open wardrobe. A four poster bed decorated with a print fabric sat facing the window. There was a dressing table with a mirror and a small writing desk with an ornate crystal ink pot, a blotter, and a powder shaker to absorb excess ink next to it. Margaret assumed the landscape pictures that adorned the walls where painted by Anna Parnell. Delia had bragged during dinner that Anna was an accomplished artist and would often come to Avondale to paint.

Margaret opened her satchel to retrieve her journal. A wad of paper fell out—the paper she had tossed in there with Michael's name written in several places. She crumpled it up again and threw it in the fireplace then sat down holding her shoulders and watched it burn. When there was nothing left, she got up, walked to the window, pulled the curtain back, and stared out into the darkness.

Chapter 6

I N THE MORNING a mist hung in the air, blotting out the valley below. Margaret put on her coat and walked around the yard and adjoining garden. The outline of trees standing guard around the estate looked like mystical giants. Margaret sat on a stone bench and stared off into the illusion of emptiness. She wondered what the future held for her. She was already feeling her life change ever so slightly, like the hour hand on a timepiece moving slowly to the next number.

Avondale would be her residence for the next few days. Then, she would be off exploring Ireland for the next month and a half. It wasn't a lot of time, only sufficient to get a glimpse, but it would have to suffice. Alex would be waiting for her when she got back. She pushed thoughts of him aside, not wanting to tarnish her new experiences with his fingerprints.

That evening the sound of voices led Margaret downstairs and into the sitting room. She assumed that Delia and Charles were discussing politics again. They seemed to enjoy bantering about the issues surrounding Ireland.

"Come in, come in." Delia patted the upholstered stool next to her. "Would you care for a glass of Madeira?" She waved her hand at Charles to pour Margaret a drink.

"No, thank you." Margaret moved toward the stool but then stopped. The man facing the window possessed dark curly hair and was about the same height and weight as Michael. The sun was just beginning to give way to the darkness outside, and it was possible that her eyes could be deceiving her.

"Have you met our famous rebel, Michael Davitt?" Delia smiled, motioning him over to Margaret.

Michael turned toward Margaret. He stroked his mustache, hiding his grin, then winked and gave her a slight bow. "Good evening, Mrs. Sullivan. It is a pleasure to see you again."

"Oh, I see you have already met." Delia arched her eyebrows, and her smile dropped to a line.

"We met on the ship coming over." Margaret nodded politely. "I interviewed Mr. Davitt for a project I'm working on."

"Shall we continue?" Charles took a draw on his cigar, then sat down in an overstuffed chair.

Margaret couldn't understand why so many people admired Charles. She found him cold, self-possessed, almost British in his snobbery.

"Michael was telling us about his idea to unite Ireland," said Delia. "It is one of the better plans I've heard, and I've listened to plenty in my day." Delia raised her glass toward Michael in salute.

"When I was a child, Mother was known for aiding and abetting a few rebels." Charles whirled the liquid in his glass. "However, now that she spends her time in America, she is denied the opportunity to stir up trouble. Not enough rebels there to socialize with, I'm afraid."

Michael's eyebrows rose at the comment. Margaret, too, knew there were plenty of rebels roaming America and spouting off about revenge, most of it talk bolstered by alcohol.

"Yes, and I recall you doing your best to chase them away. And now look at you, courting their vote." Delia replied curtly.

"Please, Mother." He slammed his glass down on the table.

"I'm sorry. Continue, Michael dear." Delia made an exaggerated pout at Margaret and then smiled.

Michael moved to the center of the room with the grace and ease of a refined gentleman. Margaret watched him as he spoke. He looked quite handsome in his dark suit and ascot, she noted.

"Ireland's freedom will come when each and every tenant can live without fear of eviction. We must stop this feudal system run by the wealthy. They are bleeding the people of any hope for the future."

"Bless their hearts. The peasants here would rather starve than lose their homes." Delia leaned over to Margaret. "These last three years have been especially hard because of all the rain. Everyone is talking about another famine. They'll have no money to pay rent, and if we don't do something, the poor dears will end up dying in the streets."

"It is time for people to stand up to their landlords and refuse to be bullied into paying their outrageous rents." Michael brought his fist down on the mahogany table close to him. "If we organize everyone to act peacefully in protest, as one body, I believe we could create the necessary leverage to change the laws to protect tenants across Ireland from these ridiculous rents."

"I agree. It is time those selfish men started treating the Irish with respect." Delia sat up in her chair, then reached for her glass and gulped down its contents.

Michael now stood in front of Charles. "If you consent to the position of the president of our new organization representing tenants' rights, it would give us a voice in government and further our cause considerably."

"I'm concerned about the motives of this organization." Charles jumped up and paced the floor. "I don't want to be associated with a group that promotes violence." He stopped and looked at Michael. "It could jeopardize my political career, and I'm not going to let that happen."

"I am not suggesting the use of violence. Quite the opposite, I assure you. If everyone refused to pay unfair rent increases or to do any business with those landlords who evict their tenants, landlords everywhere would be forced to act more justly or risk working the farms themselves. When Irishmen everywhere recognize their own power through united action, we will be able to free Ireland."

Margaret found herself fascinated by Michael's plan. "I think that is a brilliant idea," she commented. She loved being around intelligent men. It was one of the reasons she had become a journalist.

"How many people do you expect will participate?" Judging by his softened tone, apparently Charles was warming to the idea.

"I'll organize a meeting and post fliers. We will have a better idea once we see the response."

"Dear, that might draw too much attention and give the authorities a reason to arrest you again," said Delia.

"She does have a point, Michael," said Charles. "You are on probation."

"Is there some way to make it appear the ideas originated from the people, rather than you?" Margaret suggested. "It is a tactic I've seen used many times by politicians in America."

Delia leaned forward. "If we rely on Michael's reputation to bring people together and have him write the speech, I'm sure we could find someone to deliver it."

"Is there anything I can do?" Margaret started thinking of other newspapers she could send articles to.

"If you feel inclined to volunteer, I would suggest you help Delia raise money in America." Michael's eyes focused so intently on Margaret, she had to turn away.

Delia turned to Charles. "I will get your sisters involved with fund-raising." She looked at Michael. "Fanny is quite good at that sort of thing, and you know how much she adores you and hates the British. It will give Anna something to do, as well."

"I don't think women should be involved." Charles got up and refilled his glass from the decanter. "It isn't dignified, and besides, it would look like we were hiding behind a bunch of petticoats."

"Must you be so old fashioned? In America, women do all sorts of things. Look at Margaret. She has a successful career as a journalist. And Fanny is quite the poet." Delia's lips tightened in disgust.

Charles walked to his mother and lowered his face in front of hers. "I don't want women meddling where they don't belong," he said through gritted teeth.

"I agree with Delia," Michael replied, "There is much they could do. If women get involved, the men will also. Your help would be most appreciated, ladies." Michael bowed to Margaret and Delia.

Delia's nose went up in triumph. "Obviously, Michael appreciates the value of a woman."

"I still don't approve," Charles grumbled.

Margaret asked, "What are you going to call this organization?"

"The Land League," Michael replied.

In the privacy of her room, Margaret laughed. She was excited, almost euphoric about the evening. After slipping into her nightdress, she whirled around the room. She had witnessed the beginnings of an organization that could change the fate of a country. Michael would unite Ireland and lead the Irish resistance, and she would be a part of it. In a few days, she would tour the island for which she would be raising money. She would write about Ireland's struggles and solicit support from the various Irish-American organizations across the United States.

Eager to record her thoughts, Margaret flipped the pages of her journal looking for a blank page. A knock at the door startled her. She set her pen down. Clutching her robe to her chest, she walked over and opened the door.

"I wanted to say goodbye and thank you." Michael stood in the entrance looking sheepishly at Margaret. "I'll be leaving early in the morning."

"Must you run off so soon? Again." Margaret was surprised at Michael's appearance at her door, but even more confused by his tendency to run off and hers to wonder why.

"I'm sorry I ended things abruptly on the boat. You were full of questions and I was without answers."

"O'Doul?" Margaret wasn't sure what to ask.

"He was a good man. Unfortunately, he found himself in the middle of something he didn't know anything about."

She backed away from the door, and he stepped inside and closed it.

"Oh, was that Sean man part of this too?" Margaret asked.

"Sean was an informer; however, O'Doul didn't know that. An IRB member thought O'Doul might have been in partnership with Sean, and rather than hear him out, a senseless murder was committed. I had to calm things down. I couldn't have a riot break out onboard. We would have all ended up in jail when we got to port."

"I thought you weren't a member of the IRB anymore."

"Well, you were mistaken."

Having him alone in her room made her uncomfortable. "I just wasn't ready to say goodbye." Words felt foreign in her mouth. "I…" A flood of emotions left her mute.

"I hope you weren't expecting…"

An ache rose up from deep within her. "I don't know what I expected." Her voice cracked. She turned her back to him and walked to the desk. "I guess I forgot who we were, who I was. It was foolish of me."

His fingers sent a jolt through her as they touched her shoulder. "Maggie…, Margaret, please don't…"

She let go of her robe, then dropped her hands to her side. The truth had peeled her thin veneer away, leaving her emotions exposed. She had always known they could never be together. "I understand. I just…"

His whiskers touched the side of her neck. The exhale of his warm breath traveled down the peaks of her breast bringing a wave of desire over her. He turned her around, then lifted her face. His pupils dilated. She licked her lips then parted them. He looked at her wantonly. Could he see how defenseless she was? She shut her eyes hoping to hide behind her tight lids.

He brought her bare forearm up to his mouth and then dragged his soft lips slowly down the inside to her wrist. Her body quivered. She felt his warm moist tongue taste the salt in her palm, and then he gently kissed the center. "Please God, forgive me." He gave out a deep sigh. "I… I have no right to be here." Then he folded her fingers, closing her hand. "I must go now."

"Don't," she cried softly under her breath.

She heard the door close behind him.

Margaret collapsed onto the chair, shaken and unsure of what had just taken place. Putting her hands to her face she covered her eyes and pushed on her lids, trying to prevent her emotions from closing in on her. She didn't know if she should be relieved or not. Her body throbbed. His kiss had stirred up a dormant desire, and now she longed for a different life. His kiss had revealed a passion and tenderness. A passion she could only hunger for, but not feast on. Michael's kiss was a memory of Ireland she would treasure forever.

Chapter 7

WHEN MARGARET GOT off the train, a small, odd, two-wheeled horse-drawn wagon with a bench on each side for passengers was waiting to take her into the countryside. Apparently people in Ireland used such contraptions, like a poor man's trolley. Her one trunk was placed in the middle of the jaunty cart while she waited. She wore her gray travel suit and a pair of comfortable shoes in case she decided to walk. Sauntering around the cart, she chose a seat facing the left side of the road, then hopped on. Perhaps tomorrow she would ride on the right side.

The day started with all the magic and mystery Margaret hoped for. Children on their way to school waved as Margaret passed by. A long row of sturdy two-story houses on both sides of the street created a wall to the edge of town. A church on a hill sat watching over them. Everything Margaret saw appeared to be in contrast to her life in Chicago. Here people moved about slowly against a backdrop of green, instead of busying themselves with deal-making in a world of gray.

A half hour out of town, Margaret encountered barefoot adolescent girls carrying bundles of sticks on their backs. Then she passed a man with a string tied to the back leg of a pig as he guided the animal along with a switch. A donkey cart filled with baskets of potatoes passed them going the opposite direction, and several young boys pushed carts brimming with dried peat from a bog.

Off in a meadow, a flock of birds took flight. Sheep grazing in a rocky glen called to one another in the distance. Further down the hill, stone cottages sat scattered along the road. The setting was so very foreign to Margaret, as though she was walking the pages of a child's fairytale.

Over the next several weeks, Margaret explored the old ruins of castles and monasteries, walked the high cliffs of the coast, and traversed the rocky hills where the soil was only six inches deep. She watched the sky change by the hour from heavenly blue to white and gray thunderheads, and witnessed the rain go from a heavy mist to a downpour, and then disappear as quickly as it came. While on her adventure, she also ate a fair amount of fresh fish, mutton, and potatoes.

The people were friendly everywhere she went regardless of their circumstances. After they learned her name and why she was traveling, they were eager to talk and hard to stop. They filled her ears with tales of cruel landlords who owned the homes of everyone in the community.

"That place down the road once belonged to Ryan." The dark-haired man in a dirty knitted cap pointed to a stone home that looked like so many others Margaret had seen. "His landlord tripled his rent simply because Ryan, a fine man and a hard worker he is, improved it. But, like the rest of us, he couldn't afford the increase, so he was tossed out, forced to take another place down the road a half a mile." The old man scratched his whiskers on the right side of his face and scrunched his eye above. "Now he is afraid to fix anything for fear the same thing will happen again. So, the roof leaks and his floor is covered with straw to hide the mud. The place is more fit for a pig, than a man." He spat on the ground. "I guess that is how they see us—as animals, without dignity."

Over and over she heard such stories about evictions. A humble old farmer she met in Kerry told her, "A man by the name of O'Maoileoin, who was the gentlest of souls, got behind in his rent. He was turned out, and his wife and family had to seek shelter in those mountains." He pointed with his swollen and crooked index finger to the scraggly barren land that rose to the north. "This burned him up inside, and so he took his family back to his old home. As a result, they hauled him off to Tralee Gaol for three months. A neighbor took in his wife and daughter. I took in a couple of his boys. When he was released, we had ourselves a celebration. It could have happened to anyone of us." The farmer crossed himself then tipped his hat. "You tell those of us who went to America we miss them and not to forget us." He winked at her. "May God bless you and guide you home."

Margaret watched as the old farmer trudged up the hill with his dog to fetch his sheep. She climbed back in her carriage.

Margaret's thoughts turned to her relatives. Her maiden name was Buchanan. She had been told they lived in Drumquinn, County Tyrone in the north. Her mother rarely spoke about the Buchanan side of the family. Margaret had learned from her older brother that the Buchanans were Protestant and owned a successful manufacturing business. Without his parents' consent, Margaret's father converted to Catholicism in order to marry her mother. This created a rift in the family and after her father's death the Buchanan's didn't interfere when Margaret's mother packed up and departed for America

Margaret didn't know if anyone on her mother's side of the family was still in Ireland. Perhaps they were scattered like seeds in the wind to be planted wherever there was nourishment. Margaret felt like an orphan in the land of her birth.

A poster announcing an upcoming land rights meeting in a place called Irishtown was tacked up outside the bakery. After reading it, Margaret smiled. She had no doubt that Michael had a hand in organizing the event. She went inside and purchased some currant cake to eat later. On her way back to the hotel, a group of young men marched by—traveling to Irishtown, she assumed.

"Wait," Margaret called. "Would any of you gentlemen happen to be members of the IRB?" she said when she caught up with them.

They looked at her queerly. "Now why would a lady be asking such a question?" one man replied.

"Because I support land rights and happen to know Mr. Davitt."

"Ah, so you think that entitles you to the confidences of the IRB, do ya?" One man laughed, scooting his hat back on his head to reveal shiny black hair.

"No, I only want a button from the shirt of a man that has sworn his allegiance to IRB and the freedom of Ireland."

"What you want a button for?" A cocky, young blond-haired man stepped forward.

"For luck," Margaret told him.

"Well, you should be giving me something for luck if I give you my button." He yanked the black orb from his jacket, breaking the threads, and held it out for her.

Margaret searched her pocket, but didn't know what to give him.

"How about a kiss?" one of the other men suggested, pushing the boy forward.

"All right." Margaret walked over to the now grinning young man. He leaned in with his arms behind his back and she gave him a peck on the cheek.

"Woo," the other men yelled, jostling the man between them. Embarrassed, he handed Margaret his tiny button.

Laughing amongst themselves, they waved goodbye and continued down the road. Margaret examined the black button, thrilled with her new keepsake.

Though the railroad was heading toward Dublin, Margaret got off at one of the smaller stops and spent the night in a modest town. After traveling with various locals pointing out the sights, Margaret was determined to visit some of the villages and hamlets on her own, unaccompanied by a guide. She had been slowly moving her way back east and was now not more than a day or two from Rathdrum. Her trip was winding down, and she wanted to savor every moment and travel at her own pace.

This morning the sun was shining, and with hardly a cloud in the sky, Margaret felt a two-wheeled, open-air cart would be sufficient for the rest of her journey. She paid the price of the rental and promised to have someone from Avondale return it after she reached Rathdrum. A thin man in a tattered stovepipe hat put her trunk in the back and covered it with an oiled cloth. Her leather satchel sat inside the trunk for safe keeping, as she did not want to risk it falling out of the cart because of a bump in the road. If she needed to, she could always stop and access it later.

"A lady such as yourself shouldn't be traveling alone on this road." Mrs. Derby, the innkeeper's wife, stood at the door shaking her head. "What if something happened?"

"The people in Ireland are most generous and will help me if the occasion arose," Margaret insisted.

"You are both foolish and stubborn. Most ladies would want a gentleman along, at least a driver or man servant."

"I appreciate your concern. However, I'm quite capable of handling the horse on my own." She may look like a spoiled upper class woman, she thought, but she was an American and didn't need pampering. After all, she was a modern woman.

Margaret climbed into her cart and gave the horse the command she had heard her guides use, "Walk on." The horse moved forward, taking her out to the main road where she turned right and headed east.

Ancient stone walls guided her through the shadows of ruins; buildings broken apart by battles generations ago. The remnants of an ivy-covered castle stood decaying in the distance as blackbirds swirled around overhead, riding the current. Her horse continued on past gates of stately homes and through downtrodden villages on her day's adventure.

According to what she had read, the area around her had been the site of battles for many centuries, but now it lay barren and quiet. The land did not appear bountiful, but the efforts peasants made to cultivate nevertheless seemed endearing. As the cart bounced along, Margaret hummed one of the Irish ballads she had sung with Michael on the boat.

As she approached a small village she noticed the air was peppered with odors of peat, dirt, grass, manure, and something else she could not identify. Then Margaret caught a whiff of smoke. Ahead a billow of black ascended into the blue sky. The closer she got to the village, the more anxious she became and shortly the faint sound of screams and pleas found their way to her ears. She snapped her whip and the horse picked up speed.

When she arrived in the village, she found the people running through the streets and weeping. She watched in horror as the remnants of a household were flung from the entrance of a cottage. Splintered handmade tables, stools, and even a cooking pot with someone's meal lay splattered on the ground. A trail of rubble was strewn across the road as men in uniform went from one house to the next, gutting each in turn of their contents.

Angry flames reached toward the sky as they consumed one thatched roof after another. A man armed with only a broom swung at a soldier on horseback. A young boy threw rocks, desperately trying to stop the destruction. A mother fled with a crying baby in her arms. Several families carrying only what they could manage on their shoulders scurried down the road like crabs.

Spotting an officer, Margaret jumped down from her carriage.

"Stop! I demand that you stop right now," she yelled.

The thin man wearing a uniform and an officer's hat put out his arms, standing like a cross, in an attempt to prevent her from passing.

"I apologize for the inconvenience and your delay, madam," he said. "Nevertheless, you will need to wait until we are finished."

Margaret marched past the feeble barrier of his arms. "I demand to speak to the man in charge." A barking dog ran by her looking for its owner.

Two uniformed men on horses trotted over.

"Please, stop," Margaret demanded, pulling on the sleeve of one of officers. "What could they have possibly done to deserve this?" she asked.

"You know the rules. They haven't paid their rent. We are clearing them out, that's all."

The other man on horseback circled her. His face was harsh and held a scowl. "A lady like you shouldn't be concerned about these peasants." He spit on the ground in front of her as his horse restlessly shifted its weight. Then he kicked the horse in the ribs and it took off up the road.

"There must be someone here who can stop this," Margaret demanded, but she could tell from the grins of the other uniformed men that they had no intention of stopping.

Not far away, an officer pointed in the direction of several homes. He was speaking with a man and Margaret could hear their angry voices as she approached. Apparently the authorities were going to clear all the cottages lining the road. Margaret lifted her skirt and ran over to the officer. "I beg of you to stop this right now."

"We are just doing our job, mum," one of the henchmen replied from behind her.

"She's come to cause trouble," yelled another officer. "Get her out of the way." He motioned to a couple of other men.

A man grabbed Margaret by the waist and lifted her off the ground. Then she felt herself falling. She landed in a pile of muck on the side of a house.

"Ha, you're not so righteous now, are you?" The man laughed.

She leaned on a stump and pulled herself up. There was nothing else to wipe the muck from her gloves on and so she picked up a clump of straw from the ground and rubbed it between her palms until most of the dirt was off.

Margaret spotted a cottage that didn't appear to have been destroyed by the soldiers yet. Maybe she could save this one, she thought, and stomped off in that direction.

Inside, she found a single open room with a fireplace on one wall. The only light entered from the doorway and four tiny broken windows, leaving the contents of the room hidden in shadows. It appeared empty except for a couple of baskets and some trash scattered about. Margaret peered through one of the openings out into the backyard. A frightened milk cow stood against the far wall. Suddenly, a man in uniform appeared in the yard. He approached the cow, pulled out a knife, and sliced the back tendons of the poor animal's legs. Then he wiped the blade with a kerchief, climbed over the wall, and disappeared. The cow cried out in pain as it tried to stand up. Blood stained the ground. Margaret had to turn away.

There was a whoosh and blast of heat from above. Margaret froze. There was another sound she could not identify. Perhaps it was a frightened animal. She listened, but all she heard was crackling. The smell of burning grass filled her nose and her eyes began watering. There was that sound again, whimpering. Through her tearing eyes, she carefully scrutinized the room. Then she spotted a child huddled with his arms covering his head and weeping. Pieces of flaming straw rained down all around Margaret. A cloud of dark smoke gushed down, filling the room. Margaret lost sight of the child and desperately felt around for him. The flames were spreading rapidly. A cinder landed on the edge of her skirt. She smacked it with her hand. The roar overhead became louder. She couldn't see. There were voices yelling outside.

"James? James?" a woman screamed. "My son. Where is my son?"

Part of a beam crashed down next to Margaret. Orange flames closed in. She could smell her dress burning.

The room became a blur and she couldn't breathe. She dropped to her knees.

Someone gripped her arms and dragged her out.

Her lungs ached as she tried to inhale. An old man stood over her. The sleeves of his shirt were black where the fire had eaten them.

"The child," Margaret coughed. "Is the child safe?"

"Are you all right?" the man asked.

"The child? Is he…"

The man pointed.

A sobbing woman leaned over the body of the boy. The clumps of singed hair lay matted on his forehead and his arms were both red and black, blisters forming along their length.

Margaret stretched out her arms and the strange man pulled her to her feet. "He needs a doctor." Margaret frantically looked around and pleaded, "Please, someone get a doctor."

"There is no doctor here, and if there was," the child's mother peered up at Margaret, "we have no money to pay him."

"Where is my carriage?" Margaret glanced down the road of the village. The shell of stone and plaster buildings lay smoldering against the bright blue sky. A few people milled about, picking through piles of rubble in the street looking for something of value. Apparently, the soldiers had moved on, leaving these poor peasants to deal with the remnants of their lives.

A balding man with a scruffy beard and no hat appeared from behind a gutted house, leading Margaret's horse and cart toward her.

Margaret ran to him. "We must get the boy to a doctor. Do you know where we can find one?"

"Aye, I do." He wiped his hand on his britches then extended it. "Murphy's the name."

"Could you drive up there? I will pay you."

"No charge, mum. It would be my privilege to help the boy."

The child was lifted carefully and placed into his mother's arms as she sat in the back of the cart on top of Margaret's trunk. Margaret settled in next to them. The boy suffered in silence, but his mother sobbed for him. If I could only take away someone else's pain, Margaret thought. She placed her arm around the young mother, trying to comfort her. Murphy climbed in, took the reins, and they galloped off to the nearest village in search of a doctor.

Chapter 8

MARGARET SAT WITH Emma, the boy's mother, in the stark room of the medical office. Dr. Keller carefully cleaned and bandaged five-year-old James's arms. The poor child, no doubt, would carry those scars for the rest of his life. But at least God granted him more time on earth, Margaret thought, and she uttered a prayer of gratitude.

"Here are bandages and ointment. Remember to change them every day until his arms heal. Make sure his arms stay dry." Dr. Keller handed the boy's mother a bundle. When James stood up, a button from the front of his burnt shirt was dangling by a thread.

Margaret leaned over to James. "Is it all right if I keep this?" She held out the smoked-stained button between her fingers so he could see it.

He nodded.

"I will treasure it. Thank you." Margaret winked at him then put her new token in her pocket.

"I think I can find the boy a different shirt." Dr. Keller returned moments later with a worn shirt several sizes too big for the child. With his scissors, the doctor cut off James's old shirt along with the arms below the elbow of the new shirt. Carefully, he slipped the new shirt over James's bandages. Margaret then buttoned two of the buttons to keep the shirt closed in the front.

"Thank you," Margaret said to the doctor. She smiled at James. "Your arms will heal in no time and then you will be able to play again."

"Oh, mum, I don't know how to thank you for doing this for us. You are an angel sent from God." Emma's sincerity tugged at Margaret.

"I'm glad I was there to help." Margaret cringed at the thought of what would have happened had she not gone into that house.

"I will forever be in debt to you for saving my son. My husband will repay you when he finds a job."

Margaret knew Emma was telling the truth, but she couldn't allow it. "You don't owe me anything."

Margaret could tell from Emma's looks that she was frightened. Who wouldn't be afraid in her shoes? Where was she going to go? How was she going to live? She couldn't be more than twenty years old, and with an injured child her chances of finding any kind of work were slim to nil. Emma had mentioned to her earlier that her husband had gone to Dublin in search of work and so Margaret knew the young woman was on her own. Margaret sighed.

Margaret paid Dr. Keller and then walked with Emma and James to the parish church two blocks away. She decided not to go into the sanctuary and instead they went around to the side door in hopes of finding a priest to help. Margaret pounded on the wooden door until finally it opened.

"Is it possible for this woman and child to stay the night here? They have nowhere else to go."

A milk-white hand lined with blue veins poked through a crack in the door and motioned her away. "We are overflowing with people as it is."

Half a face peeked at her from behind the edge of the door. His eyes were bloodshot and his lids drooped along with the rest of his face. The old priest started to close the door.

Margaret put her hand up to prevent its closure. "Father, I beg of you. Show mercy on them. Please."

Looking down at the boy's arms, then back up at Margaret again, the priest opened the door wide so they could pass. "I'm sure we can find a place." His voice was hoarse, almost a whisper.

The priest's robe hung on him like a hand-me-down and his cross swayed as though it was a heavy weight. Motioning her to follow him, he teetered along a dark hall. The stone building smelled of mildew, incense, and candle wax. The priest pushed open a door leading to an outside courtyard.

"There is an abbey next door." He pointed to a large stone building. "The nuns will help you."

Margaret crossed the courtyard and knocked on the door. After a moment, a nun opened the door and let them in.

"I see you need help. I'm Sister Mary Joseph. Follow me."

Candles flickered, casting ghostly shadows on the wall. The sound of their footsteps echoed as they walked the stone hallway. Sister Mary Joseph stopped at an entryway. Peering inside, Margaret saw it was a large room but lacked windows. A crucifix hung on the central wall. The room felt stuffy and was cramped with people dressed in rags huddled on the floor. Children clung to their families, most of their faces gaunt from too many days without food.

"What will happen to them?" Margaret asked.

"Some will go to the workhouse and others will try to find relatives to stay with. Several will go to England in search of work there. Some, if they are lucky, the government will load into the belly of a ship bound for America," the nun answered.

Margaret dug through her pocket for money and handed the nun all she had. "Please see that they find a place to live." She gave her one of her calling cards too. "I would also appreciate it if you would notify me of their address, so that I can keep abreast of the boy's progress."

The nun nodded. "Of course. As you wish."

Margaret bent and kissed James's cheek. "You will be fine. Your mother will take good care of you." She hugged Emma. "Things will get better. I promise."

"God bless you," Emma replied.

Margaret bit her lip so as not to shed tears of her own in front of them. Feeling nauseous, she quickly ran down the hall to the exit.

She stood trembling outside, her back to the door. Taking in a breath then slowly exhaling, she regained her composure. She spied a path to the street as light rain fell. The street lamps were now lit, giving the town a gray glow. Margaret stood there in front of the church wondering what to do now. She remembered passing a hotel on the way to the church. The moisture felt good on her skin as she walked past the shops on her way to the building with the words "Moylan Hotel" painted on the front. It had been a long day, and she was looking forward to a bath and a good night's rest.

"I'm sorry, mum, but if you don't have money to pay, you can't stay here." The hotel clerk stared over the top of her wire frame glasses at Margaret.

Margaret searched her pockets again. They were empty of paper and coins. There was only the button from James's shirt inside. "I'm sure that Mrs. Parnell will cover the expenses." Margaret smiled at the woman. "You do know of the Parnells? Charles Stewart Parnell is a Member of Parliament."

The woman tapped her fingers on the counter impatiently. "You should try the place down the road. It is more for people like you." Her British accent was thick with sarcasm.

"People like me? I've stayed at some of the finest hotels." Margaret glared at the woman. "Much nicer establishments than this, I must say."

The woman laughed. "My dear, you certainly don't look like no lady to me."

Margaret looked down at her coat which was streaked with dirt. Burn holes revealed charred lace on the dress she wore underneath. The palms of her gloves were blackened with soot. She touched her head and realized her hat was missing. No wonder this woman doubted her social status. She must look horrid.

"You go along now and find yourself some other place for the night." The woman laughed again. "Maybe some gentleman will take pity on you and provide you a bed."

"How dare you." Margaret wanted to slap the woman's face. She had never been spoken to with such crudeness before.

"If you don't leave now, I'll have someone throw you out." The woman leaned over the polished counter. "Get."

Margaret stood outside on the street. She wasn't going back to the church. The only option was to try to make it back to Avondale. The man who drove her to town had left hours ago and so she would need to drive herself. She walked to where the rented cart was hitched and untied the reins, climbed into the driver's seat, and snapped the whip. The horse trotted, pulling the cart quickly back and forth over the cobblestone street several times. She had no idea which road to take.

"Excuse me," she called to a woman lingering outside of a saloon. "Could you direct me to the road to Rathdrum?" The woman approached Margaret. Her face was painted and she was dressed in a low-cut frock.

"Aye." The woman looked up at her. "Buy me a drink?"

"I have spent my last shilling, I'm afraid." Margaret couldn't believe she was speaking to the woman.

In a matter of seconds the woman leaped onto Margaret's carriage, knocking her down. Margaret could smell the woman's foul breath inches away from her face. The woman straddled her skirt, shoving her hands into Margaret's pockets. She had bitterness in her eyes.

"You ain't got no money." The woman sat up and laughed.

"Please, let me go." Margaret had no weapon to scare off the woman; her ladies revolver was locked away inside her trunk.

"Gimmie your shoes."

"My shoes?"

"Take off them shoes or I slit your throat."

Margaret rapidly unbuttoned her shoes and handed them to the woman.

"Fair is fair." The woman climbed down, grasping Margaret's shoes to her chest. "You see that lamp post there? Go past that then turn to your right. When you come to the next saloon on the corner that road will take you to Rathdrum."

Margaret followed the directions out of town, berating herself for being so naïve as to think everyone would treat her with the respect and dignity she thought she deserved. Here, she was just a tourist, and a vulnerable one at that.

As the night wore on, the rain came down harder. Why had she chosen an open carriage? She stopped and took the oiled cloth that had been covering her trunk and put it around her shoulders. The road was now muddy and difficult to travel. More than once a wheel got stuck in a rut and she had to get down and pull on the reins to convince the stubborn horse to move.

Why hadn't she looked for another place to stay in town? She was alone on a road she didn't recognize and sopping wet, and now her shoes were on some trollop's feet. The carriage came to an abrupt stop.

"Oh, not again." Margaret climbed down to take a look at the situation. The left wheel was blocked by a large rock. There was no way she could move it. Leaning up against the carriage, she brought her hands together in prayer.

"Mother Mary, you have always shown your tender mercy to those in need, and I have witnessed those suffering more than I today. Please hear my humble prayer for assistance amongst the cries of others. Amen."

In the distance there was a crack of thunder and the rain came down harder. Margaret climbed back in the carriage and snapped the reins but the horse wouldn't move. Should she continue to sit or try walking? If she walked, at least she would be moving, she rationalized. Tired, Margaret got down again into the slop. "Each step will bring me closer to Avondale," she said out loud to bolster her spirits. No more than a few hundred yards from the wagon, pebbles in the road ate away the bottoms of her stockings and mud seeped in around her toes.

As she walked, thoughts of the day occupied her mind. Evictions in Ireland were utterly barbaric. The fact that a landlord would burn his own property to rid himself of tenants didn't make sense to her. Obviously, these wealthy land owners felt no responsibility for the welfare of the people they evicted, either. She had been told of this practice, but witnessing it was startling and beyond her previous comprehension.

In the past, she had managed to distance herself from the realities of other people's lives. Yes, she wrote about them, but it was just an intellectual exercise. Nothing touched her personally. It was not that she didn't know of the conditions in which the poor lived, but poverty was still an abstraction. "I feel so ashamed. I am no better than those I scorn." Hearing the words out loud startled her. "God, forgive me for my arrogance. I deserve to be walking this road. It is the penance that I must pay for my ignorance."

Her feet now ached, the edge of her skirt was caked with mud, and she could feel wet ringlets of hair on her shoulders.

Margaret heard the sound of a horse galloping up the road. The rider was approaching. She waved hoping whoever it was would assist her. The horse came to an abrupt stop. A man in a hooded cape got down.

"Please, sir." Margaret walked toward him. A rock pierced the bottom of her foot and she tumbled to the ground. He rushed over to her.

"Are you all right?"

Her ankle throbbed with pain. "Now look what I have done." She had never felt so helpless in her life. If this man was going to harm her, she would not be able to run away. She grasped for strength from within. She was going to have to accept her fate.

"Maggie?" He pulled the hood back.

"Michael?" Tears ran down her cheeks.

"Look at you. My dear Maggie, you have become an Irish peasant girl before my eyes," Michael said with delight. He knelt down beside her.

"Oh, Michael, I am so glad you are here." Margaret threw her arms around his neck and hugged him.

"You have never looked as beautiful as you do now," Michael said, his deep voice resonant in the rain.

If she were dreaming, she didn't want to wake up.

He pulled back and smiled. "We must get you to Avondale."

She laughed. What else could she do? The whole day seemed to be upside down. Nothing made sense anymore. Somehow, the shell around her had broken open and new experiences had poured in.

"Place your arm around my shoulder and I will help you onto my horse."

"But how will I ride? I have never ridden on top of a horse before. I don't know what to do."

Michael laughed. "You will need to hoist your skirt up and throw your leg over the animal."

"But, my skirt is too full. My bustle…" Margaret was terribly aware her cumbersome clothes were a disadvantage in this situation.

"Then, my dear, I suggest you figure out how to adjust it." He stood grinning at her.

At the moment, she said to herself, practicality was more important than propriety.

"I guess I have no choice but to remove my bustle."

"I will leave that decision to you."

Margaret could see Michael was trying hard not to laugh.

"But what will Mrs. Parnell think when she sees me without it?"

"I'm afraid your appearance has already been compromised by the weather and whatever else you got into today."

"Oh." Margaret remembered the reaction of lady at the hotel. She laughed at herself.

As modestly as she could, she lifted her skirt while trying not to put weight on her injured foot. She leaned against Michael for support as she untied her bustle and slipped it off. Her ragged and muddy clothes now hung down with only her natural body to give them shape.

Michael helped her onto his horse. The rain stopped as they made their way back to the wagon. Michael rescued Margaret's satchel for her and put the oil cloth around her trunk, which would have to be retrieved later. He lifted his cape over her shoulders to ward off any further chill, then kissed her on the cheek and helped her again onto his horse. As they traveled the road to Avondale, she wrapped her arms tightly around him, knowing the opportunity may never come again.

"Dare I ask what happened to you, my dear?" Delia's eyes went from Margaret to Michael as they stood in the entrance to Avondale.

Michael held on tightly to Margaret's waist as she leaned against him for support. "She injured her ankle," he replied with a grin.

"I twisted it," Margaret said, trying to sound confident. She pushed the wet hairs from her face.

"Her rig was stuck in the mud a few miles outside of Rathdrum. Apparently, she has been through quite a bit today."

"So it appears." Delia eyed Margaret top to bottom. "Please draw a bath for Mrs. Sullivan. And find her clean clothes to put on," Delia instructed Mrs. Gaffney. "And tell the other servants we will need their assistance for Mrs. Sullivan."

Charles walked into the room dressed in a long formal coat with a tan ascot at his neck. "Glad to see you." He put his hand on Michael's shoulder. "Mr. Devoy and Mr. Egan will be joining us later. Care for a drink?" He guided Michael in the direction of the sitting room. "I wanted to discuss the details of your new organization and my role as president."

Michael glanced back over his shoulder and nodded at Margaret. Then she watched him disappear in Charles's clutches. Michael was always being pulled away from her. Charles could have at least acknowledged her, Margaret thought. She could have been a scullery maid as far as he was concerned. Why Michael thought Charles was the man to lead his new organization was a puzzle to her. Then again, she knew of other political leaders just as witless.

"Let's get you out of those wet clothes, mum." Mrs. Gaffney stood ready with the other servants to help Margaret tidy up. She knew a sponge bath would be in order before she could submerge into the warmth of a tub.

Margaret glanced back at the entrance to the sitting room. It was safe to assume that she and Delia would not be included in the men's conversation tonight.

After her bath, Margaret dressed in the nightgown and robe that had been laid out for her. To be clean again was a wonderful luxury. Margaret sat in front of the looking glass combing her wet hair. When she held the ends to her nose, she detected a slight aroma of smoke. She inspected her hairline. Perhaps she could hide the few singed areas under a hat. Her clothes had been declared rubbish and her walking shoes now adorned the feet of some harlot. But at least she salvaged the button from James's shirt and had the memory of hugging Michael.

Mrs. Gaffney brought hot tea and a plate of food so Margaret could dine in her room. Margaret was famished and sopped up the gravy from the stew with her bread, leaving the bowl quite empty. She wondered if she should ask for another.

The front door slammed downstairs. Margaret hopped over and opened her bedroom door a crack and peeked down from the balcony. Mr. Devoy and Mr. Egan had arrived. She watched the two men shed their topcoats and hats and greet Michael and Charles. Until recently, Margaret hadn't paid attention to Ireland's exiles. However, most Irish in America knew of Mr. Devoy's reputation from the articles he wrote calling for action against the British. Margaret suspected he was a powerbroker between the rebels in Ireland and those in America, and she wondered if it was even safe for him to be in Ireland. Avondale was apparently a meeting place for rebels. If her ankle had been better, she would have found an excuse to eavesdrop downstairs. Margaret looked down at her night clothes. Well, perhaps not. Without the proper clothes, she was relegated to this room.

"Margaret?" Delia called through the adjoining door. "May I come in?" Apparently Delia's bedroom was right next door.

"Yes, please enter." Margaret limped over and sat down in one of the needlepoint chairs by the fire.

"How is your foot, dear?" Delia asked from the open doorway.

"My ankle is much better thank you."

"I brought some Madeira." She held up the bottle and two crystal glasses. "I thought you might care for a drink."

"That was very considerate of you," Margaret replied, setting her legs on the footstool.

Delia poured them both a drink and sat down opposite Margaret.

"I trust you had an interesting tour of the countryside?"

"Yes, I did." She took a sip of the Madeira and enjoyed its elegant, sweet taste.

"Please, I want to hear all about it."

Margaret spent the next hour telling Delia about her adventure, but only revealing just what she needed to know. The rest was none of her concern.

"Now that you have observed the struggles of the people firsthand, I trust you still desire to get involved with fund-raising efforts in America."

Indeed, Margaret was more committed now than when she previously volunteered.

"Of course, I will do whatever I can."

"And your book, do you intend to write about Ireland too?"

"Yes, I believe I will."

"Good, good." Delia took a sip from her glass then set it down. Leaning forward, Delia looked directly at Margaret. "Now tell me about you and Michael."

Margaret looked away. What could she say—that he had captivated her heart and that she wanted nothing more than to be with him?

"I'm not blind, my dear. I've seen the way you look at him."

She wasn't about to tell Delia about her feelings for Michael.

"As a woman who has spent time with rebels, let me give you this advice." Delia took a sip from her glass. "His passion is for his country, and no woman can steal that from him, nor should she try."

"I understand your concern. However, we are merely acquaintances." Margaret swallowed hard. "Nothing more." She knew Delia was telling the truth, but she wasn't ready to give him up.

Delia stood and walked to one of Anna's landscape paintings, colorful wild flowers springing from the ruins of a cottage doorway. "My dear, you have no idea how important Michael is to Ireland." She looked out into the room then down at Margaret. "He truly understands the needs of the people. He is one of them, and because of that, they believe in him. He gives them hope, something they so desperately need."

Emma's face popped into Margaret's mind. She ached with shame and looked up at the ceiling, hoping to keep the tears from running down her cheeks.

"If we are ever going to become a free country, it will be through the efforts of men like Michael, men willing to stand up to the British."

"And Charles?" Margaret blotted the corner of her eye with her kerchief.

"Charles?" Delia shook her head. "I know he is a Member of Parliament. Unfortunately, his sisters care more about Ireland than he does. He is just a figurehead to the Irish, someone who can blend in with the British and talk politics over tea. He could never relate to the poor, not like Michael does."

"Then why not have Michael run for Parliament?" Looking down at her hands, Margaret fingered the lace on her kerchief. She must release him, she knew, all of him.

"He is the son of a peasant who was found guilty of treason, and he is out on a ticket of release. The British would never allow him to serve."

Margaret took a deep breath and looked up. "But if the people elected him, certainly Members of Parliament would listen to him. He is highly intelligent." She remembered how passionate he was about the Land League.

"Yes, he is intelligent, more so than most men in government. But the change Ireland needs will take more effort than that of one man..." Delia turned to Margaret, "...or woman."

Margaret sat up. Her melancholy fog suddenly evaporated.

"We have to help them." Delia took Margaret's hand. "You may think I'm a crazy old woman, but there is still a fighting rebel in me. I can't think of a better way to live than right in the middle of the fight for Ireland." Delia radiated confidence and conviction.

Margaret envied her courage. She was a true patriot.

"Can we count on you?" Delia looked very serious when she made the request.

"You have my word." Margaret truly wanted to help Michael in any way she could.

"Excellent." Delia patted Margaret's hand. "You didn't think I invited you here just for the scenery, did you?"

<h1 style="text-align:center">Chapter 9</h1>

O N HER RETURN voyage to New York, Margaret spent a great deal of her time writing in her stateroom. Words flowed onto her paper as she scribbled thoughts and ideas about Ireland and this mysterious man, Michael Davitt. His compassion for the people of Ireland had seeped into her, and it was bittersweet.

She carried a cup of tea to the cabin's tiny porthole and peeked out at the sea. She took a sip. The gray ocean seemed endless, with only the horizon as a guide. She thought of her time in Ireland and of her return home and wondered which story was the myth—her time in Ireland or her life in Chicago?

Margaret turned away from the window and walked to a chair and sat down. Sadness now held her in its arms. Had her experience compromised her in some way she would regret later? What about her marriage vows to Alex? Would she ever be able to go back to her old life?

Margaret bit her lip. How could she be so foolish? Why had she allowed herself to be tempted by Michael Davitt, this incredibly charming man, and his ideas for freeing Ireland? Was she so unhappy in her marriage that she could be easily seduced by a complete stranger? The truth was obvious. There was more to her temptation than her unhappiness. She was tempted because Michael was everything Alex was not. Michael was honest, generous, and compassionate; whereas Alex was manipulative, controlling, and self-interested. How could she not want to be with a man like Michael? Nevertheless, it was wrong of her to compare the two, she told herself. It was more than wrong; it was a sin. Would God forgive her for lusting after another man? Why was she torn inside? Was it because her marriage with Alex was nothing more than a charade? Were these new feelings she was experiencing for Michael real? She had never examined her feelings before now, not for anyone or anything. Feelings weren't logical and only clouded the mind. For years, she had hidden behind her carefully constructed façade, but this trip had opened her up to a cornucopia of feelings, genuine feelings that she could not deny, which was something she had always feared. Was she now destined to a life of loneliness and anguish longing for something she could never have? Would she be able to go back to being Mrs. Alexander Sullivan?

Margaret took another sip of cold tea. She picked up the papers she had written and carefully put them in her satchel, vowing not to look at them again until she had been home at least a month.

She would need to resume her old life and pining away for a man she could never be with would only bring heartache. She took a deep breath. Her time with Michael was gone. The hand of the clock had moved to another number. She had left behind the person Michael Davitt, but not his passion for Ireland and the Land League. Those she brought back with her.

Though she hid it well, the transition back to her old life did not come easily to Margaret. She wasn't quite ready to slip into her role as Alex's wife and lover, and she tried to fend off Alex's affections the best she could.

"Can't you find time for me?" Alex complained to her from the entrance to the parlor.

"Darling, I have been busy with my writing and with my charity work." She wished he would leave her alone. He was buzzing around her like a pesky wasp.

"You know I don't like it when I don't get what I want." He came toward her with his arms out like he was herding a stray animal.

"Yes. You don't have to remind me." Margaret moved around the table avoiding him.

Alex stepped in front of her, snatching her by the waist.

"Perhaps you have left me no other choice but to seduce you right here." He pulled her toward him while she scrambled to get away.

Mrs. O'Brien brought in a tray of tea and set it down on the table. She stood there with her cold dark eyes peeking out from the folds of her skin. A tight grin crossed her face.

Alex dropped his hands and stepped back.

Margaret blushed. "Thank you, Mrs. O'Brien. That will be all for now."

"I suppose you want me to sit down and behave myself?" Alex took a chair, pulled a cigar from his pocket, and dragged it along the front of his nose, inhaling its aroma.

"That would be the gentlemanly thing to do."

"Well, tell me about your trip. We haven't discussed it since your return." He leaned back, putting his boots on the needlepoint footstool her mother had given her and lit his cigar.

"You know about the Land League," Margaret said.

"That is all I know about. You have been obsessed about the damn thing." Alex blew smoke in the air. "What about Delia? How is the old broad? Pardon me. I meant to say, the charming widow."

"She is a compelling woman and highly committed to helping the Irish. She convinced me to get involved."

"Well that is good to hear." Alex stuck his cigar in his mouth and got up and poured himself a drink from the decanter. "Ireland is a good cause to get fired up about." He stood there with his back to the table and flicked the ash from his cigar in the air, letting it fall on to the oriental carpet.

"I witnessed an eviction," Margaret said softly. The thought of that night gave her a chill. "An eviction? What's that? Some poor chump got tossed on his rump for not paying the money he owed?" He sucked his cigar between his lips.

"Yes, something similar." Margaret knew he wouldn't understand so she dropped the subject.

Mrs. O'Brien appeared at the doorway. "Dinner is served."

Alex followed Margaret into the dining room. He pulled out her chair and then walked around the wood paneled room to his chair across from her. Mrs. O'Brien set out a bounty of food before them: a succulent pork roast, gravy, baked turnips, and parsnips. When Mrs. O'Brien went to pour Margaret a glass of wine, Margaret shook her head no.

"Go ahead, Margaret. Drink up. It will make your evening more tolerable." He winked, then raised his glass and took a sip of wine.

Margaret had been back in Chicago a month already. Why weren't other newspapers running her story? Certainly her articles about the Land League were of interest in Boston and New York. She inspected the papers, going through each column before she found the article condensed and used as filler in the latest edition of the *Boston Globe*. The *Chicago Tribune* ran it on the first page where people would read it. She folded the *Boston Globe* and set it back on the table with the other editions. If the *Globe* wanted any more articles from her they should think about giving her a featured spot next time or she would send her articles to a rival paper instead.

At least her fund-raising efforts were successful. Many Catholic women from Chicago, Detroit, and Philadelphia had been recruited and were helping with donations. Locally, new Irish immigrants were giving speeches at ladies luncheons, and Father Meany had spoken to his parish not once, but twice about the Land League. If she could only get more men involved, her proceeds would triple.

Margaret retrieved an envelope from the silver tray on the table where the incoming mail was kept. Glancing to see who it was from, she picked up the pearl-handled opener and sliced the letter open.

"Alex, good news," Margaret called as she carried the stationery to the library then stood at the entrance and leaned against the door frame. "Delia Parnell sent us a report on the success of the Land League. Apparently, more than ten thousand people gathered to hear Charles Parnell and Michael Davitt speak on tenants' rights." Margaret paused, then looked at Alex. "Are you listening?"

Alex peered over the top of his newspaper. "Yes, dear. I just don't see the point. How are land rights going to make a difference in Ireland?" He scooted his chair back.

"Darling, we've discussed this before." Why couldn't he understand the importance of land rights? Margaret looked around the library. Legal papers sat in neat piles on a nearby table. He understood the finer points of debate but he could be extremely close-minded when he wanted to be.

"The only way the British are going to release Ireland is by force. Any other effort is a waste of time," Alex said. He pulled out his pocket watch, opened it, and studied the numbers for a moment before snapping it closed again. He looked up as though he was thinking about something other than their conversation.

"Must you always insist violence is the only answer?" It annoyed her. He worshiped cowboys and their aggressive ways. He read dime novels that romanticized crime, and wanted posters of outlaws decorated the wall above a bookshelf. Billy "the Kid" McCarty was his favorite because the boy was Irish and their paths once crossed in the Southwest many years ago. Alex even wore leather cowboy-styled boots most of the time. Such foolishness, she thought. This was Chicago, not New Mexico, for heaven's sake.

Alex walked over and slipped his arms around her waist like she was his saloon harlot. Margaret found his affection annoying, especially while she was trying to discuss something important like the Land League.

"You know enough about how these things work from the articles you have written over the years. One has to do more. Campaigning for land rights isn't going to accomplish anything," Alex said.

Margaret tried to free herself from him, but he only gripped her tighter. "I like it when you get all wound up in a cause." His smug look irritated her. "I've noticed a flame in your eyes ever since you got back from Ireland."

Yes, she thought, my new found passion *is* for Ireland. Perhaps now would be a good time to ask. "I know I've brought this up before…"

"Yes?" he replied. His nose traveled her neck as he inhaled her perfume.

"Everyone knows what an eloquent speaker you are." Margaret chose her words carefully. "It would mean so much to me if you would consider becoming more active with the Land League."

"You women are doing a fine job without me." He let go of her and backed up. "You have collection boxes all over the city."

"Darling," Margaret said in her most charming voice, "Ireland needs the help of all Irish-Americans, not just the women. It would certainly be good for your career. Look at how many Irishmen live here in Chicago. Don't you want to be recognized for helping Ireland?"

She watched his face for any indication he was receptive to her suggestion. Unfortunately, his expression indicated otherwise.

"I have a meeting with someone from Washington. Senator James Blaine from Maine is in town. He is planning on running for President again. Would you join us for dinner tonight?" Alex grabbed her arm and pulled her toward him again. He leaned over and whispered in her ear, "Can I entice you with the possibility of an article?"

Margaret hesitated. She had planned to work on her book tonight, but an article about Blaine sounded very tempting.

"Well?" She could feel his grip tighten.

"If you insist." Her book would have to wait. Tonight, she would play the part of the quiet and dutiful wife, lending social credibility to her husband while the men discussed business. The senator would never suspect she was a journalist. It was a game she and Alex often played.

"And please wear something fashionable and feminine that shows off your *décolletage*, not that dress with the high collar and buttons you like to wear when we go out. It is too matronly. I want him to picture me as wealthy and powerful, someone he might need in the future."

"I'll see if I can find a dress that meets with your approval," Margaret replied.

He kissed her on the cheek. "Now go get ready. I don't want to be late."

When they arrived at the restaurant, Senator James Blaine was waiting for them at a table with a drink set before him that appeared untouched. The senator stood when she approached. "It is so good to see you again Mrs. Sullivan." He gave Margaret a nod and shook her hand.

Margaret had always thought the senator resembled a billy goat with his beard and narrow, droopy eyes. He and Alex had known each other for years, as Alex had spent his childhood growing up in Maine.

"Alex tells me that you have ambitions regarding the presidency again," Margaret said while Alex pulled out her chair for her.

"Why, yes. I plan to be one of the contenders at the 1880 Republican Convention if all goes according to plan."

"It was unfortunate that the Union Pacific Railroad debacle undermined your ability to rally enough support in the last election," Margaret added.

"My dear wife has an interest in politics and is well-versed in the ways of government," Alex said, as he placed his napkin in his lap.

"So I see. Might the rumor be true that you are indeed a journalist writing under a different name, Mrs. Sullivan?" Blaine sat back and smiled.

Margaret looked to Alex for a clue on whether or not she should admit anything.

"Come, my dear. I follow your articles and find them quite good. Your writing is remarkably well thought out, I must say," the senator added.

Alex nodded to Margaret. "I see no harm in revealing the truth to Senator Blaine."

"Yes, I am guilty of the sin of writing under an assumed name. Sometimes I use no byline at all. But, please don't let others know our secret." She put her finger to her lips. "It has taken me a long time to establish credibility, and I wouldn't want it compromised by rumors." She hoped he wasn't planning on exposing her to his acquaintances.

"Your secret is safe with me, my dear. However, perhaps I could request that you write a favorable article about me now and then while I am campaigning?"

"Of course, she will," Alex volunteered. "Won't you darling?"

"I… I guess I could." Margaret was unsure what would be expected of her.

"Good. I will have someone send you a letter with the contents of what I would like you to print. You can, of course, rephrase it if you wish."

She preferred to generate her own thoughts in the articles she wrote, but she reminded herself that, if Blaine did become President, he could give her access to valuable information in the future, thus helping her career.

"Now that we have settled that," Alex said. "Have you given any thought to whom you might choose as your candidate for Vice President?" Alex sat back confidently, his chest puffed out.

"Let us see if I survive the convention first, and then perhaps I will look around at who would make the best running mate." Blaine took a sip of his drink.

Margaret knew Alex had lofty aspirations, but Vice President of the United States? No, she did not see that title in his future. Perhaps a different position would be a much better fit.

Chapter 10

AFTER ATTENDING A ladies luncheon in which she spoke about the hungry in Ireland, Margaret stopped off at a bakery and bought herself a pastry. Today was her birthday, which had apparently slipped Alex's mind for there was no bouquet of roses or chocolates waiting for her this morning. She preferred that he not make a fuss. She didn't need to be reminded that she was now thirty-one years old.

When she went down the hall to the bedroom, she noticed a light under the door to her study. Margaret put her ear to the door. There were sounds of something being moved around. She did not like it when someone went in there when she wasn't home. Margaret threw the door open.

"Surprise!" Alex and Mrs. O'Brien stood there grinning.

"Happy Birthday, darling." Alex gestured to a large item on a stand next to the window covered by a cloth.

Margaret went over and lifted the corner. "Oh my goodness! It's a birdcage."

She slid off the fabric, revealing an ornate metal cage. "It's beautiful." It looked like a palace with its dome roof.

"There is a bird in there," Mrs. O'Brien added. She clapped her hands in excitement.

Margaret peeked in and looked around. "Oh, so there is." A dignified bright yellow bird stared back at her.

"It's a canary. It is supposed to have a pleasant song. I thought you would like it." Alex beamed. "It came from a birdman in England."

"I am truly surprised." And she was. Normally he gave her jewelry and flowers. A bird would be a nice companion in her study, she thought. Alex had managed to amaze her. She would never have guessed that he would have given her such a gift.

"Good. Now change into something attractive for dinner. I'm taking you out."

Margaret gave Alex a peck on the cheek. "Thank you, darling."

When they arrived at the restaurant, Alex ordered roast duck in orange sauce for both of them and he requested a bottle of champagne.

"You know dear, I can't drink champagne," Margaret pleaded. In fact, one drink was enough to make her lose control. She was ashamed to admit to herself that she had lost her virginity to Alex prior to their marriage due to the fact he had gotten her drunk on champagne and seduced her. She had lived in fear for weeks that she might be pregnant, and she even requested they move up the marriage date. Now, she was well aware that she didn't need to worry about becoming pregnant. Thank God, she thought, or otherwise Alex would keep her pregnant all the time.

"Please, darling. It is your birthday. You are too much of a prude sometimes."

Margaret finally succumbed to the idea and had a sip with her dinner. And before she knew it, she was laughing too loud and gossiping to Alex about some of the stuffy ladies she had spent the day with. During dessert she noticed that, no matter how many sips she had taken, her glass never appeared anything but full. She stared at it as if it magically refilled itself. The bubbles seemed to tickle her insides. She felt as though she had no worries at all.

Margaret leaned over to say something to Alex, sending a plate crashing to the floor. She looked around to find other diners staring at her. "Alex, I'm afraid I have embarrassed you." She giggled.

"Never, my dear. I am never embarrassed with you." He laughed and reached across the table and squeezed her hand. "Come, let's go."

Outside on the street, Alex put his arm out and Margaret looped hers through his. She needed to cling to him for support. They wandered down the street under the hissing gas lamps and past stores closed for the night.

"It has been too long since we've spent time like this together," Alex told her as they strolled along. "I thought we would walk home rather than take a carriage."

Margaret could feel the effects of the champagne as they walked. Alex stopped in front of a dress shop.

"Would you like a new dress or some silk undergarments?"

Margaret lifted her skirt to her knees, exposing the lace of her pantaloons. She looked down. Then shook her head and dropped her skirt. "I have too many now."

"A woman can never have too many gowns. Though, I would agree that women have too many undergarments. But on you they look delightful. You have a figure most women would envy."

"Do you think so? I thought I was only average," Margaret replied. She reminded herself that she wanted to be admired for her mind, not her body.

"Darling, you underestimate your beauty. Your breasts are like ripe peaches and your loins slender but firm. Your taste is that of sweet honey. The thought that you are my wife, that I can have you whenever I desire, excites me even now."

Margaret just shook her head, and when she did, the street seemed to roll under her. She clung to Alex for support. He held her and whispered in her ear. "What more could a man ask for?"

After a moment, Margaret felt better and resumed walking with Alex's arm around her waist. They came upon a saloon noisy with patrons spilling out into the street. A woman inside waved as if she recognized them. Alex tipped his hat.

"Alex?" A wiry bearded man with a wild look in his eyes stumbled toward them.

Alex just raised his hand in acknowledgement and hurriedly escorted Margaret away. When she looked over her shoulder, the man was staring at them. She thought he might be walking in their direction, but wasn't sure.

Alex turned down the road that led to the lake. The cool breeze from the water seemed to clear her head and Margaret felt much better now, but she was still intoxicated.

They talked about politicians and which one they thought would make a better leader. Margaret found herself enjoying their conversation, reminded of when they first met. Before she had encountered Michael on the boat to Ireland, Alex had been the only man with whom she could share her ideas who didn't find her odd or unfeminine. She had considered him a friend.

They stopped next to a building and leaned against it, looking out at the water and boats in the distance. Alex stroked Margaret gently on the cheek. "I love you," he said, looking into her eyes. He kissed her on the nose, then on the lips. She pretended he was Michael. She kissed him back. He kissed her again, this time more passionately.

There was a sound of footsteps nearby. Alex turned and looked around. A man stepped into view, the same individual from the saloon.

"Alex. So good to see you again." The man flipped his jacket, revealing a gun he had in his waistband.

Alex reached into his coat, pulled out a revolver, and whacked the butt of the gun across the man's face. Blood flowed from his nose.

Stumbling backward, the man brought his hands to his face as Alex kicked him in the crotch. The man doubled over. Alex smacked him on the back of the head with his gun. The stranger immediately fell to the ground. Alex pointed his weapon as if he intended to shoot.

"Please don't kill him." Margaret begged. "It is my birthday. Let this be my gift. I beg of you."

Alex stood there for a moment as if considering her request, then put his gun back in his jacket. "Come Margaret." Alex reached out for her hand. "Let's go home."

Margaret wasn't sure if what she had just witnessed really happened. She put her hands to her mouth and took a few breaths trying to clear her head. She grabbed Alex's hand. They walked the rest of the way home in silence.

When they arrived at their house, Margaret was still shaken. Alex pulled her close to him and kissed the top of her head as Margaret bit her knuckle like a child. Alex retrieved a bottle of whiskey, a couple of glasses from the parlor, and then helped Margaret up the stairs to her room. He closed the door behind them and poured the whiskey, adding water to Margaret's from the pitcher on her wash stand.

"I don't need any more to drink," Margaret told him as he shoved a glass into her trembling hand.

"It will settle your nerves."

Margaret gulped down the whiskey as though it were medicine. It burned and tasted harsh. Alex carefully undressed her, unfastening her bustle and her corset until she stood before him in her silk lace chemise and pantaloons. Then he pulled her close in his arms. "It is all right, darling. You have nothing to be afraid of." She felt the room spin. The last thing she remembered was Alex lifting her and putting her onto the bed.

Margaret awoke with a terrible headache to the sound of a bird singing. She got up and opened the door to her study. Bright sunlight streamed in through the window. She grabbed the curtain and drew it closed, blocking out most of the light. The little bird in her ornate cage had its claws wrapped around a metal bar. It looked up at her with one little eye. Hopping down to a container mounted near the bottom of the cage the bird splashed around in the water. Yes, a bath, thought Margaret. That would make her feel better.

Once clean, she returned to her room and brushed out her wet hair. Then she wound it up into a bun and secured it on top of her head. The dress she wore last night lay on a chair. Margaret pressed on her still-throbbing temples. Perhaps she forgot to hang it up. The only thing she could remember was Alex taking her out to dinner.

When Margaret went downstairs, she heard Mrs. O'Brien humming as she dusted in the parlor.

"Do you think you could make me some coffee?" Margaret interrupted.

"I take it you had a pleasant evening last night, mum?" Mrs. O'Brien tucked her feather duster in her apron pocket.

"I don't quite remember. Perhaps I drank too much champagne. Is Alex around?"

"No, mum. He was in a hurry this morning. Didn't even take a piece of toast when he left. Would you like something besides coffee? I know of a good cure for your headache."

"Yes, it would be most appreciated."

Margaret settled into a chair. She didn't feel like going anywhere this morning. Glancing around the room, she noticed a pocket-sized notebook on the table by the cupboard where the liquor was kept. She got up and retrieved it. Leafing through it, she was surprised to see it only contained jumbled up letters and numbers with notes next to them. She set it down again. She was in no condition for a book of games, which she assumed must belong to Alex.

After her coffee, a piece of toast, and Mrs. O'Brien's strange homemade remedy for her condition that tasted of vinegar and something utterly unidentifiable, Margaret went back up to her room. Today she would refrain from anything that required very much thinking, she decided. Margaret took out her box of buttons. She knew it was silly of her to keep such trivial things, but she treasured them like gold nuggets. She rummaged through them, pulling out different ones, holding them up and admiring them. Her assortment included ornate carved buttons with flowers, metal ones with animals, colored glass, and plain ones of sentimental value only. She kept a separate pouch for her mementos from Ireland. Maybe someday she would add to that collection. Perhaps she might even get one of Michael's buttons.

The sound of her new canary was now pleasant to her ears. The bird needed a name. She had no idea if her little feathered friend was a male or female. She thought for a moment, the name Beatrice came to her. When she was a child, Margaret had met a woman by that name who had a beautiful voice. So, it only seemed fitting to name the bird Beatrice.

Upon returning home from Mass the following day, Margaret found Alex in his usual spot in the library. When she entered, he quickly folded up the newspaper and opened a dime novel and set it on top.

"Is there anything interesting in the news?" Margaret asked as she reached for the paper.

Alex gripped her wrist. "Before you read that, I need to discuss something with you."

She sat in the chair across from him.

"Do you remember the night of your birthday?" he asked.

"Barely. However, I get an uncomfortable feeling when I do try to recall it."

"So you don't remember our walk home?"

Margaret shook her head.

"A man was found beaten on the shore of Lake Michigan."

Suddenly, Margaret had flashes of Alex hitting a man. "Oh, my God. You were the one. You hit him."

"There is nothing to worry about. Several witnesses gave statements claiming that they saw us having dinner together when the event took place." He leaned back in his chair.

Margaret pulled open the paper and read the article. "But these people lied."

"Come, come, Margaret. What are you going to do? Write a different article? Besides, it was self-defense. The man had a gun."

"But it says here that he almost died from a blow to his head."

"Well, he should consider himself lucky. If it hadn't been your birthday, he would have died. Apparently you don't remember, but his life was my gift to you. I could have just as well shot the bastard."

"I don't know how you can live with yourself."

"If I had done nothing, the man could have killed both of us." Alex scowled at her.

Margaret sighed with resignation. He was telling the truth.

Chapter 11

MARGARET PULLED THE heavy, velvet drapes across the window in her study to smother the night wind and to keep the cool air from giving her a chill. During the day she had a view of the tree in the yard and the sidewalk below. But it was dark now, and the wind was blowing across the lake and into her neighborhood. Tonight she was attempting to work on her book about Ireland, but that was proving to be a challenge.

The scent of old dusty rose petals in the bowl by the window was no longer noticeable. It had disappeared along with the color of the dead flowers long ago. She had not heard a peep from her canary for hours. Several oil lamps cast their shadows on flowery wallpaper as she sat at her desk searching for words and inspiration. It had been days since she had an opportunity to write. Margaret dipped her pen into the crystal ink well and tapped the tip lightly on the edge. Holding the pen between her blue stained thumb and forefinger, poised to touch the surface of the vacant paper lying before her, she hesitated. Why were the words eluding her now? She set the pen back in its silver holder. An assortment of research papers and letters filled the outer edges of her desk. Wrinkled papers littered the floor like broken structures.

Margaret sat back in her chair, then leaned over and picked up the rose patterned china cup that had been sitting there for what may have been minutes or hours. She couldn't remember when she last heard the clock chime.

Mrs. O'Brien must have brought in the tea. The dear woman took such good care of her. Perhaps giving her a little something extra to spend this month would be a nice thing to do. God knows the woman deserved it. Putting up with her and Alex could not be an easy task.

Her last maid had run off. Margaret came home one day and found the woman gone. Though he swore otherwise, Margaret thought Alex had something to do with her departure. When Margaret inquired around for a new maid, she was initially resistant to the idea of hiring Mrs. O'Brien. The old woman was Alex's choice. One of his associates from the Irish club highly recommended her.

"Have a heart, Margaret," Alex had said. "The woman's husband died fighting for Ireland's freedom. It is the least we can do for her. Her current employers are moving to San Francisco and decided not to take her with them."

"Yes, but can she clean and cook?" Margaret had asked. Now she couldn't imagine having anyone other than Mrs. O'Brien run her house.

Margaret stirred the amber tea, churning up brown flakes from the bottom. Resting the silver spoon in the saucer, she stared into the cup. Her inspiration was now as cold as her tea.

Margaret opened the journal from her trip and flipped through the pages, looking for something she could use.

April 10th, While traveling through the countryside, I passed weather beaten grandmothers, matronly women, and young maidens trudging through the dirt in their bare feet. Their skirts were ragged and their shoulders covered only by soiled remnants of fabric. Many are from the rural districts and are poor beyond imagination.

April 15th, I walked the hallowed ground of Connaught and Munster. The earth beneath my feet was wet with tears from the sorrow that had seeped into the earth. I heard murmurs in the berm, the sounds of hearts breaking in the tide of the ocean. I felt the breeze rush past me carrying prayers across her barren moors and up to the summit of the mountains.

April 14th, Today, I looked into the faces of the peasants standing at their cabin doors, speaking with their eyes, wondering if I've come to rescue them.

April 16th, Along both sides of the road lay ruins of what had been a village. Once these were homes of hard-working men and women, but now it's only rubble. Here, ghosts of blue-lipped children shiver, forgotten amongst the broken-hearted.

There was a knock at the door and Alex stepped in. He had his topcoat on and held a hat in this hand.

"Margaret, I'm going out. It may be late when I return, so don't wait up."

"You'll be home before I'm finished." Margaret motioned to her blank page.

"You are much too demanding of yourself, my dear." Alex smiled. "I have the utmost confidence you will come up with something wonderful. You always do."

"I want to tell the world the truth, but right now my words are failing me." She put her hands in her lap and shrugged.

"You are a brilliant writer. I don't know of anyone who could do a better job than you of furthering the cause of Ireland with words. Now, I must go. There are several gentlemen that I need to discuss a few important things with."

He kissed her on the cheek then left.

She sighed. She had no idea where he went when he left for his meetings, perhaps to one of the Irish saloons or private men's clubs. With his departure went her struggle for ideas, as though the lace of her corset had been loosened and she could breathe easily again. Lately when Alex was home, worry would grab her and shake her, though she hid it well. She had no explanation for it, just a strange unsettling feeling.

The house was quiet. She took a deep breath, sat back in her chair, and closed her eyes. She rubbed her left temple with her index finger. Her mind wandered from her task and thoughts of Michael drifted in. His laugh, his smile, and his touch...

Her eyes jerked open. She pulled out a new sheet of paper and began to write:

Dear Mrs. Emma O'Neil,

I hope this letter finds you in better circumstances. Please write me of James and how he is doing. I've enclosed some money to help with rent and food. You must not give in to feelings of despair. Many people are working to improve your circumstances. Things will change. I promise you.

Chapter 12

ETTERS FROM DELIA Parnell now arrived at least once a week with news regarding the Land League. Both daughters, Fanny and Anna, were organizing women across America, and Delia informed her that Michael had arrived, and that he and Fanny had set up an office for the American branch of the Land League in New York. A man by the name of Collins in Boston was appointed Land League President. Fanny was thrilled to be managing things for Michael, Delia said in her latest letter, but they needed more support from the press. Would Margaret be willing to help?

Margaret daydreamed about working next to Michael, and she wondered what excuse she could come up with to travel to New York that wouldn't raise Alex's suspicions.

Then one day, Margaret received a telegram from Delia.

Dear Margaret,

I am pleased to inform you that Charles will be arriving in America soon. He and Mr. Davitt plan to go on a lecture tour for the Land League. I am sure you will share my

*enthusiasm when I tell you that they have chosen Chicago
as one of their destinations. Could you please ask your
dear husband Alex to make the arrangements for them?
I plan to accompany Charles at least as far as Chicago.
I am looking forward to visiting with you when I arrive.*

*Graciously yours,
Mrs. Delia Parnell*

Margaret folded the telegram in half, took it with her to the parlor, and sat down. Margaret did not know how to take the news. She had prayed to see Michael again, but here in Chicago? No, that was not how she imagined it. Looking around the room, she pondered the idea. Yes, of course she would ask Alex, she thought as she studied the wallpaper. Maybe a different color wallpaper would be better, something less elegant. Would Michael be coming to their home, she wondered? No, he would not stay in Alex's house, not if she had a say in the matter, and any entertaining would take place elsewhere. But should she attend? Both Michael and Charles would be speaking about the Land League, she reminded herself. This was not a personal visit, after all. Besides, she had been working diligently, raising both awareness and funds for their organization. She would be expected to write an article about the event. Then why was she apprehensive? What did she think would happen? Delia would be accompanying the men and Margaret hadn't seen her in a while. This was a professional visit, and she was a journalist and not some silly young girl. Margaret pushed down any feeling she had about seeing Michael and carried the message to the library where Alex sat reviewing legal papers.

"Alex, I have a telegram from Delia. Charles Parnell and Michael Davitt are coming to Chicago," Margaret said, struggling to suppress a tremor of excitement that was trying to surface in her throat.

"They need my help, I presume?" Alex closed his folder and looked up at her.

"Yes, it would be most appreciated." Please, she thought. Margaret placed her hand on Alex's arm. "It would help the Land League tremendously."

Alex picked up Margaret's hand and kissed it. "If it will make you happy, I'll take care of the arrangements."

Margaret leaned over and kissed the top of Alex's head. Everything will be fine she told herself.

Margaret pushed open the oak door to the *Chicago Tribune* building. She detected the faint smell of machine oil and ink from the print room. Tomorrow's edition was running. Lifting her skirt, she quickly climbed the stairs to the third floor. The front desk was empty. She checked her message slot and picked up her letters then headed back to her office. Everyone must be out working, she thought as she walked down the hall, peeking into the open doors. Delany's desk was a mess, as it always was. The new man, she couldn't remember his name, Edwards or Edgar, wasn't there, either. Turning one of the letters over in her hand, she noticed that the return address was Dublin, Ireland. Margaret carried the envelope down to her office and closed the door behind her. She set her satchel on her desk and pulled out a letter opener from the drawer. She ripped open the letter.

My Darling Margaret,

I hope this letter finds you well. I know I shouldn't have written and it is presumptuous of me to think you would welcome any contact. Nonetheless, I am counting the days until I will be in Chicago and can see your face again, if only from a distance.

Fondly,
Michael

Margaret smiled. Containing her feelings suddenly became an impossible task. She read the words again. He wants to see *me*.

Her hand felt around for the key hidden on a hook underneath the top drawer of her desk. After retrieving it, she went to her oak filing cabinet against the wall and unlocked the bottom drawer. In the back behind her files was a scrapbook. Setting it on top of the cabinet, she opened it to a blank page and placed Michael's letter inside with the articles she had been saving about him from various newspapers. She had been telling herself that the secret articles were for research and she was only interested in him profession-ally, but right now they felt like kisses from afar. Then she locked the scrapbook in its hiding place again and returned the key to its hidden spot.

Chapter 13

"DARLING, HOW GOOD it is to see you again." Delia kissed the air on both sides of Margaret's face. They then proceeded down the hall of the Palmer House Hotel to the restaurant for lunch. It was the nicest hotel in Chicago, and Alex had booked rooms for the Parnell party's stay. Michael and Charles's speeches would be taking place here tonight, as well.

In the restaurant, several large crystal chandeliers hung from the ceiling, giving the room an opulent feeling. It was a popular place amongst the well-to-do, and many of the tables were taken. A waiter led them to one of the white linen-covered tables in the middle of the room. He pulled out the chair for Delia and another waiter did the same for Margaret.

"May I suggest the salmon?" the waiter said.

"Is it fresh?" asked Delia. "I only eat fresh salmon."

"Of course, madam. The Palmer House spares no expense in providing you with the freshest fish available."

"I'll have the salmon, then."

"I'll have the salmon, as well." Margaret smiled.

"Alex is such a dear, and so charming. It was nice of him to help organize the lecture for us and to pick up the bill. You be sure and let him know how much we appreciate his generosity." Delia smoothed the napkin sitting in her lap. "And thank you too, my dear. The articles have been wonderful. How is that book of yours coming along?"

"It is taking longer than I thought, I'm afraid." Margaret was still struggling with what to include in her book about Charles's and Michael's efforts. She didn't want to appear too biased.

Delia glanced around the room. "I see there will be quite a few Fenians in attendance tonight." Delia picked up her fork and poked at her food inquisitively, then looked up at Margaret. "I take it Alex invited them?"

"What exactly do you mean?" Margaret looked around at the men in the room. A few nodded and smiled at her. "Alex is well known in the Irish community, and he belongs to an organization, but I wouldn't call them Fenians."

Delia held her teacup between her fingers then brought it to her mouth. Hesitating, she stared at Margaret over the rim. "What would you call them, then?" she asked.

"I believe Alex refers to them as the *Clan na Gael*." Those were Irish Gaelic words meaning "brotherhood." She thought the title signified a common ancestry, nothing more.

Delia reached over and touched Margaret's hand.

"You watch. They have a way of greeting one another, a certain handshake. They are part of a secret organization."

Margaret looked around the room, puzzled. "I don't understand." If Alex was a Fenian he would have told her, she thought. Yes, he was spending a lot time recently with his male associates, but he was an influential man.

"It is all right. Don't worry about it. We need everyone's support," Delia replied.

"No, please tell me." Margaret wanted to know what this meant: that the men around her were Fenians, that her husband must be the one to have invited them. How could she have missed the fact that her husband had such associates? She was a journalist and should have recognized some sign that would have alerted her to this information.

"I just assumed you knew. The Fenians have been around since the end of the Civil War."

"Yes, I was aware that a group of Irish hooligans that called themselves Fenians organized a militia and set out to attack Canada, but that was years ago." Margaret remembered reading about them but she assumed the organization no longer existed.

"Well, Fenians in this country are much like the Irish Republican Brotherhood in Ireland. They never completely died out here, though they have gone through several leaders since they began, including Mr. John Devoy," Delia said then took a sip of her tea.

"Aren't they a militant group?"

"They talk like they are, but they haven't achieved much. If they had accomplished a fraction of what they proclaim they wish to do, Ireland would be a free country right now. Maybe Alex can do something about that, get them more organized. They have been suffering under poor leadership for years."

"I can't believe my ears. I thought you were in favor of freeing Ireland through peaceful means?"

"I am in favor of freeing Ireland any way we can." Delia cut a piece of salmon, slid it into her mouth, and swallowed. "Aren't you?" she asked, as she delicately blotted her lips with her napkin and smiled.

Margaret looked around the room but didn't see Michael's face amongst the men waiting to enter the lecture hall. Her stomach fluttered with anticipation. There was an abrupt tug on her arm, and Alex pulled her through the crowd. Soon she was face-to-face with the man she had been looking for. The shock was wonderful. There he stood, two feet away from her.

"I would like you to meet my dear wife." Alex presented her to Michael.

"It is a pleasure, Mrs. Sullivan." Michael bowed. When his eyes came up, they fixed on hers, and everything else faded around her. Margaret let out a small sigh. Don't faint, she told herself. To do so would embarrass everyone. Breathe. She inhaled. Then she held out her hand to be kissed, but then quickly pulled it back again, nodding instead.

"Who would have guessed that after a trip to Ireland my wife here would become such a patriot," Alex commented. "Did you know that she has been campaigning diligently for your Land League since her return?"

Michael's eyes sparkled as he lowered his head a little to one side and stroked his mustache, trying to hide his grin. "So, I've heard from Mrs. Parnell."

Margaret noticed Alex's eyes inquisitively dart from her to Michael. Alex's smile dropped at the corners, ever so slightly, and he became stiff.

"Well, Mr. Davitt, we need to move on. I will talk with you later, no doubt." Alex grabbed Margaret's arm. "Come, dear."

"I hope you enjoy the lecture tonight," Michael called to her. "Again, it was a pleasure, Mrs. Sullivan."

As she looked back over her shoulder, Margaret saw that Michael's eyes followed her.

Alex pulled her to the corner of the room. "I take it you've met before," he said in a low stern voice as he gripped her arm tightly.

"Yes, briefly at Avondale. Mr. Davitt came to visit Mr. Charles Parnell to discuss the possibility of his involvement in the Land League." It was not a total lie, Margaret told herself.

"I wished you had mentioned that before. I had no idea. You embarrassed me." He squeezed her arm tighter.

"I am truly sorry, but I didn't think it was important," Margaret replied. "Let go. You are hurting me." His brutish ways were uncalled for. She wasn't a disobedient child in need of punishment.

He released his grip. "In the future, please let me know about the men you have fraternized with or I will need to curtail your travels." His voice held a touch of anger.

"Of course, and I apologize." She had no intention of telling him who she met and when. It was none of his business.

Together they strolled to the front of the crowd and chose seats before the stage. Alex waited for Margaret to sit down then walked off, leaving her alone. For a few moments, Margaret sat back and replayed the image of Michael. As wrong as it was, she had to admit that she was still enchanted by his presence and hopelessly enamored with him. Tonight she would relish in listening to him speak.

Someone scraping their chair behind her brought Margaret's attention back to the lecture hall. The room was starting to fill up with men in top hats, bowlers, and caps milling around in small groups. A few men she recognized lined the wall. Which ones were members of the secret Irish organization, she wondered? Was it Mr. Durbin? Perhaps Mr. McBride? She knew little about the background of either man other than that they avoided her whenever she tried to interview them. When he noticed Margaret staring at him, Mr. Woods nodded and she gave him a polite smile in return. Did Michael know there were Fenians here tonight? Did he know any of them personally?

After a few minutes, Alex took the stage and stood behind the wooden podium. "I would like to introduce two distinguished men from Ireland who have traveled here in the hopes of gaining your support for their organization," Alex said. He bowed toward Michael, who was standing near a side wall. "Our first speaker will be Mr. Michael Davitt."

Margaret's heart skipped a beat in anticipation of hearing Michael's speech. She hardly noticed when Alex took his seat next to her. The crowd jumped to their feet with wild applause as Michael walked to the podium. Some men chanted, "Free Ireland. Free Ireland..."

"I want to thank you all for coming out tonight, and for your belief in and support of the Land League," Michael bellowed to the crowd in his baritone. "Because of the many generous donations made by Irish men and women across America, we have been able to provide legal services and funds to help poor evicted tenants all around Ireland. I want you to know that our efforts have been so successful that they have coined a new word for our method of resistance. 'Boycott,' is now the term used to describe our united peaceful action, and we are staging boycotts on a regular basis throughout Ireland. Many landlords are now agreeing to roll back rents and to do away with unfair rent hikes. In combination with the work Mr. Charles Parnell is doing in Parliament, we are taking great strides toward a free Ireland. But, we still need your financial support."

Michael looked down at Margaret and smiled at her briefly then continued with his speech. Her heart ached. She was proud of him and of all the good he was doing.

Charles, who was not as articulate, took the stage after Michael and spoke of his plans for Ireland as though he were its future leader. Maybe he hoped to someday be their king, Margaret thought.

After the speeches, many men in the audience lit their cigars and ordered drinks from waiters, who suddenly appeared to take their orders. While the ladies headed for the exit to return home, men milled around discussing Irish politics. It was not long before the room took on a din as voices grew louder, bolstered by alcohol. Alex drifted off to join a group of men. Margaret could see that Michael was preoccupied and wouldn't be able to speak with her, and so she made her way into the lobby. Delia had also disappeared, and thus she had no one to talk to.

A bellhop suddenly appeared in front of her with a tray perched on his palm. "A message for you, Mrs. Sullivan." A small envelop was sitting on top. Margaret opened it.

> *If you can get away, meet me in an hour in room #516.*
> *The door's unlocked. M*

She gazed at the card then folded it and put it in her dress pocket.

"Hi, darling," Alex came up from behind her. "Do you think you could see yourself home? There are several people I still need to speak with and I didn't want you waiting around for me."

"Why yes, of course." Her guilty heart pounded loudly in her ears.

When Margaret reached the fifth floor of the hotel, she began to tremble. Surely she would burn in the fires of hell for even thinking of being here, much less actually making the journey, she told herself, but her temptation was stronger than her resistance. Pulled by an invisible string woven of curiosity and longing, she moved down the hall. With each step, her heart beat louder. The closer she came to his room, the more anxious she became. What would she do when she got there? Margaret panicked at the sound of someone opening a door. She quickly turned, and walked back down the hall toward the stairs.

"Margaret?" Delia's voice called. "Were you looking for me, dear?"

Margaret took a deep breath, spun around, and calmly strolled toward Delia. "Why, yes, I wanted to tell you how impressed I was with Charles's speech tonight." Margaret was almost relieved at this unexpected escape from her dilemma.

"Come in." Delia motioned Margaret into her room. "Would you care for a drink?"

Stepping inside, Margaret nervously glanced around the room. It was elegantly decorated with sky blue brocade wallpaper, the ceiling painted with virgins and cherubs. A plaster statue of a Greek goddess sat poised on top of the fireplace mantel. It all seemed fitting for a guest such as Delia. Margaret took a seat on the rose-colored velvet settee.

Delia sat facing Margaret in an upholstered high back chair. "May I ask how you and Alex are coming along?"

"I beg your pardon?" Margaret blushed and lowered her eyes.

"With your fund-raising efforts?" Delia asked.

Margaret could see Delia's intense blue eyes staring at her. "I've been able to raise a fair amount of money from many of the Catholic groups here in Chicago." Margaret caught herself speaking too fast. Slow down, she told herself then forced a smile. "Alex has been busy, too. He attends quite a few meetings. I am sure he will forward the funds to the League's office in New York."

"I understand that your husband is trying to make a name for himself."

"Yes. He is quite ambitious." Margaret coughed softly.

"I hope you are guiding him in our direction."

"Of course." Margaret didn't want to be reminded of Alex's pursuits at the moment. Her opportunity to see Michael was slipping away and the urgency of the situation was churning up her nerves inside. Certainly the devil had her in his clutches. A moment ago she had been glad Delia had unwittingly intervened, but now…

"Forgive me, but I must go." Margaret stood up. "It has been a long day, and you must be tired. I know I am." Margaret set her untouched drink on the table. "It was so good to see you again."

"I appreciate you dropping by." Delia kissed Margaret's cheek. "*Au revoir. À la prochaine fois.*"

"*À la prochaine fois,*" Margaret replied.

Once out in the hall, Margaret slowly walked down the corridor, stopping in front of room number 516. She wanted desperately to speak to Michael alone. Glancing around to make sure that no one else would see her, she nervously placed her hand on the doorknob and turned. It was unlocked as the note indicated it would be. The urge to enter was almost unbearable. No, she mustn't, she heard her mind saying loudly. What was she doing? The devil must be laughing at her. Could she so easily be led astray? Please, Heavenly Father, help me resist this temptation. She released the knob and jerked her hand back. Quickly she headed for the stairs. A door opened behind her. Margaret didn't look back. She didn't want to know who it was.

Upstairs in her bedroom, Margaret took off her shoes then went over to her dressing table. Unclasping her necklace, she noticed her image in the mirror next to her jewelry box. "Oh, Michael, I truly wanted to spend time with you." She frowned. "You will never know how much." She pulled the pins from her hair, allowing her curls to fall to her shoulders. She attempted to smooth out the evening's waves with her brush, but after a few strokes she threw the brush across the room. Margaret brought her hand to her quivering mouth. Lifting her head, she sniffed back her tears. The pain burned deep within her. She wished Michael had never come. What was she supposed to do? They were so close and yet still an ocean apart.

She changed into her nightdress then pulled back her blanket and climbed into bed. When she finished patting the pillow to fluff it up she sat back and pulled up her knees to read. Margaret picked up the book of poems by Thomas Moore that she kept next to her bed. Her finger traced the lines as she read the words to the poem out loud that Michael had recited to her on the ship. She kissed his card, placed it in the book, and then blew out the lamp.

Michael's image was the last thing she wanted to remember before she dropped off to sleep.

Later in the evening, Margaret was awakened by a loud noise downstairs. She quickly lit the lamp and sat up in bed. The sound of footsteps stopped outside her room. As it swung open, her door hit the wall with a bang, startling her.

"Is it Ireland that excites you, or is it the men who talk about saving her?" Alex demanded.

Like an angry bear, Alex clumsily made his way toward her, bumping into a chair which he shoved out of his way.

"I don't know what you are talking about?"

"You went to his room didn't you?" He stood there, swaying back and forth.

"Whose room are you referring to?" Her own guilt swirled around her.

"That Irish pacifist Davitt, that's who."

"Of course not. How could you think such a thing?" She should have left the hotel immediately after Alex spoke to her. She was not thinking straight at the time, she reminded herself.

"I saw the way you looked at him tonight."

"You are mistaken. I was just enchanted by his speech." Had her admiration for Michael been on display or did Alex merely assume it was?

"Speech?" He raised his voice. "You didn't think anyone would notice when you climbed those stairs at the hotel did you?" He tapped his chest. "I have friends and they tell me things."

"I went to visit with Delia. If you distrust me, then ask her. She will vouch for me. I have done nothing wrong." Margaret clutched her blanket tightly to her breasts.

He picked up the book of poems from her table. "What's this?" Alex turned it over bringing it closer to his face.

Her body tensed. "You know I like to read before I go to bed." She held her breath, praying he wouldn't open it.

Alex walked around the room holding the book his hand and then tossed it onto her dresser.

Margaret exhaled. "Please, Alex, go to bed. You've had too much to drink," Margaret said, doing her best to not sound alarmed.

Alex approached and hovered over her for a moment. Then he reached down and roughly removed her blanket and snatched the front of her nightdress, clutching it tightly in his hand. "You care for me don't you?"

"Of course I do," she said. "You are my husband."

With a snap of his arm, he jerked the front of her cotton gown, ripping it, exposing her left breast. Margaret's hand went to her mouth and she turned her head as she squeezed her eyes closed. With the other hand she covered her breast. She waited.

A long moment later she heard the sound of his footsteps as he stumbled down the hall to his bedroom, and then she heard the door slam. Margaret burst into tears. Thorns of anger, guilt, remorse, and shame pierced her, punishing her for ever having thought that she and Michael could be together. Margaret crawled out of bed and found her rosary then climbed in bed again. Her tear-filled eyes focused on the crucifix in her palm. She touched the brass body of Jesus with her forefinger. Was life only about suffering? Then she let go of the cross and found a bead. She needed something to hold onto.

Chapter 14

MARGARET GLANCED AT the large school clock on the wall in the foyer of the *Chicago Tribune* offices. She had plenty of time to work on her article for Sunday's paper.

"Good morning, Mrs. Sullivan." Delany stood up as she walked past him. "How are you this morning?"

Margaret strolled back to his office. The sleeves of Delany's pin-striped shirt were rolled up, indicating he had been there a while. Several newspapers lay scattered around the heavy wooden desk where he was working. A crude circle enclosed one article and words were scribbled on a piece of note paper next to it. She tried reading it but couldn't make it out from her angle.

Margaret smiled. "Busy, thank you."

"How is the book coming?" Delany sat down on the corner of his desk, blocking her view of his mess. He pushed his wheat-colored hair to the side.

"It is nice of you to ask." Margaret pulled on the fingers of her gloves then slipped them off. "It will be completed soon." She liked Delany. He always showed support and treated her with respect.

"I hope you are going to use your real name." He folded his arms across his chest.

"Yes, I intend to." Margaret smiled.

"Good for you."

"Mrs. Sullivan." Edwards approached to join the conversation. "Is it true you are writing a book?" he asked.

Edwards was a short man with a bulbous nose and a brown mustache and beard. He was a recent addition to the *Chicago Tribune*, having come from a paper back East. Margaret didn't care for him or his yellow journalism.

"Yes, it's about the situation in Ireland," she replied.

"Isn't there enough information floating around about the plight of poor old Ireland with all the rags the rebels are printing?" Edwards stroked his beard and grinned. "I hope your husband didn't put you up to it."

"Careful, now." Delany stood up, putting his body between his fellow co-workers. "Those are fighting words for Mrs. Sullivan. In case you weren't aware, she is a staunch Irish nationalist."

"Well, just keep it out of the newsroom," Edwards remarked. "There are other things to report on…"

Delany interrupted. "I think it best if you keep that opinion to yourself around here."

"It's quite all right, Delany. A little criticism has not stopped me yet," Margaret said. She smiled then playfully reached over and smacked Edwards chest with her gloves. "Apology accepted," Margaret said, knowing he had not offered her one. It was best to disregard insults from people like Edwards. She did not need enemies at work.

"I admire your dedication," said Delany. "I don't know how you do it." He gave Margaret a bow. "Who could imagine, may I quote, 'One of the best journalists around,' according to the *New York Times*, is actually our own Mrs. Margaret Sullivan?"

"They can't be serious. Pardon me, Mrs. Sullivan, but with all due respect, they must have made a mistake. I know of several men who deserve that honor," said Edwards.

Margaret knew the compliment irritated Edwards. She had been around men like him before. They preferred their women ignorant. But she was used to being underestimated, which made it all the more rewarding when she beat them at their own game.

"That may be true. However, Margaret is the one who was mentioned. Well, under her alias Joseph Brown, of course," Delany added.

"Unfortunately, my dear woman, you'll never get any real credit in this business," said Edwards.

"Secrecy works well to my advantage. So does being a woman. It allows me to move about freely without suspicion, unlike some men who work here."

"Last time I inquired, saloons and backrooms at Chicago's men's clubs were off limits to women."

Margaret didn't know how long she could listen to this drivel. Edwards's sarcasm was getting on her nerves.

"Margaret has to leave us some topics to write about." Delany winked at Margaret. "Otherwise we'd be out of a job."

"I seriously doubt that a woman can hold her own against a man for very long, much less understand the intricacies of finance and business. If it was up to me, you would be relegated to writing about society teas and fashion." Edwards walked around Delany's desk, avoiding eye contact with Margaret. "So, my dear, if you want to be taken seriously, I would suggest you use a man's name on that book of yours."

"Regardless of your opinion on the subject, I have made my decision," Margaret said firmly.

"Well, Madam Sullivan, I hope it gives you the attention you...' Edwards turned his head and picked through the papers on Delany's desk. "Have you started that article on the mayor yet? I want to talk to you about that," he said looking toward Delany.

Delany shook his head and shrugged his shoulders then turned his attention to Edwards.

In her office, stacks of British and Irish newspapers filled the perimeter of her desk and boxes on the floor. She made it her business to follow every detail of the Land League and to keep the topic in front of American readers.

Margaret retrieved a piece of raisin bread from her satchel and set it before her on a napkin. She pulled out all the raisins and popped them into her mouth one by one.

She leafed through a stack of telegrams, hoping to find something she could use. Several were from London and one was from Delia in New Jersey. Margaret pulled Delia's out and read it as she broke off pieces of bread and put them in her mouth.

Apparently Michael was worried that the British would soon be rounding up men who supported the Land League. Did this mean he was in danger? Margaret hated being so far away from everything. She read further down the telegram. Delia mentioned that Michael had suggested a women's group be formed to take over if something happened to the men. He thought Anna Parnell would be the perfect choice for the Ladies Land League in Ireland. Margaret shoved a piece of bread in her mouth. Then she sat back and smiled. Charles Parnell wouldn't be very happy about his sister running things.

When Margaret finished her article, she dropped it in her editor's box. Another two copies were placed in the outgoing mail to be sent to Boston and New York. Pleased with herself, she left for the day.

A month later, when Margaret checked her message slot on the wall in the entry, there was a telegram from the London. She carried it along with her other mail to her office and sat down. Suddenly, she found herself uneasy about this message from England and didn't want to open the telegram. It wouldn't be good news, something told her. Finally, after going through her other mail, she forced herself to read it.

> *February 3rd, 1881–Michael Davitt was arrested while crossing Carlisle Bridge in Dublin. He was brought under heavy guard to London where he was committed to prison without a trial to serve out the remainder of his fourteen year sentence for treason. More than five thousand people gathered in Trafalgar Square in London in protest.*

Margaret read it a second time. Her insides tightened and she choked back her tears. Why Michael? Hadn't he suffered enough? She put her hands together in prayer and placed her fingers under her chin. "Dear God, please give him the strength he will need to endure, one more time."

After several moments, she sat there staring blankly at the ceiling as if a miracle should occur. She had hoped an angel would appear and somehow make the truth vanish. "Michael didn't deserve this," she said to the heavens beyond. There must be something she could do.

Suddenly Margaret jumped up, grabbed her satchel and rushed out the door.

Edwards stood in the hall blocking her way. "What's the hurry, Mrs. Sullivan? On the trail of a story?"

"Please, leave me alone." She pushed his shoulder so that he would get out of her way and stormed past him.

When Margaret arrived home, Mrs. O'Brien greeted her at the door.

"Good afternoon, mum. An urgent telegram from Mrs. Parnell just came for you." Mrs. O'Brien held it out.

Margaret took it from her and quickly read it.

Margaret, I am sure you have heard the terrible news. Please remain in Chicago. Darling, you can do more good there than anywhere else. I would like it if you and Alex could find it within yourselves to increase your efforts and pull everyone in America together during these unsettling times. Mrs. Delia Parnell.

What does she mean by, "pull everyone in America together"? Margaret was confused. How could pulling everyone together possibly help poor Michael? She had written articles and collected money for the Land League. What else was she expected to do? She thought for a moment. Her book, that's it! Delia wanted her to finish her book, and Alex needed to put more effort into organizing the Irish community. That was the message Delia was conveying. They mustn't let Michael's organization die. She would do everything in her power to see to it that the Land League would go on. Now, she just needed to convince Alex.

"Mr. Sullivan requested that I inform you that he is holding a meeting in the library." Mrs. O'Brien smiled then went back into the kitchen.

"Thank you." Margaret removed her hat and gloves and set them on the table in the hall. She noticed a calling card with the name Dr. Cronin in the silver dish. Who's Dr. Cronin? Was Alexander ill? She went to the library door and leaned against it in an attempt to hear what was happening inside. She only heard muffled sounds of the scraping of chairs on the floor and low voices. Grasping the crystal doorknob with one hand and knocking with the other, she turned the handle.

"Sorry to intrude," Margaret called out as she walked in. Next to Alex stood a handsome man with a full head of hair and a mustache.

"Are you ill?" Margaret rushed to Alex's side.

"This must be Mrs. Sullivan." The man eagerly extended his hand to her. "I'm Dr. Patrick Cronin."

"Pleased to meet you, Doctor. I saw your card on the entryway table and…"

"Hello, dear." Alex kissed her on the cheek. "I'm quite well."

"This isn't a medical visit. No need to be concerned about your husband." Dr. Cronin placed his hands on his hips.

"Forgive me." Margaret raised his calling card in the air.

"Dr. Cronin just moved to Chicago and we were discussing how I might be of assistance to him." Alexander nodded in Cronin's direction.

"Your husband is most generous in his offer to introduce me to some of his acquaintances regarding employment, and to provide me with an introduction so that I may gain membership in several clubs."

"Yes, I thought Cook County Hospital could use a distinguished physician like Mr. Cronin."

Margaret admired Alexander's willingness to help fellow Irishmen get ahead. He was well-connected and had made arrangements for many men in a variety of positions throughout the city. In fact, the Chicago police force was made up almost entirely of Irishmen, thanks to Alex and his friends.

"Are you a supporter of Ireland?" Margaret asked. She was curious about the doctor's convictions and if he would be someone they could count on in the future.

"Most definitely. I am not just a supporter. I'm willing to do whatever is necessary to further the cause." Dr. Cronin threw back his head and stood up straight as though he were a military officer.

Margaret was surprised by his answer. Was he one of those Fenians Delia had spoken about, she wondered.

"I heard he has a fine tenor voice, too." Alexander smiled. "He'll make an excellent addition to our local organization."

"I look forward to an invitation to hear you sing," Margaret replied and then asked, "Is there a Mrs. Cronin?"

"I'm afraid not." He smiled and leaned back.

"I would think a handsome doctor such as yourself should have no trouble attracting the attention of many single ladies in Chicago." Flattery often worked to her advantage. She never knew when she might require a favor.

"That is very kind of you. However, I'm not in the market for a wife at the moment."

"Well, I'm sorry I interrupted you," said Margaret. "Please, go back to whatever it was that you were discussing."

"Actually, I was about to bid your husband goodbye," said Dr. Cronin. "It was a pleasure meeting you, Mrs. Sullivan. I hope to see you again soon."

"Mrs. O'Brien will show you out." Alexander gestured to the hall.

"Good day to you both." Dr. Cronin took his hat and left.

"You gave me a fright there for a moment," Margaret said to Alex, though her thoughts had returned to Michael. How awful to be in prison again. Poor Michael.

Alex stood behind her. He put his hands on Margaret's shoulders and kissed her on the neck. "I'm surprised you are concerned about me." He let his hands slip down to her elbows then placed them around her waist. "With your obsession with the Land League, I didn't think you found time to worry about me. But, I could tell from your expression when you walked in that you are, and that tickles me."

"I was indeed worried," Margaret told him. Dare she mention Michael's imprisonment at the moment? No, she told herself. She would need to find another way to broach the situation.

"Alex, is it true that you are a member of a Fenian group?"

"Why do you ask that, my dear?"

"When Mrs. Parnell was here, she mentioned noticing men giving each other a secret sign and handshake. She thought you might be involved with a secret society."

"If you are referring to the *Clan na Gael,* I do hold a membership card." He nuzzled her ear.

Margaret was uncomfortable with what she was about to ask, but she was willing to do whatever it took to help Michael and the Land League. "I'm not objecting to your involvement. I was just wondering if you would or… have… ever considered becoming an officer or perhaps one of their leaders?"

He spun her around. "You are full of surprises today, my dear. First you are concerned about my health and now this. You are not only endorsing my membership in this so-called subversive group but suggesting that I might lead such an organization. Is that correct or are my ears deceiving me?"

Margaret bit her lip. "Yes, that is correct."

"Perhaps you've finally realized that just raising money for charity isn't enough. Maybe what Ireland really needs is help from abroad; help from a strong leader."

What was he talking about? She only wanted him to support her efforts in holding together the Land League. What did he think she meant by her suggestion?

"Would you find me more attractive, my dear, if I became a powerful force in the Irish cause?"

She swallowed hard. "Of course." It was the answer he wanted to hear.

Chapter 15

T HE GATHERING WAS small, only about fifty people, but Margaret was thrilled just the same. She wore her
cream-and-prune silk dress with a plunging neckline and a
large bustle, and the new pearl necklace Alex had given her set it
off nicely. She felt like a princess going to the ball. Although, when
she told Alex how she felt, he said she was more a queen than a
princess, his Irish queen.

A large crystal chandelier hung from the ceiling of their private
room at the Palmer House Hotel. Lavish paintings of maidens covered the walls. A poor imitation of classical art, Margaret thought.
However, it was the best Chicago had to offer and most people
weren't as critical as she was about such things. To Margaret, the
room embodied superficial elegance. At the moment, this fit her
mood perfectly, for now her confidence was waning and she felt out
of place. She wasn't a great novelist or a trained historian, merely a
journalist trying to educate the public. Nevertheless, she had worked
hard to present an accurate picture of the problems in Ireland.

"I would like to present to you this evening, Mrs. Margaret
Frances Buchanan Sullivan and her new book, *Ireland of Today;*

The Causes and Aims of Irish Agitation," announced a tall, thin man with a top hat, as he stood in the center of the room. Margaret nervously stepped forward to the accompaniment of applause. She wasn't a skilful orator like Alex, but she had never aspired to be one, either. Margaret cleared her throat and began the speech she had memorized.

"Ladies and Gentleman, I want to thank you for coming. You may wonder why I wrote about Ireland. How could I not write about our homeland? Everyone here tonight, no doubt, has heard stories of our brethren in Ireland and the hardships they must endure. What some of you may not know is the history of Ireland and how it came to be that so many people fell under the control of the British. After reading my book, you will have a better understanding of why we need to continue the fight to set Ireland free," Margaret said. Then, as an afterthought, she added, "The number of evictions must stop and stop now. Organizations like Ireland's Land League need your support." The audience politely applauded and she continued, "Please, I ask that you purchase this book and give it to your family and friends so that we can spread the word and come together as one in our commitment to save Ireland. Thank you."

Alex joined her and gave her a kiss on the cheek. "My charming wife," he said, thrusting his arms out toward Margaret and bowing to her. He took Margaret's hand so they could both bow to the people gathered there.

The band started playing and Dr. Cronin's magnificent tenor voice filled the air.

"May I have this dance?" Alex held out his arm and led her to the center of the room. "You were excellent tonight." He smiled. "My Irish lass."

People watched as he waltzed her around the room.

"Tonight is your night, darling."

Margaret was surprised. Alex seemed genuinely proud of her. Together they whirled around and around. Margaret felt everyone's eyes upon her. Those gathered, she assumed, must think them to be a lucky high-society Irish couple. Alex was a distinguished attorney and a member of Chicago's best men's clubs and she, his charming wife, was now an author. Margaret wondered how many people here knew about her career as a journalist. Did they whisper behind their hands about how scandalous it was that she had a job instead of a house full of children? She wondered why these people had come. Were they here because they wanted to celebrate her accomplishment or because Alex asked them to attend? She wished her mother or her brother, or perhaps Michael could have been here to celebrate her victory instead of these people, whom she barely knew.

The other guests joined them as they waltzed around the dance floor. In the corner, a bartender poured drinks and soon everyone appeared to be having a good time.

When the musicians stopped for a break, Alex took a bottle of whiskey and a glass from the bartender and led Margaret to where her books sat on a linen-covered table decorated with fresh flowers. Alex opened the bottle and filled his glass then raised it. "To you, my dear." He took a sip and then set it down.

Alex stood next to Margaret as people filed by with copies of the book to congratulate her.

"It is a pity that they only used your initials as author." Mrs. Clarey pushed a book in front of Margaret to autograph. "Seriously, though, who would purchase a book about Ireland if they knew it was written by a woman?"

Margaret had heard that comment many times and had, in fact, struggled with the decision. She wanted to publish it under her own name, but when the time came, she realized putting her name to it would doom its success and her goal was to rally people in support of Ireland. Keeping her identity a secret was only a matter of using her initials rather than her first name. Alex, however, insisted she use the last name of Sullivan.

Margaret dipped her pen into the ink and wrote M. Sullivan in cursive across the inside cover then handed the book back. She reached out and took a book from the next person.

"I don't know who is the bigger fighter for the cause: you or your wife." Mr. MacKaye playfully nudged Alex with his elbow as Margaret signed a book and handed it back to MacKaye.

"Tonight, my lovely wife is." Alex gave Margaret a slight bow. Then he poured himself another glass of whiskey.

"I want to thank you for writing this book." Mrs. MacKaye placed her hand on Margaret's. "Now people will understand why we care so much for Ireland."

Margaret's pride bubbled up after hearing the comment.

"Mrs. Sullivan, I want to congratulate you for including Mr. Michael Davitt in your book. He is a good man. Too bad he couldn't be here tonight."

"Yes, she does admire him." Alex gritted his teeth and smiled. "A pity he is being detained in prison," Alex said, as he fiddled with one of his cufflinks.

Margaret added, "The book contains information on several notable Irish men including Mr. Charles Stewart Parnell." Alex was not pleased when he found out Margaret devoted so many pages to Michael, but she decided it was the right thing to do. Michael was one of Ireland's martyrs and many people would have been disappointed if she had not mentioned him.

Alex leaned over and whispered, "I trust in your next book you will write a section all about me and what I've done for Ireland."

"We shall see." Margaret grinned.

Outside their house, Margaret watched as Alex fumbled with the door key. He made such a clatter that he awoke Mrs. O'Brien, who eventually opened the door in her robe. When Alex stepped inside, he shed his coat, letting it drop to the floor. Upon entering the parlor he bumped into an end table, sending a vase crashing to the floor. He stepped over it and picked up a bottle of whiskey off a tray, and then made his way down the hall to the library.

Margaret followed him.

"Do you think another drink is necessary?" Margaret asked.

"To my wife." He raised the bottle then poured himself a drink in the crystal glass.

"I think you have had enough." She lunged for the bottle, but he raised it out of her reach.

"The queen of the cause." He gulped down the contents of the glass he was holding in his other hand.

It was obvious he wasn't going to listen to her. "I am tired. I am going to bed." Margaret was about to leave.

"Aren't you going to thank me?" He swayed back and forth. "Wasn't it I who let you go to Ireland in the first place? Wasn't it I who let you have a career as a writer? Wasn't it I who put on this party for you tonight?"

"Yes, and I appreciate all you've done for me. It was most thoughtful of you."

"Most husbands wouldn't let their wives do a speck of what I let you do." He filled his glass again.

"I am well aware of that." Must he always bring that up? She wished he would stop drinking so much. "Let us save this discussion for the morning."

"Come here." He motioned her over with his hand.

She had no intention of going to him. "Darling, I am tired; I'm going upstairs to bed."

"Come here," he shouted.

"No." She turned to walk out the door. "I don't like it when you behave like this. You are drunk." When she stepped into the hallway, she heard the sound of his glass hitting the wall next to her. She didn't turn around but instead climbed the stairs to her room. In the morning Alex would, no doubt, act as though he hadn't spoken an unkind word to her, moaning like a child because of his headache and hoping for her attention.

Laden with disappointment, not only with Alex but with the whole evening, Margaret closed her bedroom door and locked it. What had she expected? Did she think her life would be any different after the book was published; that somehow everyone would understand its importance? She had poured her heart into it, but perhaps the emotions were lost in the words hidden so far down no one would notice. Unlike music, whereby the listener can experience the depth of a sorrowful tune, words don't easily evoke such emotions. Perhaps poems do, or a letter from a lover, but not her book. It contained only depressing facts about a country, or as Michael told her once, an island of rock and dirt shaped by the hand of God. Did anyone in Chicago, besides her, truly care about the people of Ireland?

Margaret took out a sheet of paper to write to Emma, her link to the truth about Ireland. The suffering Margaret witnessed that awful night of the fire had penetrated her soul. It drove Margaret to get involved and motivated her to keep striving to make a difference. She had done what she could for Emma's family, sending Emma money each month to improve her circumstances. Still, Margaret felt like it wasn't enough. There had to be something else she and Alex could do to change the course of history.

PART 2

The Clan na Gael

1881

Chapter 16

MARGARET AND ALEX'S cab slowly approached the corner of State and Monroe where at least twenty horse-drawn carriages were lined up like ants outside the Palmer House Hotel. The driver maneuvered around those departing then took a place in line. Margaret looked out at all the men dressed in black jackets and waistcoats swarming the entrance.

Alex had made special arrangements with his friend and hotel owner, Mr. Potter Palmer, for this year's *Clan na Gael* convention. Apparently, they expected over one hundred and sixty delegates representing camps from across America. According to Alex, extra precautions were being taken and no one who wasn't pre-approved would be allowed in. There would be two check points inside and proper passwords were required. Thinking about this made Margaret uncomfortable. Why all the secrecy? What would they be discussing in there?

When Margaret looked back at Alex, who was sitting across from her, he appeared relaxed and confident in his new black suit and vest. He was wearing the gold cufflinks with the engraved four-leaf clovers she had given him for his birthday. Margaret thought he looked more like a priest with his short, neatly cut hair and his clean-shaven face, than a man who might become the leader of a rebel organization. This was an important night for Alex. He was running for President of the Clan and she had heard rumors he was expected to win.

The horse pulling their cab suddenly moved ahead to the front of the line. It was now Alex's turn to depart.

"Thank you for accompanying me this far," Alex said, then leaned over and kissed Margaret on the cheek. "I treasure your support, darling." He winked and climbed out of the carriage.

As the cab moved away, Margaret waved to Alex, watching him as he occasionally stopped to shake hands with acquaintances and friends. At the next intersection, the carriage turned right to take Margaret home.

Thoughts of this mysterious organization swirled in her head. There had been a constant stream of new activity taking place behind the library door. Margaret never knew what to expect when she arrived home. Often, through the sheer curtains of the parlor window, she could see shadows of strange men parading back and forth smoking their cigars. When introductions were made, she was only told their assigned number and not their real names. They all seemed very polite. Though skeptical, Margaret soon warmed to the possibility that intellectual men were coming together to work on solutions to the Irish problem. After all, Alex told her that the *Clan na Gael* was nothing more than a private men's club for Irishmen, a fraternal organization similar to the Masons, the members helping each other succeed. At the moment, she had no reason to doubt him.

One particular member became a frequent guest. Margaret was allowed to know his name. It was Henri Le Caron. Margaret thought Henri an odd-looking fellow, almost rodent-like in his appearance with his spikey, long, black waxed mustache and his little dark eyes. Alex and Henri often dined together after work at a restaurant and then returned for a nightcap in the library. Margaret grew to like

Henri, a good man who was very polite, a pharmacist and medical adviser. From the looks of him, she would have never guessed that he had been part of the Fenian rebel group that attacked Canada after the Civil War. Henri also claimed to have fought for the union in the war. He didn't look like the military type, she thought. Instead, he looked more like someone afraid of his shadow than a man who had touted a gun. However, Alex insisted the stories of Henri's army service were true.

When Margaret inquired as to why someone with the last name of Le Caron was involved with a secret Irish organization, Henri replied, "My mother was Irish and my father French. They were both strong Irish sympathizers. My mother was a rebel at heart, and I grew up listening to stories of oppression. I can assure you that you won't find anyone more committed than me when it comes to helping Ireland."

Margaret thought his explanation sounded reasonable, and it seemed to satisfy Alex as well, for he stood by Henri whenever the subject was brought up.

The carriage stopped in front of her two-story house. Margaret got out and paid the driver. The lamp in the parlor was lit. Thank goodness, she thought, there were no shadows moving across the walls tonight. The room was empty and the house would be quiet for a change. She climbed the front stairs. Mrs. O'Brien's eyes peeked at her through the little window at the top of the wooden front door. The woman had been told not to open the door to strangers unless they gave the secret knock.

"Good evening, mum," Mrs. O'Brien said after she had opened the door and stood poised to take Margaret's coat.

"I hope it is, Mrs. O'Brien," Margaret replied.

"I beg your pardon, mum?"

"Oh, forgive me. I was just thinking out loud."

Margaret could not shake her uneasy feeling. She was having second thoughts about suggesting Alex run for President of the

Clan. Had she done the right thing by encouraging him to become more active in this secret organization? Would she regret this later? She hadn't done it for Alex, after all, but for Emma and all the poor tenants in Ireland. There had been no other choice. With Michael in jail, there was no one else to generate the funds to continue the progress of the Land League. Her only hope lay with Alex.

After Mrs. O'Brien retired to her bed, Margaret went in search of a strong drink to help her relax. The decanter was empty in the parlor. With all the men coming through her house these days it was difficult to keep it full. In the kitchen, Margaret opened a few cabinet doors but found nothing. She had no idea where Mrs. O'Brien kept the spare bottles. Leaving the kitchen, Margaret wondered where else she might look. She remembered that Alex always kept a bottle of port along with whiskey in the library. It had been months since she had been allowed in there unaccompanied. He would never know, she told herself.

The crystal knob to the library door resisted when she turned it, but there was a slight gap indicating the door had not shut properly. Leaning into the door, she gave it a shove and it opened. There was a lamp near the door on top of a cabinet. She lit it and carried it to Alex's desk. She tried the bottom desk drawer, where Alex normally kept an extra bottle of port, but it was locked. She tried the top drawer to see if the key could be found, but it too was locked. A sheet of paper poking out from under a book sitting on top of the desk caught her attention. She set the lamp down. Carefully, she slid the paper out. Holding it up to the light, she could see it had a long column of numbers. At closer inspection, it appeared to be a balance sheet. Total receipts were listed at $91,453.57 for the year. The expenses column included several items that made no sense to Margaret, such as $23,345.70 for a submarine vessel.

Further down the list, next to lines of figures, were jumbled letters of the alphabet and no explanation. Then she saw the name Davitt with a corresponding number of $1,532. Perhaps the Clan sent money to London to help Michael, she reasoned. Then Margaret realized she was looking at something she might regret later. She wasn't supposed to know any of this. Certainly, she wouldn't be able to investigate the list further without risking trouble from Alex. This was most likely secret Clan business. Still, she was curious. What did they discuss in here? What did this list mean and what were these mysterious expenditures? No, she mustn't think about this, she reminded herself. It would only make her crazy. Her only option was to block such questions from her mind and pretend she had never seen this list. Margaret placed the paper back where she found it. Returning the lamp, she blew it out, closed the door, and pulled it tight behind her.

In the dark hall, Margaret heard someone.

"What were you doing in the library?" Mrs. O'Brien's concerned voice rang in Margaret's ear.

Margaret was flooded with guilt. She defensively replied, "It is not your place to question me."

"Sorry, mum. Mr. Sullivan gave me orders not to let anyone go into his library." The old woman hesitated as if considering whether to speak further. "Especially you, mum. He asked me to tell him if you ever went in there."

Margaret bit her lip. She couldn't have Alex find out. He would be furious with her.

"He did, did he? Well, this is my house, too," Margaret replied. She needed to convince Mrs. O'Brien not to say anything. "I was merely looking for something to drink. I couldn't find where you keep the wine, and I knew Alex had some port in his office."

"I'll show you where I keep the wine, mum. If you will just follow me…" Mrs. O'Brien lit a candle and led Margaret to a lower cupboard in the kitchen pantry where she pulled out a bottle.

"Would you like me to open it for you?" she asked.

"Yes, that would be fine. Thank you." Margaret was worried. "Mrs. O'Brien, I would appreciate it if you didn't tell Alex about this. I can assure you, I only went for some port."

"Of course, mum."

"I take it you won?" Margaret could smell whiskey on Alex's breath and his hair reeked of cigars. The crystal glass in his hand was half empty. Apparently he was still celebrating.

"Indeed, I did." He surveyed the papers spread out on her table and the notes on her writing pad.

"I'm sure you will do an excellent job." She stood up from her chair and shook her hand, trying to get the circulation to return. It was cramped from writing. She had been working on an article about Ireland's current situation.

He picked through her papers, turning them so he could read what they contained. He pulled out *The Irish News* and glanced at the article on Anna Parnell and the Land League. He held it up and smiled. "You know, I have always admired independent women." He winked at her.

Margaret looked at her clock on the table by the window. It was two o'clock and she had already eaten a mid-day meal. It wasn't like him to visit her this time of day. He was still in his wine-colored robe and gray silk pajamas. Obviously, he was in no hurry to go anywhere.

"Yes." She smiled. "It is one of your better traits."

"Just as long as you understand that, now that I am president of the Clan, I may have to do some things you may not agree with."

She stared into his face. What was he talking about?

He set down his drink on the edge of the table and picked up her writing pad and read it. "I may need you to compose some articles."

"Of course." A knot was beginning to form in her stomach.

"Good. Then I can count on you to *not* write anything that might undermine my efforts." He picked up the pearl-handled letter opener and turned it over and over restlessly in his hand.

"Need you ask?" She was confused. Was he expecting her to compromise her role as a journalist?

He flung the opener, which tumbled through the air and landed upright in her leather-top desk. He grinned, apparently pleased with his dexterity.

"Oh, and one more thing..." He moved directly in front of her. She stepped backward and he followed her. The back of her bustle touched the wall behind her and she bumped a table, sending a glass figurine crashing to the floor. Alex reached over and placed his hands around her throat. He leaned over and whispered in her ear. "I don't want you meddling in my affairs."

"Let go of me."

"Ha, my lascivious nationalist wife." He pulled his spread hands across the sides of her neck then he put his thumbs together at its base. "Swear to me you won't do anything foolish." He poked on the small hallow under her wind pipe.

"I have no intention of doing anything to jeopardize your position." She detested his aggressiveness. "Stop it. You're frightening me."

"Good." He kissed her on the cheek and let go of her. He had made his point. She would need to be careful in the future.

The next day, Margaret found a letter from Emma waiting for her on the silver tray by the front door. She carried it upstairs to her room, tearing the side of the envelope along the way.

The letter indicated that James was doing better and his arms were healing nicely. A pencil drawing was included, one he had made for her. Margaret smiled at the heart he had drawn with her name in the middle. She traced it with her fingers. Memories of the fire and the homeless people filled her mind. She sat down at her desk, haphazard piles of Irish newspapers still scattered about. The letter opener stood like a knife protruding from her desk. She yanked it out and threw it across the room.

There was a knock. Mrs. O'Brien poked her head around the half-open door.

"I was meaning to ask you, mum, if you would like me to take care of your bird for ya. I know you don't like anyone in your study when you're not around."

Margaret looked over at the pile of feathers on the carpet and the hardwood floor, then back at Mrs. O'Brien. "Yes, and if you could keep on top of the feathers too, I would appreciate it."

"Mind if I come in now?" Mrs. O'Brien pulled on the bottom edge of her apron. It had bunched up around her middle.

"No, please do." Margaret went through the side door to her adjoining bedroom. When she turned around to go back and retrieve James's drawing, Margaret found Mrs. O'Brien had set her waste basket on the desk and was rummaging through its contents.

"What are you doing?" Margaret had no idea the woman went through her garbage.

"Sorry, mum, I was looking for paper to line the bottom of the birdcage."

Margaret thought about it. "Perhaps you can use newspapers from downstairs?"

"Of course." Mrs. O'Brien looked down at the pile of papers then back at Margaret.

"Go ahead, but in the future, I would prefer you not use my discarded notes."

Margaret skimmed her fingers through the holy water in the stoup at the entrance of Holy Name Cathedral. She made the sign of the cross. Then, slightly lifting the fabric of her skirt in one hand, she moved to a center pew, genuflected and sat down, and placed her satchel next to her. The church was empty of visitors and utterly quiet. Prayer candles flickered, sending requests to heaven. Particles of dust drifted in a ribbon of sunlight streaming through a stained glass window. Closing her eyes, Margaret inhaled deeply. The aroma of incense from morning Mass still hung in the air. In the stillness, ghosts of martyrs and saints whispered messages in her ear, empowering her with the strength and courage to rise above her mortal human weaknesses. The light of her conviction filled her with heavenly passion. Her purpose on Earth was to help others and her sacred vocation was to educate; her pen was her instrument. This she believed without question.

Margaret gazed at the statue of Mary, then knelt and prayed.

"Mary, Mother of God, look with tender mercy on all those who bear the indignities of injustice everywhere. Guide our minds to a meaningful understanding of the problems of the oppressed so we may help them. Sharpen our intellects to pierce the pettiness of prejudice so that we may perceive the beauty of true human brotherhood. May we hunger and thirst after justice always. Amen." She hesitated for only a moment before continuing.

"Also, please watch over and protect Michael. He is a good man, but he is a mere mortal and needs your help."

Margaret slid back into her seat. She savored the moment and then slowly let out a breath. Gathering up her satchel, she left her seat, genuflected, and hurried out the door.

Outside the church, a light breeze tugged at her hat. The bright sun and the noise of a city bustling with activity brought her back to her daily life. She hailed a cab andthe coachman helped her climb in. She needed to drop off her article at the *Tribune.*

Chapter 17

"THEY ARRESTED CHARLES Parnell." Delany dropped the telegram on the pile covering Margaret's desk.

Edwards leaned against the door frame with his thumbs in his pocket and a grin on his face as if amused by the news.

"He is a Member of Parliament." Margaret shook her head in disbelief.

"Says it right here." Delany pointed to the lettering. "On Thursday, October 13th, 1881 Charles Stewart Parnell was taken into custody at the Morrison Hotel. Read it for yourself." Delany lowered his body into the chair across from her desk. "Apparently, he and several other members of the Land League were arrested and thrown in the Kilmainham Gaol in Dublin without a trial."

"Oh, this is not good news." Margaret tapped her fingers nervously on the wooden arm of her chair.

"Their treasurer managed to slip out of the country before the British could grab him or the League's funds. He most likely went to Paris, I would estimate," said Delany.

"This means that Miss Anna Parnell is now in charge," Margaret replied.

"A woman?" Edwards said while stroking his beard. "What can they do? Forgive me, Mrs. Sullivan, but I just don't see how they are going to be able to accomplish anything without the men to tell them what to do."

"These women are quite capable of carrying on the organization." Margaret wondered the same thing, but wasn't about to admit it. At the very least, Anna had a serious challenge before her.

Over the next six months, newspapers from abroad piled up in boxes on the floor in Margaret's office. Malicious articles condemning Anna and the Ladies Land League filled the British newspapers. The Irish news countered with articles of unfair treatment and Anna gave speeches pleading for support. The British threatened to shut the Land League down.

Margaret found herself restless and frustrated whenever she came to work at the *Tribune*. She had doubled her efforts in soliciting funds for the Land League, even going so far as to pay for ads herself from the money she hid from Alex. But, she wasn't satisfied. She pestered Alex to ask for more money to be sent from the coffers of the Clan to the people in Ireland.

"Darling," Alex said. "I am impressed with your efforts. However, you are wearing yourself out with all your fretting over this nonsense in Ireland."

"Someone needs to help these women."

"Yes, but must it be you?"

Margaret glared at him. "I don't see you stepping forward."

Alex grabbed her by the arm. "I am doing my part and don't you ever question my participation."

"Perhaps you could make it more visible?"

"Well, if that is what you want." He let go of her, grabbed his coat and hat, and slammed the front door on his way out.

By mid-April, Margaret had decided that going to Ireland was the right thing for her to do.

"I am appalled at the level to which the British authorities stoop. Let me read you this from the *Irish World*." Margaret followed Delany into his office.

"In their efforts to arrest the women involved, and hoping to damage their reputations, the women of the Ladies Land League have been declared prostitutes. If it hadn't been for a measles outbreak in the prison, the jails would have been overflowing with women." Margaret placed her hand on her waist. "At least they had the good sense to not risk the health of these women. I wonder what else the British will come up with to destroy the League's reputation."

Delany just smiled and shook his head politely. "Margaret, I sympathize with you, but most men don't have much respect for what these women are doing."

"I can't believe they are printing this rubbish." Margaret threw the paper across the room, stormed down the hall, then knocked on the door to her editor's office.

"I want to go to Ireland and write about what's happening," said Margaret.

"No, I forbid it," Mr. White said, folding his arms across his wide body. The smoke from his cigar curled into the air next to him. "I will not risk your safety for this story."

"These women are being treated unfairly." Margaret paced back and forth.

"I understand your concern, Mrs. Sullivan, but I won't allow you to traipse over there. Besides, these women have chosen to put themselves in harm's way. This crazy woman, Anna..." White flicked his cigar ash in the air.

"Parnell," said Margret in a loud voice.

"She is responsible, and she should send these women back home to their husbands."

"I am a woman. Do you think I should be home with my husband too?" Margaret folded her arms across the front of her dress while tapping her foot impatiently on the hardwood floor.

"The only reason I publish your articles is because you are the best writer I have." White glared at Margaret. "It is not because I endorse unfeminine behavior in women."

"I thank you for your patronage." Margaret took her satchel and left in a huff.

Margaret instructed Mrs. O'Brien to bring her travel chest to her room. She had made up her mind; she was going to help Anna in Dublin.

"Would you be so kind as to take care of my bird while I'm away?" Margaret asked. "Perhaps bring her downstairs to the parlor so she won't be lonely?"

"Of course, mum. I'll take good care of Beatrice for you."

"What is going on here?" Alex stood with his hands on his hips at the entrance to her bedroom glaring at her.

Margaret knew he was annoyed. He never liked it when she did anything without asking him. "I'm going to write a firsthand report on the situation in Ireland," she replied.

"No, you are not." Alex lunged toward Margaret in hopes of frightening her, no doubt.

"Don't threaten me, Alex." She glared back at him. "I'm not one of your Clan lieutenants."

"Margaret, you promised me you wouldn't get involved," he said through his clenched teeth.

"I'm a journalist and someone needs to report what these women are doing besides the British and Irish press."

When Alex attempted to grab her, Margaret picked up the letter opener and pointed it toward him. If he made another move she was prepared to lunge at him. She wasn't going to let him intimidate her this time.

Sensing that his bullying tactic wasn't going to work, he put his hands up and backed away.

"I do love you. I would do anything for you. Please, Margaret." He was using his softer charming voice.

"Then let me go to Ireland," she demanded.

"No." He hit the table with his palm causing a slight leap in the glass figurine.

"Then I will go without your consent."

She could see the veins on his neck protruding.

"Margaret, you wouldn't get very far. You know I have friends everywhere. They would just bring you back here." He opened and closed his fists.

Margaret pondered her choices. He could be bluffing, she thought.

"Trust me." He leaned toward her. "We have the same goal. We both want Ireland to be free. I am working just as hard as you are toward making that happen."

She stared at him. Doing what? As far as she could tell, all he did for the cause was go to meetings. Perhaps he and his friends sat in saloons singing Irish ballads all night. What he did to help Ireland was a mystery to her.

"Truce?" He extended his hand toward her.

She put the knife down and reluctantly took his hand, but she hadn't given in.

Chapter 18

THE JOURNEY BY train to New York took two days, and it would be a nine day voyage to Liverpool. Margaret had been paid in cash for her articles over the last several months, and Alex hadn't inquired about her income so she had plenty of money to cover her trip expenses. Prior to boarding the ship, Margaret telegraphed Anna that she would be traveling under an assumed name and that she could be reached in London at the Bentley Hotel where she would be staying for a few days. There was someone she wanted to visit before she departed for Dublin.

Once on the ship, Margaret spent her entire voyage hidden in her room which gave her time to think about her actions. Alex may have men looking for her; then again, there was the possibility that he may not. She decided she would take the risk and do what her heart was telling her to do, regardless of the outcome.

Standing outside the station of the train that had transported her from London to Weymonth, Margaret looked around for the man who would take her the rest of the way. Everything was gray, the cobblestone street beneath her feet, the walls of the buildings, even the air itself. It was almost impossible to tell what time it was, for there was not enough light to indicate if it was just before dawn or dusk. If she hadn't worn a timepiece, she might have guessed wrong. The ghost-like fog curled around the streets, leaving the town veiled in mystery. It was as though the mist around her was hiding something. Something she wanted to know, but could not clearly identify. It lurked in the shadows of her soul.

The gas lamp hissed on the corner. The diffused glow of the approaching carriage's lantern appeared almost otherworldly. She called out and the driver spotted her, bringing his horses to an abrupt stop in the middle of the road.

"Are you the woman looking for a ride to Portland Prison?"

"Yes, and I have all the necessary forms." Margaret waved the papers in her hand.

She was fortunate to have made arrangements her first day in London. Apparently many men had been refused. She had convinced the authorities that she was a journalist for a ladies magazine writing a column about Ireland's rebels. The bald man she had spoken with seemed intrigued that she would want to travel so far just to see the criminal, Mr. Michael Davitt.

"I can't believe that American women would be interested in our Irish villains," the man had said, while lifting his hat and scratching the top of his bald head. She assumed that he had been wavering on his decision whether or not to approve her request.

"Just curious, that is all." Margaret had given him her best flirtatious smile.

"Something to gossip about over tea, I take it?" She remembered his eyes traveling up and down her body.

"You are so clever, Mr….?" She had edged her gloved hand across the counter toward him, just avoiding his hand.

"Preston. Mr. Preston." He had tipped his hat and grinned mischievously at her.

"Apparently you now know our secret." She had covered her mouth with her hand trying to look coy.

Soon she found herself walking out the door with the necessary papers in her hand while the bald man behind the government desk helped the next person in line. When dealing with men, flattery often worked for her, when logic failed.

Margaret glared at the carriage that would be delivering her to her destination. It looked scuffed and worn. She didn't want to think about its previous passengers and what their motives might have been for making the trip.

The driver climbed down from his seat and held out a lantern to inspect the signatures and necessary stamps that gave her permission to enter the prison. Once satisfied, he handed them back and helped her to a seat inside. The damp air followed her into the carriage where she detected an odor of mildew and tobacco. The road seemed long, and they appeared to be the only visitors going in that direction. As they made their journey, Margaret peered out the window. Fog blew by in wisps, revealing the rock formations that dropped down on one side of the road into a smoke-like abyss. Margaret could hear the sound of the ocean crashing on the cliffs below as the horse made its way up the steep road to the outline of the fortress on the hill.

Margaret's thoughts strayed to Michael. How many years altogether had he spent locked away in a place like this, unable to see his beloved homeland? Nine years? He was not guilty of murder. Why was he treated as such? He was a political prisoner, whose only crime was caring for the people of his country.

How lonely he must be, she thought. What did he think about in his cell all day? How could he survive in this closed-in world of gloom, not seeing the green valleys, the forest, the waters, or the stars in the sky? She had been told this time he wasn't even allowed a newspaper, his letters were rarely delivered, and gifts were out of the question. How was he able to find peace with only his thoughts to keep him company? What kind of person risks his freedom not once, but several times for an idea, for others? Margaret had never known such a man before.

Portland Prison was like a citadel, large and impersonal. Was Michael well, she wondered? This couldn't be good for his health. When she arrived at the main gate, her papers were scrutinized, and her satchel was searched for weapons. Her driver was given a nod and they proceeded to the stable inside where he would wait for her return.

Margaret was escorted into the prison building and down a hall by men in uniform. Several doors had to be unlocked before she entered and were again locked after she was through, and then there were more halls until she arrived at a large room deep within the structure. There, her papers were read and stamped. The prison officials obviously didn't consider her a threat or they would have sent her away, she reasoned, or perhaps they thought Michael would reveal some secret plot to her. She could not guess their motives; she barely understood their legal system. She waited on a bench. Inside, the prison was as dark and damp as the air around it. The walls were empty of anything reminiscent of the world outside. It occurred to her that her decision to come here was not just rash but insane. Confined within these walls were prisoners, after all, and not all of them here for political reasons. Some were indeed dangerous. Why was she here? If Alex suspected that she would even attempt such a thing, he would not only destroy her life, but Michael's as well.

Finally, two guards arrived and accompanied her down a long hall. Its dank and musty smells followed her, trailing behind her fears and apprehensions. What if Michael didn't want to see her? What if she only imagined his interest in her, that he was only flattered by her schoolgirl crush? She needed to know.

Michael rose when she entered the room. His hair was cut short, but he looked handsome as always. He was dressed in a plain tan prison uniform. There were no metal restraints securing his legs, giving him free movement about the tiny room. A worn narrow table sat between them with a wooden chair on each side. The two guards stood outside the door discussing something that Margaret didn't care to know, as she was only focused on the man in this room.

"When they told me you were coming, I felt truly blessed. I never imagined that I would see you, and yet you are here before me, a vision from heaven. I know it may seem only a small thing to someone else, but to me, your visit means so much more."

Her eyes overflowed with soft tears. He had lit a flame within her that the wind of others could not extinguish. He reached for her gloved hand. She peeled away the tight laced fabric and then extended her hand, yearning to feel his warm lips on her skin. The moment they graced the back of her wrist, she shivered. Honesty filled her with emotions she had kept for nights alone in her room. She bit her lip, trying to stop the feelings from poking through her resistance.

The expression on his face was of a lover yearning for his mate. The intensity of their unspoken feelings filled the space between them. His eyes traveled straight through her, caressing her silent dreams—a reminder of another season, one of lightness casting away the darkness of others.

The guards stepped back into the room, breaking the spell. Embarrassed, Margaret sat down in the chair across from Michael. She quickly slipped back into her disguise of the visiting journalist, there to write a story of a man imprisoned because of his affiliations. Michael took his cue from her and slipped into his role as Ireland's latest martyr.

"Well, Mr. Davitt, do you feel any remorse for the choices you have made?" Margaret asked, trying to sound professional.

"If one is to live an honest life, he must stand by his choices and take responsibility for them, however they play out."

Margaret was taken aback by his response. Those words would no doubt haunt her later.

"Is there anything you would like the world to know?"

"I have always been interested in the peace and welfare of Ireland. I stand by the actions of the Land League and all their efforts to ease the suffering of the victims trapped in the clutches of cruel and unjust landlords. I call upon others to listen to their heart, to come together peacefully and do what is right and fair for Ireland."

Margaret scratched notes on her pad, leaving the real story of her visit hidden from future readers. Her time with Michael evaporated in an instant, and she was reminded by the guards that she must go. Michael bowed slightly. Her eyes lingered, trying to avoid the inevitable. Her heart ached as if ripped in two. The guards escorted her out. As the door closed and the key turned, she felt the prison lock snap shut around her feelings, again.

Chapter 19

O N THE TRAIN to London, Margaret vowed to carry on Michael's efforts while he was in prison. It was the only thing she felt she could do to demonstrate her love for him. He had sacrificed so much for others, whereas all she had done was compose articles.

There were a couple of other people she wanted to see before going on to Dublin, and after she checked into her hotel, Margaret took a cab to the east end of London. She got out in the Whitechapel district and made her way along a dark ally, passing stinking garbage piled high in the street and an occasional noisy bar with ladies of the evening adorning the entrance. A dog growled at her as she stopped to reread the address under a hissing gas lamp.

"Tis that Margaret Sullivan?" an old lady in rags called to her.

"Why do you ask?" Margaret looked with suspicion at the crone approaching her. The woman had a dark tattered shawl covering her head and most of her white hair. She was small, almost shrunken looking, and hunched over from a curved spine.

"Emma wanted me to watch for a lady by that name. Might that be you?" The woman placed her hands on her hips. "I've come to show you the way."

Margaret relaxed. Now she would have an escort. "Yes, I am Margaret Sullivan."

"Come, dear. I'll take you to where she lives." The woman waited for Margaret to join her.

"Emma says her boy wouldn't be alive today if it wasn't for you." When the woman smiled Margaret could see one of her front teeth was missing. "I'm Mrs. Mooney. I watch James when Emma fills in at the factory. Sometimes they need extra workers and then Emma needs me."

"Pleased to meet you, Mrs. Mooney." Margaret didn't know what else to say. She was never good at idle conversation, especially with someone from Mrs. Mooney's social class. After a moment, Margaret asked, "How is James doing?"

"Quite well. He is as spirited as most boys his age."

"I'm happy to hear that." Margaret was looking forward to seeing him.

Margaret followed Mrs. Mooney down the street to a boarding house. "Emma and James are on the second floor." The woman pointed up at a window. Margaret handed Mrs. Mooney a coin and thanked her then went inside the run down building and climbed the creaking stairs to the landing on the second floor. Margaret knocked loudly on the door. After a few moments she heard a voice.

"Who's there?" a voice called from behind the door.

"Margaret Sullivan."

The door opened and Emma stood, wiping her floury hands on an apron.

Margaret felt awkward and wasn't sure how to greet her. She extended her gloved hand, but Emma threw her arms around her and gave her a hug, leaving traces of white power on the front of Margaret's dress.

"I'm so glad you came. I didn't know when to expect you. I've been baking cakes every day in hopes it would be the day you would arrive." Emma pushed her dark curly hair back from her shoulders. "Please come in. Take a chair. I'll get you some tea. You do want tea don't you?"

Margaret could tell that Emma was as nervous as she was.

"Please don't put yourself out," Margaret replied.

"Sit, please." Emma removed some papers from a chair next to the fireplace. Margaret assumed it to be reserved for her husband, as it was the only one with padding in the room.

James sat on the floor in the corner playing with broken pieces of wood.

"Come." Emma motioned for James to come over. He reluctantly got up. "Say hello to Mrs. Sullivan. You remember her, don't you?"

James just looked at her curiously. He was eight years old now and had grown quite a bit since the night of the fire. Margaret could see that he had a couple of pink scars on his head where the skin had been burned. His arms were covered with the sleeves of his shirt. She assumed he had scars there, as well. He had big eyes like his mother and when he finally smiled, his face lit up. Oh, he was such a precious child, she thought. Margaret wanted to take him in her arms, but was hesitant; she didn't want to frighten the boy. From her pocket she produced a small wrapped box. "This is for you."

He tore at the paper and opened the container.

"Oh, James, it's a wooden top," Emma gushed with enthusiasm. "Here let me show you how it works." Emma wrapped the string around it and pulled the end. The top went skidding across the hardwood floor, bumped into the wall, and wobbled back and forth, then eventually came to a stop. James grabbed it and slowly wound the string back around the toy and then jerked on the end like he had seen his mother do. However, the toy just sputtered a few times and toppled over.

"Don't worry. You will master it with practice," Emma assured him. "Thank you, Margaret. That was very thoughtful of you. Would you like some tea now?" Emma poured water into a china teapot, set a tea cup on a tray along with a slice of cake and a fork, and handed it to Margaret.

"Don't you want any?" Margaret asked.

"No, I've eaten enough already. I've been baking cakes for days."

"Will your husband be home soon? I was looking forward to meeting him."

"No, I'm afraid not. Between work and going to his meetings Peter is rarely home. He has joined the IRB, and I'm worried sick that he might get himself arrested for being seen with them. With Mr. Parnell's and Mr. Davitt's arrest, the IRB men seem to be in a quandary about what to do. Not that they are up to anything, mind you. At least Peter has assured me they are not."

Margaret could sympathize with Emma. Though she wanted Ireland free, like Emma, she did not want her loved ones punished for the actions they took to make it happen.

After her tea Margaret felt more relaxed. Emma was a charming young woman, and James was such a well behaved child. He showed Margaret a few of his drawings and recited some of the things he had learned in school. Margaret felt proud that she was contributing to his welfare and future. She hoped he would go on to do something important in his life, perhaps even go to college. If he chose to do so, she would do whatever she could to help pay for it. She wished Michael could meet young James. Maybe someday he would. James was as close as she would ever come to having a son.

The time went by quickly, and soon Margaret needed to end her visit. Emma went next door and asked her neighbor, Mr. Dunne, to escort Margaret to a safer area, so that she could catch a cab back to her hotel. Margaret hugged both Emma and James goodbye. Tearfully she left with Mr. Dunne, not knowing when she would see Emma and James again.

Chapter 20

MARGARET WAS READY to become a full-fledged member the Ladies Land League. However, when she arrived on Upper Sackville Street in Dublin, she didn't know what to expect or how to help. She eyed the brass plaque with the name *Land League* on the wall next to the door. From the outside it was a tall narrow brick building like so many others, but inside it was a hub of rebel activity. Right now the League was run by women committed to doing something worthwhile that might even change the course of history. Margaret smiled to herself. She was about to become one of them.

Margaret knocked on the door. An older woman opened it a crack.

"Who are you?" she asked.

"Margaret Sullivan. I wired Anna Parnell that I was coming."

"Welcome. I'm Miss Lynch." The woman opened the door and Margaret stepped in. "I understand you are an American journalist and an acquaintance of Mrs. Delia Parnell."

Miss Lynch's full skirt rustled as she led Margaret down the hall past several offices. Margaret had been informed by Delia that the elegantly dressed spinster was Anna Parnell's assistant and the office manager of the Ladies Land League.

"I have had the pleasure, on several occasions, of meeting Miss Anna's mother, Delia Parnell. And yes, I am a journalist. I write under several names." Margaret smiled. "Male names, I'm afraid."

"Here you can write under whatever name suits you." Miss Lynch motioned Margaret to follow her up the stairs to the second floor.

Margaret was relieved. If they wanted her to write she would surely do so, however, perhaps a new name would be in order. "J. Morrin. I will go by the name J. Morrin." She hadn't used that name before.

"We appreciate you coming all the way here to help. Anna is trying to do everything herself and the poor woman can't be everywhere at once."

"Will I be able to go out and see all your good work for myself?" Margaret lingered in front of a small room stacked with boxes.

"I'm sure that can be arranged. Would you like to accompany Anna, or would you prefer I give you a list of names of women to contact on your own?" Miss Lynch asked.

"Whatever you think is best will be fine. I don't wish to be any trouble," replied Margaret.

"As you can see, though we are a small group, we try to run a professional operation. Our publishing department consists of an editor and someone to check the proofs, and of course we have someone to handle the records. We don't print our fliers or *United Ireland* here, everything is sent to a different location. It is safer that way. In fact, if the British continue to interfere, we may have our printing done in France. We conducted a trial run to see if we could smuggle the papers under the nose of the British government."

"Did you succeed?" Margaret asked.

"Yes. We hid the newspapers by attaching them to our bustles, and wore them like petticoats under our skirts. Unfortunately, they were a bit heavy. You couldn't sit down very well."

Margaret thought that sounded imaginative and exciting.

"Please let me know if you need anything." Miss Lynch gestured to the desk in the little room. "Someone will bring tea later, unless of course, you prefer coffee."

Margaret settled herself behind the worn and scratched desk, which wobbled when she touched it. One leg was being propped up by a wooden box. On top of the desk sat a stack of paper, pencils, pens with extra nibs, and a container of ink. Wooden boxes on the floor overflowed with papers. There were notes scribbled on a cracked chalkboard on one wall. An old map of Ireland hung off kilter on another. A dirty window, facing out upon the main street, was dressed in delicate lace. Margaret smiled. Somehow this shabby room felt right.

A shallow box sat on the floor next to the desk. Margaret pulled out a handful of assorted pages and set them before her. She retrieved a pen and a clean piece of paper to jot down notes and observations. Margaret then read through someone else's hand written notes which indicated that the No Rent Manifesto was being carried out across Ireland. She didn't understand the logic behind not paying rent. If everyone refused, the idea might work. Unfortunately, the idea didn't appear to have the results they were looking for, however, because according to another note, tenants refusing to pay rent were being arrested and held without a trial. The way things were handled in Ireland seemed truly foreign to her. Apparently the British could arrest whomever they wished for little or no reason at all.

She set those papers aside and read through another. The numbers were stunning. The total evictions recorded for the previous year came to 27,000. No wonder Michael and the others felt such a strong need to do something now. Americans needed to know how wide spread this problem was.

Margaret prepared her notes for both the League paper and newspapers back home in America. She worked until late, losing all track of time. When she finished, she sat back and bathed in her feeling of accomplishment; wishing all her articles could produce this sensation of doing something beneficial and worthwhile.

The following day after a light breakfast of currant scones and strong coffee, Margaret decided she would walk to the Land League office. It was a couple of blocks from her hotel and only a light sprinkle of rain was falling. She opened her umbrella and strolled past several small businesses and a flower vendor, taking in the quaintness of Dublin along the way. At one street, she carefully crossed, dodging carriages and avoiding the droppings in the road. While waiting to cross another, she noticed a small crowd gathered on the opposite side of the street outside of the office of the Land League. Margaret closed her umbrella and made her way through the crowd to get a better look.

Men in uniform carried boxes out to the police wagon. Several women Margaret had just met the previous day were being led away in handcuffs. Fortunately, she didn't see Miss Lynch amongst them. Margaret had been warned that the police might raid the place; however, she didn't consider the possibility that it could happen while she was there. What should she to do now? Go back to her hotel and wait for someone to contact her? Certainly going to the League office wasn't a good idea. Yes, she would go to the hotel, she decided.

Margaret spun around and came face to face with a man with narrow eyes, a small mustache, and a bowler hat. "Mrs. Sullivan?" he raised his hat slightly as he stepped forward as if to grab her arm.

How would he know her name? She poked him with the end of her umbrella and pushed him back a pace. "You are mistaken, sir." Margaret moved around him then lowered her umbrella and hurried away.

"I need to speak with you, Mrs. Sullivan," he called to her.

People glanced at her as she hurried passed them. Her heart raced. She was unfamiliar with Dublin and had no idea where to hide. Up ahead was a book shop. She stepped inside, hoping the stranger would not pursue her, but the man followed her in. She moved toward the back behind rows of books. Someone who looked like a clerk, or possibly the owner, was standing on a ladder pulling out a book from a shelf high above. Margaret quickly searched for an exit. Spotting a door, she unbolted it and stepped into an alleyway. Her shoes echoed as she ran between the buildings. To her right was another alley. Holding her umbrella under her arm, she tried several doors before one opened. She stepped inside, closed the door, and slammed the bolt, locking it behind her.

"That's not the entrance." A tall blond-haired woman in a multi-colored ruffled gown rushed past her. The woman checked the lock to make sure it was secure. "Why did you use that door? Have you no manners? Are you a thief?" The woman looked Margaret up and down. "Possibly not. I doubt a thief would wear as nice a dress as this." The woman stared at her. "Were you trying to run away from something? The police, perhaps?"

Margaret was out of breath. "I don't know," she managed to respond. "Someone was following me and I... Forgive me, please. It was rude of me," Margaret replied. "My name is..." Margaret hesitated. What name should she give this woman? "Mrs. Morrin."

"May I ask are you with the Ladies League?" the woman inquired, setting a hand on her hip as she spoke. "Don't be afraid to tell me. I am Mrs. Dolan, and I support the League."

"I suppose I am. I was going to their headquarters just now and found the police arresting people."

"Oh, how dreadful. It is a good thing you got away. Are you all right, my dear?"

Margaret wondered how much to tell this woman. She did seem eager to help. Perhaps she could trust her. "A stranger on the street called out my name. My real name that is. I didn't know what to do, so I ran."

"You go by more than one name?" Mrs. Dolan's smile flattened and her eyebrows went up.

Margaret explained to the woman that she was an American journalist traveling under an assumed name and that she was writing an article on the Ladies Land League.

"So, how does this strange person know your name?"

"I have no idea." Who knew she was here?

Mrs. Dolan reached over and pointed to the front of Margaret's dress. "Dear, you have a button missing. Let me find you a replacement." Margaret glanced around at bolts of fabric leaned up against the wall and realized that she was in a dressmaker's shop. Mrs. Dolan led Margaret to a cupboard with many drawers. Mrs. Dolan opened a drawer and held up a button.

"I think this one will do."

Margaret's eyes widened. "Would you mind if I picked out a second button as a souvenir?" she asked.

Margaret stood outside and peered in the window of her hotel. Several men in overcoats and hats were standing around in the lobby. She quickly opened her umbrella and held it out in front of her. She peeked over the edge so that only her eyes and hat showed. She could see one man leaning against the paneling on a wall, eyeing a well-dressed couple coming down the stairs. Was he looking for her? Now every stranger was suspect. She stood outside on the steps debating whether or not to enter. When the door opened, she ducked behind the umbrella. Why did she choose one of the most expensive hotels to stay at instead of one Anna had suggested? She was such a fool. There must be a more modest hotel she could stay in.

Margaret walked to the corner and found an urchin with his hand out.

"Could you tell me where I might find another hotel?" she asked the boy.

He pointed to a place around the corner and indicated that it was two blocks down.

"Thank you, and one more thing..." Margaret dug in her pocket and found a pencil and a scrap of paper. She wrote a note and paid the boy to take it to the dressmaker's shop. "There will be another coin and sweet for you after I know you've delivered the message."

She was hoping Mrs. Dolan could pass on the message to Miss Lynch about her new location. She hailed a cab and left, hoping she wasn't followed. However, for precaution, she had the driver take her down the main street and back in case she was. Once she checked into the new hotel, she made the necessary arrangements to have her luggage transferred. Then she took the key and went to her room. There she would wait until someone contacted her.

Margaret heard a loud knock at her door. She had waited hours in anticipation for someone to inform her of what to do. She wasn't about to turn around and go back home without doing something to help the ladies of the Land League.

"Mrs. Morrin? It is Anna Parnell."

A young woman with Delia's features, but a stronger chin and intense blue eyes, stared back at her when Margaret opened the door. Anna was dressed in a plain gray wool skirt that only came to her knees, showing off her Wellington boots, as well as a traveling cape, a hat, and black gloves. She looked to be Margaret's age, but in the lamp light Margaret could see worry lines across her forehead and in the corners of her eyes.

"Would you like to join me on my rounds? I thought you might want to see what I do."

"I would indeed." Margaret scrambled to get ready. After seeing what Anna wore, Margaret chose a high button-up blouse, a practical warm skirt, her walking shoes, and a long coat. She also put on a medium brimmed hat and tied a scarf over it to keep it from sliding off.

"I don't think you will need that." Anna pointed to Margaret's satchel.

"I don't go anywhere without it," said Margaret. "Besides, I keep a revolver in it for safety."

"You might want to get one of these instead." Anna hoisted up her skirt, revealing a thigh holster strapped to her pantaloons. "I'm sure you can find one in Chicago. I got mine in New York."

"I will keep that in mind when I return home," said Margaret.

Margaret and Anna boarded a train headed for a small village outside Dublin. When they got off at their stop, a young farm boy was waiting for them with a wagon filled with hay.

Under the cloak of the night, the eye of the moon, and the heavens above, Margaret and Anna journeyed between farm communities in the wagon secretly laden with flyers hidden in the hay. Throughout the evening they were met by both women and men eager to help. In one little hamlet Margaret and Anna left the wagon behind to walk across fields and ditches, traveling from farm house to farm house delivering bundles of fliers until Margaret was sure she had carried the weight of several fat pigs.

While they walked, Margaret and Anna chatted.

"I am surprised that you don't have more women from the estates around Avondale involved with the Ladies League," Margaret commented after realizing most of the people they had met tonight were from more modest backgrounds.

"We had a falling out years ago when I criticized my dearest friend for her stupidity in choosing to follow in her mother's footsteps and pursue a husband rather than develop her mind. It was a real shame."

"I suppose the choices were rather limited for women such as yourself," Margaret commented.

"Limited is not the word. Marriage to a society man, either in America or abroad, offers women nothing but a life of misery. Take my sister Sophy, for example. She supposedly married well. However, she was so unhappy in her marriage that she attempted to take her own life. Can you imagine the misery of being tethered to someone you detest? The thought alone gives me indigestion. At least my sister Emily married for love; unfortunately our father disinherited her for doing so. Apparently, one loses either way."

"I was unaware that you had other sisters. Delia only speaks of you and Fanny."

"Mother only cares about Ireland. That is all she ever talks about. Even when she is staying in America, she is obsessed constantly with what is happening to free Ireland."

"What about you? Are you happy being married?" Anna asked Margaret.

"Not especially, however it does have its advantages at times." Margaret replied. In truth, she was starting to wonder what the advantages were. Oh yes, access to politicians and businessmen. Maybe if she were as flamboyant as Delia or Anna she would be looked upon with amusement by those she wished to interview, and they would go ahead and grant her access anyway. It was a charming thought, even if it were beyond the realm of possibility.

"According to Mother, every woman must, forgive the expression, sell herself to get what she wants. I am doing my best to avoid having to service any man for favors, but one never knows their future do they?"

Margaret was surprised by Anna's vulgar statement. Nevertheless, she could not help but think it true.

"Good evening, Miss Parnell." A handsome gentleman with reddish hair walked up. "Here, let me take those." He reached over and took a bundle of flyers from her and tucked them under his arm.

"Thank you. How are you tonight, Brian?" Anna asked. "This is Margaret." Anna turned to Margaret. "Is it okay to tell him your real name?"

"Yes, of course. I'm Mrs. Margaret Sullivan." As soon as she said it, the words felt dry in her mouth.

"Would either of you care for a nip?" He brought out a flask and held it out.

Margaret wondered what it must be like to have the freedom to be kissed by other men. She harbored the dream of kissing Michael one day. Perhaps Anna was bringing to the surface Margaret's discontent with her own life. Being here in Ireland, she questioned not only her marriage but the reasons why she chose to hide her true feelings from herself, as though it were a sin to feel them.

"Thanks for the offer, Brian. However, we have more to do before we can stop to celebrate." Anna waved him off and he disappeared behind a stone wall.

As they walked, the conversation drifted to their current situation. Anna told Margaret of all the work she had been doing to help the Land League. She spoke of the checks she had written to cover the cost of rent for over two hundred evicted families, the dwellings she had built, and the rooms she rented for the homeless to stay in.

"It is still not enough." Anna shifted the bundle of flyers to her other hip.

"I admire your efforts." Margaret remembered overhearing conversations between men in power where debates raged over what proper action to take. But once they agreed, little was ever done to implement their solutions. Here was a woman who had taken it upon herself to make something happen, rather than just talk about it. She should be canonized as a saint in Margaret's opinion.

"We tried to get more people to come together, but each week it gets more difficult. The authorities are doing their best to scare the ladies and evictions have increased."

Margaret remembered James's burnt arms. "I am here to do whatever I can." Margaret picked up her skirt with her free hand and stepped around cow droppings in the road.

"Charles has begged me to give up my work, but I don't intend to." Anna sat on a stone wall and threw her legs over the other side. "How could I, when everywhere I look there is so much to do?"

Margaret envied Anna; the woman had the courage of her convictions. She could imagine the two of them becoming friends and sharing ideas, just like her experience at the convent where women could speak their minds freely. Margaret missed having an independent female friend to confide in. Anna was a woman who wasn't a slave to a husband; she was smart and exploring life on her own. She was just the type of woman Margaret looked up to.

The night quickly passed and the moon faded in the west. Singing birds announced the coming of a new day as light sprouted in the east. Their empty wagon bounced and swayed down the road toward a new destination. Off in the distance, the outline of a two-story dwelling became more pronounced as they lumbered closer.

Margaret and Anna were met by a servant who showed them to a guest cottage containing two small beds where they could rest. After removing her dress, and rinsing her face and hands in the bowl perched on the pine dresser, Margaret fell into bed, content. Exhaustion quickly beckoned slumber, and all sounds ceased around her.

Margaret awoke to the smell of eggs, bacon, and potatoes.

"Up, ladies. There is work to be done." A round pleasant-faced woman with wiry orange and white hair poking out from under her bonnet handed them both a cup of coffee. She had set down a tray containing plates of food for Margaret and Anna to eat on a table by the window.

Anna introduced Margaret to Mrs. Mitchel, a Protestant home-owner who wanted to do her part for Ireland. Her husband was off on business in London and Mrs. Mitchel had volunteered to help Anna while he was away.

Margaret picked up a plate, and while balancing it in one hand, slid her fork into the potatoes. She was famished. Before she knew it, she had eaten all the food on her plate.

"Margaret, if you don't mind, today I will have you go with Mrs. Mitchel and some of the other women." Anna went to the little mirror on the dresser, pinned up her hair, then secured her small hat with a decorative hat pin and tied the ribbon under her chin. "However, please be careful." She turned to Margaret with the look of concern on her face. "A girl was imprisoned last week for merely going into town. She had as much right as anyone else to be there. Unfortunately, when the constabulary suggested she leave, she refused and was sentenced to a month in prison," Anna warned.

"Yes, but we can't let them scare us off, now can we?" Mrs. Mitchel replied. "Or we'll never be free."

Margaret stood next to Mrs. Mitchel and waved goodbye to Anna. They watched as Anna's now empty wagon bounced down the road to some unknown destination. "I wish you luck," Margaret said, though Anna was too far away to hear.

Turning to Mrs. Mitchel, Margaret smiled. She was ready to participate in something new. The woman motioned to Margaret to follow her around to a wagon waiting next to the barn. Clutching her ever-present satchel, Margaret climbed in and took her place next to Mrs. Mitchel on the front seat. A tan horse swished its dark-colored tail while it waited for its command.

"This is my charity work, and I guess right now it is yours, too." Mrs. Mitchel beamed.

Margaret hadn't thought of it as charity work. To her it felt more personal.

"Today we will be collecting baskets of food and clothing. Then we'll drop off the donations and go join the movers," Mrs. Mitchel said, snapping the reins. "Walk on." Chickens scurried out of the way as the horse trotted the path to the main road and turned left.

Happy faces ran out to greet them everywhere they stopped. Women handed them baskets of eggs, bread, cabbages, and bags of potatoes. One man gave them two live chickens in a wooden cage and a container of cheese. After everything was carefully packed in the wagon, Margaret and Mrs. Mitchel headed off to deliver the donations. When they drove up, Margaret could see peasants waiting outside the stone church in a long line. Some carried young children; others assisted the crippled and the elderly. Most were barefoot. A few boys wore dresses, so as not to be snatched by fairies and carted away. The only protection their superstitious mothers had to keep them safe. Unfortunately, the dresses wouldn't keep the hunger from gnawing at their stomachs.

Margaret made the sign of the cross as they trotted past. May God have mercy on them. "Do you think there is enough to feed them all?" Margaret asked. She had never known hunger, but doubted the few baskets they had brought would feed more than a few dozen.

"Jesus fed the multitudes with only a few loaves of bread," Mrs. Mitchel replied. "Let us pray Father Duffy can do the same."

Several bone-thin boys in ragged clothes helped pass the bundles of food and the cage with the chickens to Father Duffy.

"God bless you," Father Duffy called out, as Mrs. Mitchel turned their now empty cart to the main road.

"Walk on," Mrs. Mitchel told the horse. "Now for our other task of the day: moving those poor evicted families."

Margaret and Mrs. Mitchel traveled down the road in their wagon to a clearing where they were met by several other women waiting with carts to be pulled by swayback horses and mules. Mrs. Mitchel pointed out each of the ladies and told Margaret their names.

"Mrs. Flynn is the woman there dressed in her Sunday best. She is the wife of a wealthy merchant, and not one to boss around. She hates the British and is known to pick fights just to see if they dare arrest her. Miss McCabe, the young woman with brown hair and a Bible in her hand, is the daughter of a Protestant preacher. She is here to do God's work. Miss Jacob, on the other hand, is a suffragette and here to prove a point. Those two ladies are Miss S. Byrne and Miss M. Byrne, old maid sisters here to further the cause. And the lady over there standing next to the gray horse is Miss Alicia Flood, the rebellious daughter of a wealthy landlord, here to protest the unfair treatment of tenants everywhere."

Margaret was thrilled to be part of the group.

Once all the ladies were accounted for, they proceeded in a caravan down the road. When they arrived at the village, neighbor helped neighbor load each other's belongings onto the carts. Children rode high atop piles of furniture, kitchen utensils, and farm tools, while men walked alongside. They would be putting their things in the barns of strangers who had volunteered to keep them dry and safe until they could be collected and moved to a new residence.

The sun was low in the sky by the time all evicted villagers' belongings were stored and the carts returned. The evicted families set up camp in one of the farmer's fields for the night. They would have to move on in the morning in search of another place to sleep.

Margaret joined the other women on foot as they proceeded to walk to a nearby eatery and celebrate the day's accomplishments. She swung her satchel next to her as she walked.

"I'm having ale tonight so don't lecture me about the evils of drinking," Miss Jacob told Miss McCabe. Margaret decided ale sounded good to her, too.

"A lemonade would quench my thirst," said Miss McCabe, and several ladies agreed.

Up ahead was the constabulary with a wagon. Several officers leaned against it with their arms folded, waiting. Margaret's group of ladies put their heads down and marched forward.

"What might you good ladies be up to this evening?" one of the men asked as he approached them.

"It is none of your business." Mrs. Flynn pushed past them. The others followed her lead and kept moving.

"You aren't causing trouble and stirring up the locals are you?"

"The only trouble here that I can see, are you and your men," Mrs. Flynn replied.

"Well, there will be no loitering or gathering for rebel meetings in this town."

"We are here to seek out a meal that is all." Miss McCabe waved her Bible at them.

"I'm afraid you will have to come with us first," said a tall man, who appeared to be the head constable.

Margaret didn't say a word. She wanted to witness how these men treated the ladies of the Land League. As things progressed, she couldn't help but find humor in the event. Several officers tried herding them like geese into a pen. One man lifted Miss Alicia Flood into the wagon. Another chased Miss Jacob in circles while she stayed just beyond his grip. Margaret watched as the men put the different women in the wagon only to have them climb out again.

"Ladies, ladies. Your behavior is that of juveniles. Please, come peacefully or we will have to restrain you."

Mrs. Flynn walked up to the man in charge and put her wrist together. "Take us in chains if you must. Let everyone see how you treat the fine women of your community."

Someone tapped Margaret on the shoulder and when she turned around an officer snapped cuffs onto her wrist. It never occurred to her that she might suffer the same fate as the other women. She clutched the handle of her satchel tightly; she had never been arrested before. Going to the local jail would be exciting and patriotic but she knew they wouldn't dare keep her once they found out she was an American. Margaret smiled. This would make a great story.

"Get into the wagon, mum." His dark eyes peered at her from just below his helmet.

Margaret sat in the back of the wagon on a bench facing out so she would watch what was behind them. Once all the ladies were in the wagon, the horses pulling it trudged slowly down the road. Margaret watched the uniformed man trailing behind on horseback. She tried smiling, but she was only met by his blank, possibly disapproving, stare. She wondered what was going on in his mind. Was he merely doing his job or did he think these women were going to start a revolution?

They traveled past several stone dwellings and turned near a blacksmith shop. Margaret noticed something move behind a barrel. Two men with blackened faces ran and hid behind a building.

Ahead, a drunken man staggered out in front the police wagon and they came to an abrupt stop.

"Get him out of the road," the officer in charge yelled. Two men dismounted and approached the inebriated old man. The officer Margaret had been watching rode up ahead to assist.

"Drag him to the side."

While watching the drama, Margaret felt someone put a hand over her mouth and pull her quickly from the wagon. She was lifted from one man and passed to another, then placed under a cloth in the back of a strange cart containing damp hay. The horse lunged forward, and gathering from the sounds she heard, her absence had not been detected yet. Was this how all the ladies would be rescued, she wondered? Perhaps Anna had a hand in this. It seemed amazingly creative. She decided to keep quiet, at least until they had traveled some distance and it was safer to speak. Her hands were still in metal cuffs that rubbed on her wrists, and she quickly became uncomfortable with the cloth over her head.

After some distance, that could only be measured by counting the clip clops of the horse's feet upon the ground, they stopped.

"I think this is the place." It was the first voice she heard since she was plucked from the police wagon.

The rag was thrown back from her head. A man with a sooty black face lifted her out and indicated with a nod for her to go into a crumbling stone building. It was now dark and she could see stars starting to appear through the broken thatched roof. A couple of sheep huddled nearby in the corner, watching. It was then that she noticed there were no other women, only her and the two men with darkened faces.

"Excuse me. Where are the other ladies? Have you not rescued them, also?"

"No, I'm afraid those ladies will be spending the night in a cell instead of here with us."

"I don't understand?" Who were these men? Why had they only taken her?

"Sit down." One of the men pointed to a crude stool next to a pile of hay.

"Not until you answer my questions."

"You don't need to know anything so just get comfortable. It may be a while before someone comes for you." He lit a lantern that cast shadows on the broken stone wall.

"You want a drink?" said a chubby little man with red sideburns that grew down to his chin. The cheeks that weren't covered with hair were smeared with coal dust and grease. He wiped off the opening of the bottle with his sleeve and reached out to hand it to her.

"She's a lady. She won't drink from a bottle, especially with your mouth all over it." The tall dark-haired man with a devilish grin winked at her.

"Sorry, ma'am, don't have a glass." The red-haired man lifted his stove top hat and gave her a slight bow.

"Give it here," The dark-haired man grabbed the bottle and took a couple of gulps then handed it back. He pulled at his belt, then stuck his hand down the front of his pants and walked over to Margaret. "You are a fine-looking woman." He touched the side of her face with his free dirty hand. "And you smell good too." He wiggled his hand in his pants. "I'll bet that isn't all that's good about you."

How dare he say such a thing to her? Margaret prepared to smack him with the side of the metal cuffs. She eyed him to see what his next move would be.

"Ay, leave her alone. You want to get us both killed? She is not to be harmed, or did you forget that part of the deal?" The red-haired man shoved the devilish man away. "Sorry, madam. He's not from around here and doesn't have any manners."

Margaret didn't know if she should be frightened or not. Perhaps they only wanted to scare her, but then these men obviously had taken her for a reason and it wasn't to rescue her from the police. Had they been following her and the other ladies? Perhaps they had planned to take her all along. She had no idea what value she held for them. Only a few people knew who she was. Who was coming for her?

Certainly, the ladies would have noticed she was missing by now, but then again, maybe they assumed she escaped and they weren't alarmed by her absence. Under these odd circumstances, there wasn't anyone they could report her disappearance to anyway.

Neither man appeared to have a weapon. Margaret sat down on the stool and set her satchel on the hay next to her. If she could only get to the revolver inside. She stared at the two buckles holding the satchel closed. Would the men notice if she tugged on them? Margaret looked over at the men and was met by their grins. Perhaps she would wait until later.

Margaret tried engaging them in conversation, but the dark-haired man licked his lips, wagged his tongue at her, and made lewd expressions with his face. So Margaret turned her head and kept quiet.

Other than her kidnapping, her day had been fulfilling. Margaret looked up at the stars through the hole in the roof and thanked God for allowing her to walk side-by-side with the ladies of the Land League, the true crusaders of the cause. How could she hope to convey the circumstances under which so many lived here in Ireland without sounding like an annoying evangelist? Perhaps it was her mission to do so, whatever the cost to her.

After the men had finished their bottle, they started singing sad Irish songs of battles long ago. They sang until their words slurred into mumbles. Soon the red-haired man was fast asleep.

Margaret waited for the other man to pass out, too. She caught him staring at her. He stood up, wandered over by the door, and went outside to relieve himself. He returned carrying a rope.

She watched him as he came over and stood in front of her. Grinning, he reached down to grab her hand. Margaret swung her arms, striking him on the side of his face with her cuffs and he fell backwards. He rolled over and she felt his hand around her ankle, yanking her to the ground. With her hands clamped together, she struggled to hit him again but he rolled on top of her. She could smell his disgusting breath as he pawed at her. She squirmed, thrashing about, kicking her legs. He tried pulling up her skirt. She bit his ear and he yanked away. Then he came at her with the rope but stopped.

Margaret thought she heard horses pulling a carriage. Would they go on by, she wondered? She heard the carriage come to a stop. The dark-haired man dropped the rope, scrambled to his feet, and backed away.

Could this be the person coming for her? She listened to the movement outside.

Moments later, to her surprise, Margaret recognized the person standing in the doorway pointing a revolver.

"Come with me, dear." Delia spoke in a loud, authoritative voice, wakening the red-haired man from his sleep.

"What?" The red-haired man struggled to stand.

"You gentlemen go home now, and I won't tell the constable about this."

Their mouths hung open like they were waiting to be spoon-fed.

"I know how to use this gun, so don't test me." She pointed it at the dark-haired man.

Both men dusted off their trousers. The dark-haired man picked through the hay until he found his hat, then placed it on his head.

"Oh, and please wash that disgusting muck off your face." Delia pointed to the red-haired man's cheek.

"Yes, mum." He wiped his fingers across his face and looked at them.

"Hey, what about our money?" The dark-haired man approached Delia.

"I suggest you take that up with whoever arranged for you to kidnap this poor woman."

"Come, dear," Delia motioned Margaret outside. A man servant took Margaret's satchel from her and placed it inside, then helped Margaret climb in the carriage. Delia followed.

"They didn't hurt you did they?" Delia examined Margaret's face.

"No." Margaret shook her head in bewilderment.

Delia looked at Margaret's handcuffs. "I'll have one of the men remove those when we get back to Avondale."

"Who were those men?"

"Just hired men." Delia flicked her hand as if to shoo away a pesky bug.

"Why did they want me?"

"I'm sure they had their reasons." Delia reached over and touched Margaret's hand. "Let's not dwell on them. Would you care for a drink?" Delia smiled then produced a bottle and a box with two glasses wrapped inside from a compartment under her carriage seat.

"Thank you for your offer, but I would go right to sleep if I did."

"Well, maybe that is just what you should do. You are safe now with me. And God knows you must be tired after all you've been through today."

Delia put a glass in Margaret's cuffed hands and poured her some Madeira.

"You poor dear. Drink up and go to sleep if you need to. I'll quit my chattering."

The drink was comforting, however, Margaret's mind couldn't let go of the incident in the barn. There certainly were more questions than Delia was willing to answer. Margaret waded through different possibilities. Maybe Anna had conveyed to Delia her whereabouts and Delia had come to say hello; then again, how did Delia know Margaret was in that barn? It was possible that someone saw them leave and followed behind. The men didn't appear to be terribly bright and could have given away their plan in advance. Then there was Alex. Margaret dismissed that thought. He couldn't have known where she was. He was clever, but how would he know where to look for her? Besides, he would kill any man that attempted to touch her.

Chapter 21

MARGARET AWOKE TO the sound of a knock on the door. One of the servants brought in tea and toast and what appeared to be mulberry jam. Another servant dragged in her travel trunk and put it in the corner.

"Lady Parnell had it delivered. She thought you might appreciate having your things."

"Why yes, thank you," Margaret pondered the thought for a moment. Apparently, either Anna or Delia knew that she would end up back at Avondale. Whoever it was, they guessed right. She did plan to pay a visit while in Ireland. Perhaps there were no secrets in the Parnell family.

Downstairs, Margaret found Delia in the sitting room staring out the window.

"It is a beautiful place, wouldn't you agree?" Delia commented.

"Yes, Avondale is quite picturesque." Margaret joined her at the window.

"No, I was speaking of Ireland." The corners of Delia mouth curved into a frown.

"Yes, I know, it has captured my heart," replied Margaret.

"You and thousands of others." Delia let out a sigh. "I just wish there was more we could do to make the wretched British let her go."

"I believe we are all trying to make that happen."

"That reminds me, dear. Charles and Michael have been released from prison. I expect them to be here shortly."

"That is wonderful news." Margaret glowed with excitement.

"I wouldn't be celebrating just yet."

"What do you mean?"

"Let us wait and see what the men intend to do before we hail them as heroes."

Margaret stood outside waiting. She had dreamt of this moment. When Michael rode up, it was as if her lover had returned from a long journey. She wanted to run to him and hold him close to her. In her imagination, they kissed. But here, out in the open at Avondale, she would have to show restraint, it was expected of her. She did not want to jeopardize the precious time they did have together by embarrassing him, or by arousing suspicions about her attraction to him.

"Maggie, you look lovely," Michael called to her as he leaned forward on his horse. He got down then handed the reins to the stable boy. "Come, let's go for a walk."

Together they strolled down the path around the side of the house to the back. A lawn of green rolled out to the edge where it dropped off into a garden below. Just being in his presence gave her butterflies.

Michael came to a sudden stop and looked over at her. "I've so much to say, yet I feel dumbfounded, for the words are only sounds and cannot convey what is in my heart."

Margaret hungrily waited in anticipation. But, the words went unspoken.

He turned away. "I am sorry, I… I mustn't burden you with my desires."

"No, please. It is all right." Margaret reached out and touched his face.

Michael kissed her hand then held it against his cheek. He sighed. "I can't. It would not be right."

An arrow of regret shot through her hopes. "No, of course." She withdrew her hand. "I'm sorry that I was unable to join you the night of your speech in Chicago," Margaret said, choking back her unhappiness.

He looked at her as though he didn't know what she was referring to. "I didn't expect you to."

Margaret was puzzled. "But you left me a note to meet you in your hotel room."

"Maggie, I don't mean to disappoint you, but I never wrote you a note. I had known before I arrived that we wouldn't be able to spend more than a brief moment together." He studied her face.

She turned away concealing her true feelings and replied, "Of course."

Over Michael's shoulder she saw someone standing in the window, watching. "I must go." Margaret ran up the path to the house, leaving Michael behind. How foolish of her to think her love for him could change anything. It hadn't and it wouldn't. He may call her Maggie, but she was still Mrs. Sullivan to him.

From the entryway, Margaret could hear Delia's voice. Margaret went to the sitting room, stood at the entrance, and glanced in.

"When are you going to tell your sister Anna?" Delia paced back and forth in front of the window waving a pearl-handled lace fan in front of her face.

"Mother, please stay out of this!" Charles poured himself a whiskey from the decanter on the silver tray. "This is none of your business. I told you not to meddle. We appeared disreputable and reckless by allowing women to get involved. Even the Catholic Church condemned us."

Delia looked at Margaret. "Margaret, dear. I think it best if we leave him be. I am disgusted with all this talk of the future of the Land League and what is going to happen next." Delia tossed her fan in the air in a fit of anger. "Charles can be very unreasonable at times." She glared at him. "Maybe Michael can talk some sense into him."

At that moment Michael entered the room, "Good day, ladies." He bowed to both of them.

"It is so good to see you again." Delia kissed the air on both sides of his head. "I hope your prison stay wasn't too uncomfortable."

"It was a great improvement over my previous visit." He winked at Margaret.

"Still, any time confined must be terribly unpleasant."

Margaret couldn't help but admire his conviction. What makes one person put their life in danger while another hides behind the bravery of others? It was a mystery to her.

Michael turned to Margaret. "Mrs. Sullivan, I understand you have been busy helping Anna with the Ladies Leagues."

"Yes, and it has been quite interesting." After her experience, she now carried an even deeper feeling of empathy and hope for Ireland's future.

"Come, dear." Delia motioned Margaret to follow her. "Let's leave them to discuss things."

"I want to thank you for all you've done. It is most appreciated." Michael smiled then bowed again.

Margaret lingered at the door. Delia shook her head in disgust and left Margaret to listen on her own.

"Women have done more harm to the movement than good." Charles walked to the window with his glass and looked out into the garden below.

"Excuse me? I beg to disagree with you." Michael touched Charles's shoulder. "The evidence of what they have achieved is in the resignation of Forster, the dropping off of coercion, and our release."

"Rubbish." Charles turned around then lifted the drink to his lips.

"The women kept the Land League alive while we sat in prison. Anna and the other women should be praised for their work."

"I ordered Anna to stop her nonsense. She disobeyed me."

"Look at all the good she accomplished by providing rent and homes for hundreds of people."

"She stirred up trouble. The newspapers accused us of using women to do our work and putting them in harm's way."

Margaret clenched her jaw while her pulse raced. Charles's narrow mindedness was appalling. He had no idea how hard the women worked for them while he and Michael sat in jail.

"It was the British who used force on them. The ladies committed no crime."

"There will be no more Ladies League." Charles slammed down his glass. "I am cutting off all their funds."

"I do not understand." Michael stood there with his feet apart and his hand on his hip.

"I'm also dissolving the Irish Land League," Charles stated.

"We have made so much progress. Why do you want to abandon the tenants now?" Michael flung his hand in the air.

"Prime Minister Gladstone promised me that he would take action to help the tenants."

"Gladstone?" Michael backed up, distancing himself from Charles.

"He will introduce a substantial measure of relief for small tenants in arrears on their rent, and in exchange, I agreed to end the tenant protest and to cooperate with the Liberal Party."

"You made an agreement with the British government without consulting me and the other members?"

"I will be dissolving the current Land League in the near future."

Pompous ass, thought Margaret. What about all the money that was raised? Was this just a political ploy for Charles?

"I plan to form a new organization that will support my position in Parliament."

Michael stormed past Margaret and out of the room.

"Mr. Davitt," Mrs. Gaffney called as she came running from the front door. "An urgent message has arrived for you and Mr. Parnell."

"What could it possibly be? Perhaps they made a mistake about my release," Michael said sarcastically.

"No, sir. Lord Frederick Cavendish and Mr. Burke have been murdered. Happened in Dublin. Someone stabbed both of them," Mrs. Gaffney announced.

"Who were they?" Margaret asked, joining Michael in the entrance hall. She hadn't recognized the names.

"Lord Frederick Cavendish was the new Chief Secretary. I don't really know much about him," Delia replied from behind. "Burke, however, was out to put every Irishman who didn't fall in line in jail. That man deserved what he got."

"How can you say such a thing, Mother? Neither man deserved to die. This is an outrage." Charles stood with his hands on his hips.

Michael studied the paper then handed it to Charles.

"Do they know who did it?" asked Margaret.

"The message says the authorities suspect it might be rebels, possibly Land League members," replied Mrs. Gaffney.

"The Land League?" Margaret's voice went up an octave. "Why would they think that? Did they arrest a member?"

"I'm not surprised they would accuse the Land League," replied Delia. "The British have been trying to discredit the League with their lies from the beginning."

"We can't have people believing the Land League would approve of such a crime. We must write a statement condemning this action immediately," Michael said, looking at Charles.

"Yes, indeed. I don't want anyone to think I had anything to do with this," Charles added.

"I'll have to notify everyone to refrain from any rebellious activity. It would mean a certain bloodbath for anyone the British suspected might cause trouble," Michael announced.

"Of course, dear," Delia said. "Please be careful. The last thing we want is for them to arrest you again."

Michael looked over at Margaret. "I have no intentions of going back to prison."

"But, you just got here." Margaret was sick inside with worry. What was he going to do when they came for him again? He had just spent time in prison for what amounted to nothing, and now he was going to risk everything again to try and save a few hotheads from being baited into a confrontation with the British authorities. What drives a man like him to do such a thing? Did he enjoy being in the middle of the controversy? She bit her lip. She would never understand. Now that Charles had decided to dissolve the Land League, what was Michael going to do? His dream for a peaceful and united rebellion had just been beaten down by a man he trusted, and yet he still treated the traitor as a peer and friend. She was frustrated by his actions and yet loved him for what he stood for and who he was.

Charles and Michael headed to the library to work out the composition of their statement for the British press. Margaret joined Delia in the sitting room.

"I'm worried about Michael." Margaret had to say it.

"Yes, it is unfortunate." Delia stared out the window. "But Charles does have to deal with the British, and he has never been one for rebel activity."

"What about Anna?" Margaret asked. She knew this would be a terrible blow to her. It was hard enough to understand how Charles could do this to Michael, but betraying his own sister? Did he think he could just toss away all the good they had done? What about the people they served, the hope they had given them. Who would help the people now? Margaret wanted to spit in his face. How could he call himself a patriot for Ireland?

"This will not sit well with Anna, I'm afraid." Delia gave out a heavy sigh. "I don't know that she will be able to forgive him. He is such a fool."

Margaret had tremendous respect for Anna. Certainly this experience would add to Anna's dislike of male behavior. "Whatever happens, please let Anna know I wish to keep in touch with her."

"Yes, dear. Of course."

"Well, ladies. I'll bid you farewell now, as I'll be leaving shortly." Michael stood in the doorway.

It took all of Margaret's will power not to go to him. She would be going back to Chicago and probably wouldn't see him until... when? Without the Land League, nothing would tie them together. Would he just disappear from her life? The thought of not ever seeing him again made her numb with sadness.

Margaret rose from her chair and followed him into the entry hall. She watched as Michael put on his coat and slipped the correspondence in his pocket. She bit her lip when he opened the door. Michael was leaving. He hesitated then said, "Good bye." He set his hat on his head and went out into the night.

Margaret stood at the entrance watching as the stable boy brought a horse out for Michael. Not being able to control herself, she hurried out the door after him. He had his foot in the stirrup and was about to climb onto his horse. "Wait." Margaret went to him. "A button. Can I have a button?" She wanted not just his button, but all of him. She trembled at the thought of losing him.

Michael let the reins fall out of his hand and tugged at a button on his vest. Margaret reached into her pocket and pulled out a tiny pair of sewing scissors. Her intention was to ask him for one earlier, but the timing wasn't right. If he had left, she would've never forgiven herself for coming home without the keepsake. Michael stood with his chest puffed out and Margaret leaned in and clipped the threads. He caught the button and then kissed it. She opened her hand and he placed it in her palm, closing his fingers around hers. He lifted her hand to his mouth. She shut her eyes, focusing on the sensation of his whiskers as they brushed across her hand. When she opened her eyes, he was smiling.

"Well Maggie, hopefully I will not be rushing off next time we meet." Michael climbed onto his horse and trotted out the entrance way. He lifted his arm in a wave.

"Be careful," she yelled. Margaret watched as he disappeared down the road. Something inside told her it would be a long time before she would see him again. The thought filled her with unbearable grief. Tears rolled down her cheeks. She ran to the back of the house, sat down on the stone bench, and wept. Wrapping her arms around her shoulders, she rocked back and forth, sobbing. Oh what had she done? Why had she let herself fall in love with a man she could never be with? She had deceived herself into thinking that it didn't matter, but it did. Margaret wiped her eyes with her sleeve. Up in the night sky, stars shone like needle pricks in her wounded soul. She had never felt such pain. Her weeping began again. She tried taking deep breaths instead of shallow ones to gain control of her sadness but she was powerless and couldn't hold back her emotions.

Through blurry tear-filled eyes, she saw what appeared to be Delia approaching. Margaret dug her nails into her palms in an effort to divert her mind. Delia mustn't see her like this. Margaret sat up straight and sniffed. Quickly she wiped the wetness from her face with her sleeve again.

"There, there, dear." Delia handed Margaret a clean kerchief. "It has been hard on all of us. Charles can be such an ass at times." Delia placed a shawl around Margaret's shoulders. "Why don't you come inside and take a hot bath and have a stiff drink? Don't think about all of this now. You will have plenty of time to sort everything out on your trip back to Chicago."

Chapter 22

O N THE TRAIN to Dublin, the stabbing of the new Chief Secretary of Ireland, Lord Cavendish, and that of Thomas Burke, the head of the Irish Civil Service, was on everyone's lips. Margaret overheard the two gentlemen sitting across from her discussing the event and the possibility of more murders being committed by the unknown rebels. She also heard whispers from other passengers; the killings were in retaliation for the arrest of Michael Davitt and Charles Parnell. Could these rumors possibly be true, she wondered, and if so, who ordered the assassinations and why? Didn't these criminals realize they would be undermining all the good work that Michael had been doing? Hadn't it been agreed upon amongst the IRB that no violence would be used against the British? Perhaps Michael's dream of uniting everyone was only an illusion? Her head throbbed from all the questions. She was tired of thinking about Ireland's problems at the moment. She had her own pain to deal with.

When the train arrived in Dublin, police were milling around the railroad station. One officer tipped his hat as he walked past Margaret. She could see that these officers were eyeing both departing and arriving passengers as they walked up and down the platform. While the officers were looking for possible trouble makers, Margaret was looking for peace, some solace in her overturned world. She shook, trying to shake off the heaviness of her thoughts. She motioned for someone to assist her with her luggage and headed toward the exit.

Delia had suggested the Morrison Hotel as a place she could rest before her long trip home, and since Margaret had stayed there before, the idea appealed to her. When Margaret spoke with the clerk, he told her there was a room available on the third floor. She secured a reservation for one night. Tomorrow, she would board a steamship heading for New York.

Fatigued, Margaret decided it might be wise to get a bite to eat before retiring, and so she asked the bellboy to deliver her luggage while she went to dinner.

Feeling a little better after a cup of tea, Margaret spread out the newspaper to read while she waited for her food to arrive.

The news was not good. A mob had attacked the Irish quarter in Brighouse, England in response to Lord Cavendish's death. Apparently many Irish were badly beaten and their houses destroyed. The rest of the Irish fled the town, afraid there would be further outrages that could escalate into mass killings. No wonder Michael was in such a hurry to warn the Irish.

Several articles speculating about the recent murders filled the paper. Besides blaming the Land League, there were rumors that American rebels had been involved. Margaret thought both ideas were ridiculous. The Irish in America would never attempt such a crime. Why were they printing these wild lies? When she read further, she found the newspaper hinting it would pay for information. That explained these mad accusations. It would be a while before the truth would be known. She would be back in Chicago before this crime had been solved.

Perhaps Mr. White would be expecting her to telegram him about the incident. However, she had no idea what to write. Crime reporting was not her forté and someone else could cover the murders. She was not interested in chasing that story.

After dinner, Margaret climbed the stairs to her room. Her body was sluggish and her mind numb from all she had been through the last couple of days. The idea of returning to Chicago depressed her, but there was nothing of significance for her to do here. Ireland, the Land League, and even Michael had become tiresome burdens. Burdens she would be dragging back to Chicago with her. If she could only discard these thoughts like a worn out gown, perhaps she would be better off.

The lobby was nearly empty when Margaret retrieved her room key. She unlocked the door and set the key on the table. She removed her hat and pulled the pins out of her hair, then shook her head letting her curls fall onto her shoulders.

In the dark, Margaret unbuttoned her shoes, slipped off her stockings, and unfastened her bustle and corset, then stepped out of her pantaloons. Dressed only in her chemise, she hung her dress on a hanger in the wardrobe. Then she heard a sound. Someone was in her room. Panic rose in her.

In the corner near the wall, a match was lit.

"You knew I'd come for you."

Margaret flinched at the tone of his voice. "You startled me," she said.

He tossed the consumed match to the side. His shadowy outline approached her.

She froze. Can I not hide from him? Does he know me too well?

Alex lit a lamp. He set the flame low so it barely brought light into the room. Margaret turned her back to him. She was tired and had no fight in her.

He walked over and stood in front of her. "I was worried about you." His long fingers touched the nape of her neck. She felt pressure on her wind pipe from his thumb as he slid it up and down her throat. "Running off when I told you not to."

"I…" What was she to say? It was useless even to pretend. She didn't have an excuse prepared. Her mind was void of cleverness.

"I've missed you." Alex reached over and untied the front of her chemise, her veil of protection. "You've missed me too, haven't you?" The question hung in the air, demanding confirmation.

"Yes." She choked back the truth in her throat.

Alex slipped his hands under the fabric, pushing it off her shoulders. It dropped into a limp pile at her feet.

"There, that is much better." He stood back admiring her naked body in the semi-darkness.

She tried covering herself with her hands but he pushed them away.

"You disappoint me. How long have we been married? Six years? Yet you act as if I've come to steal your virginity. Perhaps you've grown tired of me and would prefer someone else?"

She stood numb. How could she so easily desire the touch of Michael and yet detest her husband for wanting the same thing? She sighed, knowing the inevitable was going to happen. What mood was he in tonight? Would he be forceful, or would he merely go about his business?

When he touched her bare skin, a wave of annoyance rushed through her. His invasive hands moved about as if she were his toy: stroking, pinching, and fondling her. His touch was neither soft nor gentle. It was not filled with tenderness. It was the touch of someone she was familiar with whom she did not love. He would have his way with her and there was nothing she could do about it. She was his wife, after all.

He put his wet lips to her breast, then with his teeth, lightly bit down. When she jerked and tried to back up, he put his hand behind her, holding her firm while he suckled her as if he could drain some nourishment out of her. But she wasn't his mother and had nothing give to him.

Pleased that he had free reign to do as he wished, he motioned her onto the bed. Margaret crawled in and clutched the blanket around her, watching him unbutton his pants, exposing his pride and joy, his gluttonous instrument. Once undressed, he yanked the blanket from her grip. She turned her head and shut her eyes as he manipulated her into the position he wanted. Soon he would be done with her, and then she could reclaim her body.

When he finished, she rolled away from him and curled into a ball. Aching from pain and overcome with sadness, she cried quietly to herself. Hoping the grief that burned deep inside would someday heal and scar over.

She stared out at the misty sea as the ship carried them back home. Melancholy had snuck in with the early morning fog and was refusing to dissipate within her. Somewhere the sun was shining, but it wasn't here. All she and Anna and the other members of the Land League had worked for was in ruins. Moisture hung like unshed teardrops all around her.

"I'm sorry the Land League didn't work out the way you had expected." Alex rested his arms on the railing next to her.

"If you could have seen the looks in the eyes of the peasants…" The waves rose and fell on the milky surface like the hopes of Ireland. Would they ever be free? Would she ever be free? "It is tragic. So many of us tried."

"No doubt you did." He put his arm around her and kissed the top of her head. She had given up all resistance to the world at the moment. Having always held her feelings at a distance, she was a stranger to the ways of the heart. Now all she wanted was the feeling of numbness to replace all the pain.

"I feel betrayed by Parnell. So many believed he would be able to convince the British to let Ireland go."

"Hmm, perhaps Mr. Parnell isn't the right man for the job."

Margaret thought of Michael and how he always put the people of Ireland first. Unfortunately, now he was caught in the web of others.

"What will become of things? I cannot hope to guess." She was wrapped in the cocoon of her own anguish.

Alex whispered in her ear. "Maybe it is the beginning of something better." She felt him hug her tightly against his chest as if he could somehow protect her from her inner thoughts.

She had forgotten how generous he could be in supporting her. Years with him had taught her his intentions were often sincere. Unfortunately, it was his means of carrying them out that were unpredictable.

"You shouldn't always look to Ireland for your heroes."

She had a feeling that she might not ever see Michael again. Alex was right. She would have to figure out how to live her life at home and not let her hope eat away at her.

She arrived in Chicago to rumors the Land League would fold. The article Margaret had written about the effort of the Ladies Land League was useless. No one wanted to read about the lost cause of a group of women. Her editor, Mr. White, told her she would have to write about something more relevant to what was happening in Ireland, like the Phoenix Park murder investigation. Margaret couldn't bring herself to fill his request. Delany suggested she write about Parnell and how he let the Land League down. However, she found herself resisting the idea.

"Margaret, I've never seen you like this. What happened to that tough woman who wasn't afraid to bark at anyone?" Delany closed the door to Margaret's office.

Margaret put her elbow on her desk and rested her chin on her hand. "I broke my rule and let myself get emotionally involved."

Exhaling loudly, she leaned back in her chair and folded her arms across her chest.

"Politics is a tough profession. You know that. One minute one man is on top, and the next someone else is," Delany said.

"I thought we were making a difference." She sighed loudly.

Delany put his hand on Margaret's desk and leaned toward her. "You did for some people, and you can still make a difference. You're a journalist and one of the best around. Write about what you know regarding the situation. It's better than sulking and wishing things were different."

Margaret looked up at Delany and smiled. "I can always count on you to perk me up. Thank you."

He dragged a chair over and sat across from her. "Now, what new strategy do you think the Irish will employ?"

Chapter 23

MARGARET WOULD BE attending the official announcement of the dissolving of Michael's Land League in Philadelphia. Shaking off her disappointment in the way things had turned out was still a challenge for her. After all, she and Michael, along with many others, spent almost four years raising money and organizing people for the now deflated League. Alex, on the other hand, saw this as an opportunity. He and fellow Clan members put together the charter for a new organization that would absorb the Irish-American membership of the Land League.

"I want you to write an article covering the event." Alex stood at the door to her study with a cigar in his hand.

Margaret was reluctant. "Darling, can't you find someone else to do it?" She moved the papers she had been working on to the side of her desk.

"No, you are the best writer for this. Perhaps your memory has failed you, but you promised me you would write articles when I asked." He bit off a piece of the end of the rolled tobacco and spit it out on her floor.

Yes, he had bullied her in to agreeing she would write articles for him. "All right, but don't expect a large article," Margaret replied.

"Why not?" he asked. "This is a big event." He lit the end of his cigar and sucked on it until the ash glowed then blew smoke in Margaret's direction. He walked over and stood in front of her desk like the imposing presence he was, fouling the air around her.

Arguing with him was futile. "Whatever you want." She was annoyed at how he thought he could manipulate her every time he wanted something. "And get that disgusting thing out of here. I told you I don't like it when you smoke in my rooms. It isn't good for Beatrice."

"Oh yes, the bird." He went over and snapped his finger on the top of the cage. The startled bird flew around banging against the side.

"What do you have to do to get it to sing?"

"It only sings when it wants to, not when you scare it."

Alex leaned over to the cage and said, "Pardon me."

Alex stood up, took another draw on the cigar, and exhaled. He walked over to where Margaret was sitting. "As the new leader of the Irish National League of America I plan to put more emphasis on educating people about Ireland's problems. I want to create sympathy, rally more interest. Can you find it within yourself to write about that? Of course you can. That's my gal," Alex said.

She gave him a disgusted half smile. Her room would stink with his smell for hours.

"Besides, I've made arrangements to have several crates of your book shipped to the hall in Philadelphia." Alex puffed out his chest and grinned. "I wanted it to be a surprise."

Margaret raised her eyebrows. "That was most considerate of you." It wasn't like him to share the spotlight with anyone else.

"You worked hard writing it, and I thought this would be a good opportunity for you to sell more copies," he said, holding out his arms, expecting her to rush to him, no doubt. Perhaps give him a big kiss. She got up from her desk and made her way to him. She gave him a slight hug.

"Do you think it would be too much of me to ask if you could show me a little more enthusiasm than a mere polite hug?" He pulled back and inhaled, then blew out a puff of smoke around her. "Or are you holding onto your affection for someone else?"

"Alex, that is ridiculous."

"Is it?" He flicked ashes in the air.

Margaret was simmering inside. "I'll write your article. Now please, let me get back to work." She slid back into her chair and arranged papers in front of her, avoiding his glare.

The vestibule was alive with activity when Margaret arrived at the hall. She wore her best smile as she strolled confidently into the room. Alex had arrived earlier, giving her more time to prepare. Hundreds of Irish-Americans spilled around her. The lilt in their voices rose and fell depending on their years away from their homeland. Margaret knew some left Ireland willingly; others had no choice and were dumped on the shores of America by the British trying to get rid of them. Some had not seen the valleys and moors since childhood, others not at all, having been born in America. It was their rite of passage to be here. They all had stories to tell, and with enough ale they would talk to Margaret until dawn about the good and the bad of the isle of Erin.

Margaret glanced through the open door to the grand hall. Amongst the mustaches, red beards, and brown and gray mutton-chop covered faces she searched for the only Irishman she cared about. But only a sea of strangers and acquaintances were gathered before her.

To the side, out of the main cluster of activity, Alex stood talking to a woman. From her vantage point Margaret could only see their profile. The woman was dressed in a dark green gown with a large bustle and many folds, to hide things in, no doubt. They appeared deep in a private conversation. The woman held a fan to conceal her face. Upon closer inspection, Margaret realized it was none other than the grand dame herself, Mrs. Parnell. Margaret wondered what they were discussing that required hiding behind a fan.

Margaret raised her fingers near her cheek and was able attract Alex's attention. He nodded then pointed to some men nearby, indicating he would be joining them.

Delia Parnell broke away from Alex and wandered over. "Margaret, darling, it is so nice to see you again." Delia stretched out her arm, the closed fan dangling from her wrist. "I was just telling your charming husband how lucky we are to have someone as intelligent as him willing to take up the fight for Ireland." The old woman's steel gray eyes sparkled, indicating her admiration for Alex. "We need a strong leader after the unfortunate demise of the Land League." Delia then added, "The British apparently emasculated all the rebels in Ireland after the Phoenix Park incident. It was as though they staged the murder themselves just to suppress any progress we had made."

"Certainly you don't believe that." Margaret doubted that the British were capable of such a stunt.

"Let's just hope the wrath of God rains down upon them for squashing our efforts." Delia raised her chin then nodded ever so slightly to someone in the distance that Margaret didn't recognize. "Excuse me, dear, but I must go find a seat before all the good ones are taken." Delia tilted her hat and then disappeared into the crowd.

Margaret spotted the two seats reserved for her and Alex up front. She slipped into hers and looked up at the men scurrying back and forth on stage. Several captain's chairs were placed next to the podium. Officers from the American branch of the Land League filed in and sat down facing the crowd. The chair she assumed was for Michael remained vacant.

"Please be seated, everyone. We are about to begin," a short man in a long beard yelled from the side of the stage.

Alex patted Margaret on the shoulder and sat down next to her. He looked relaxed and confident with his clean-shaven face and persuasive smile. "Wish me luck," Alex whispered in her ear.

A tall, slim, balding, gray-haired man in a dark waistcoat climbed onto the stage and waved a kerchief for attention then took his place behind the podium. People quieted down and scrambled for the remaining seats.

"With great sorrow I regret to announce the disbanding of the Land League," the orator began. "Mr. Charles Parnell, the former President, has decided that Ireland's efforts would be better served by a new organization with a new charter. So, with great pleasure, I wish to announce the formation of the Irish National League of America. This organization will act as the umbrella under which Irish organizations across America and abroad will come together as one unit to work toward securing the freedom of our beloved Ireland."

Cheers rang out around the room.

"I'm sure everyone signed the membership petition when they entered tonight and placed a ballot in the voter's box. So, without further delay, let's read the winners for the new board of directors. Will the men vying for that position please come forward."

It was no surprise to Margaret when Alex was declared President. The *Clan na Gael,* no doubt, used their influence to sway the American members of the Land League. When Alex took the stage, applause erupted, men jumped to their feet, and cheers filled the room. Alex gave his acceptance speech, and then to Margaret's surprise, he made an announcement.

"I want to thank everyone for showing your support, especially my wife, Margaret." Alex gave her a quick nod. "Before you leave tonight, I have a book over on the back table I would like everyone to purchase. I believe it will give you a better understanding of the reasons why we must continue to fight for our beloved Ireland. Thank you again, for your confidence."

A group of singers and a band made up of a fiddle player, an accordion man, and a flutist took the stage and started playing. Soon there was clapping and stomping to fast-paced tunes. Margaret hadn't heard such music since her first trip to Ireland.

Alex was swarmed by a crowd of admirers eager to congratulate him, and so Margaret went to the table containing her books. One of Alex's appointees by the name of Thomas was busy collecting money for her. He smiled at Margaret when she came over and stood by his side.

"I would be happy to answer anyone's questions regarding information in the book," Margaret announced proudly.

One man picked up a copy and looked at it. "Why didn't Alex use his first name?"

"Because, he didn't write it," Margaret replied with a smile.

"Who did? You?"

"I am quite knowledgeable about the events in Ireland that led to the current situation." It annoyed her that it never crossed a man's mind that a woman could be capable of commenting on something other than children, food, or fashion.

"Patrick, here's the book Alex wrote about Ireland." Another man motioned his friend over.

Several men flocked to the table. Thomas looked over at Margaret. "Why don't you leave the sales to me, mum? They might not buy the book if they know you're the one who wrote it."

Don't be angry, she told herself. At least they were purchasing her book. Margaret looked around for Delia. When she spotted her, Margaret left the table and made her way through the sea of people.

"You must be bursting with pride." Delia beamed. "I can't think of a better man to pick up the lance for Ireland."

Margaret was amused by her choice of words. Delia certainly had no problem sounding like a rebel herself. "A few years ago I would have never imagined him in this role." The Land League was

Michael's idea. It felt strange to think Alex was now head of the new version of the League.

"You underestimate him, my dear."

"It is unfortunate that Mr. Davitt couldn't be here." Margaret hoped to draw out some information about Michael.

"Yes, but wouldn't you agree that it would have been unwise of him to attend?" Delia tilted her head in Margaret's direction. "Considering we have a new leader now…" she said, "Your husband." Delia threw her head back as if some foul smell had crossed her way.

"You are quite right. I was just wondering about his health."

"Indeed." Delia leaned in and looked directly at Margaret. "My dear, I would suggest you let go of any romantic notions of ever seeing that man again."

"I was merely being polite. I wasn't…"

"How silly of me to assume. Of course, you weren't." Delia pulled back. "A married woman like you would never entertain such a thought."

Margaret was taken aback by Delia's comment. Perhaps she suspected something had gone on between her and Michael. Delia had warned her before to stay away from Michael with all that patriotic talk of him belonging to Ireland. Still, Margaret couldn't help but wonder about him. What was he going to do now that he was no longer involved with the Land League? What she honestly wanted to know was if he had inquired about her.

Delia nodded to one of the other newly elected officers. "It was nice seeing you again, dear." She flicked her fan open then strolled off to join the man.

Margaret felt out of place. Even with all these Irish men and women around her, somehow the essence of Ireland was missing.

"How does it feel to be married to the most powerful Irishman in America?" Henri Le Caron surprised her from behind.

She turned and smiled at Henri. "Is he? I suppose I'll get used to the idea." It was the first time she realized that Alex had spent years laying the groundwork for this occasion. When Senator Blaine pointed out to Alex that he could never be a contender for Vice President of the United States because Alex had been born in Canada, Alex turned his aspirations to helping Ireland. Becoming the president of the Irish National League of America was quite a coup for Alex, she had to admit.

"I am so glad they chose him." Henri beamed.

"Does this mean a position for you?" He was a dear man. Certainly they could use his services in some way.

"No, not me. I prefer to just assist wherever I can. I'll serve on committees but I'll leave the decisions to others. I don't want the responsibility. Being a doctor and running my pharmaceutical business is enough for me."

"Yes, I would assume that with leadership comes added work and responsibility." It was hard to believe that Alex was now head of both the secret *Clan na Gael* and the public Irish National League of America. The thought that Alex would be making decisions regarding Ireland's future seemed abstract to her. What did he actually know about Ireland's politics? He had been born in Canada, not Ireland. As far as she knew, Alex had only set foot once on the island to retrieve her at the hotel in Dublin. Unlike her, he had never gone out into the countryside and met with the Irish people or seen firsthand the conditions in which they lived.

A gray box containing an amethyst necklace was waiting for her in their hotel room. It contained three stones in a gold filigree setting and hung from a gold choker chain.

"Did you pick this out?" Margaret held up the necklace, carefully inspecting the stones. "It is too extravagant for me." Sparkles of spurious privilege glittered around the room.

"If you must know, Delia helped." He chuckled. "She thought you might enjoy feeling like my queen." He bowed to her.

"I can't wear this." Margaret set it back down on the bureau. "It must have cost a fortune." The money could have fed many families in Ireland.

"Please, wear it." Alex picked it up and placed it around her neck. "I want people to know that I am a man of means." He nuzzled her ear as he snapped the latch closed. "Besides, we are going to the opera tomorrow night." He backed away to admire her. "There will be important people sitting in the audience and I want to show off my beautiful wife."

"Is this really necessary?" Margaret felt pressure in her new role as wife of such a powerful man. She reached up to remove the necklace. Alex grabbed her hand. "Do it for me, please."

"If you insist." It was important to him, she told herself, and she needed to show support even if she didn't want to.

"I also want you to wear the new gown I bought for you. I'll send for a dressmaker to do the alterations. "

Her eyebrows went up. "Did Delia pick out the dress, too?' Margaret was disgusted at the conspiracy to turn her into a socialite. Delia could be a peacock if she wanted but no one would be making her decisions for her.

The Opera House was crowded with men in top hats and women in expensive evening gowns. Both local and visiting couples of means were attending the performance. On Alex's arm Margaret would be admired and whispered about, whether she liked it or not.

Recognizing Alex, some men nodded and tipped their hats as they strolled past. Others looked on, curiously wondering who he was. Margaret doubted anyone knew she was the person behind all the recent articles about the Land League. Here, she was only Alex's wife.

Faces blurred together as Alex presented her to one man after another. Most had women accompanying them and a few did not. Many ladies, not knowing what to talk about, would inquire about the children that Margaret did not have. She was used to the embarrassed faces when she told them that God had not blessed them with any.

"What is your view on the current political situation in Ireland?" Margaret asked the wife of one man, but she was only met with a blank stare in return.

Alex leaned over and whispered to Margaret, "Don't be too hard on them." Then he chuckled and went back to his conversation with the woman's husband.

Glancing around, Margaret recognized some faces from Alex's new organization at the event. She also spotted Delia on the arm of a distinguished-looking elderly gentleman. Delia approached Margaret, leaving the gentleman to continue his conversation with two other men standing nearby.

"I must say, that dress is stunning on you, my dear," Delia said, "and the necklace… Perfect."

"Thank you. I understand you helped Alex pick them out." Margaret was still annoyed at Delia's involvement in dressing her for the evening.

"Men never are very good at that sort of thing. I merely guided him in the right direction, that's all. He just wants you to look beautiful. You can't fault him for wanting to show you off, can you?" Delia was obviously trying to be modest. "You make such a nice-looking couple. Too bad there isn't one of those photographers here tonight to capture your image." Delia looked around as if she expected a photographer to suddenly appear. "Well, maybe another time." Changing the subject, Delia asked, "Did you happen to sell many books? It was most thoughtful of Alex to mention them. He wants you to succeed too, my dear."

"Yes, we sold all we brought and received orders for more." Margaret was grateful for the money. However, she didn't like the idea of Alex getting credit for her book and he did nothing to dispel the myth either. She overheard him telling people that education was the key to Ireland's future and that he might even take up a collection to build better schools in Ireland. How could he say such things? He was sounding like a politician making promises that would never be kept.

"Good, good. You must be pleased. You worked very hard on the book's creation. I haven't read it yet, mind you. But, I plan to," Delia remarked.

From the side of the room a group of four men pushed themselves in her direction. Margaret recognized John Devoy in the middle as he marched over to Alex.

"This looks menacing," Delia commented, flicking her fan to cover her face.

"Good evening," Alex said, giving Devoy a slight bow.

"It was, until I was told you were in the building." Devoy stood planted right in front of Alex.

"Please, let's not upset everyone with our personal differences." Alex smiled and glanced around at the people who were staring at him.

Margaret cringed knowing Alex did not take well to being criticized, especially in public.

"You sent secret invitations to members of my organization to join your Irish National League." Devoy took off his coat and handed it to one of his men.

Alex just shrugged his shoulders and put his hands out to his side. There was laughter in the crowd.

Devoy drew his fist back but several men jumped him from behind before he could take a swing at Alex. Devoy was quickly escorted to the exit by several large men. Members of his party trailed behind while onlookers whispered to each other, speculating about the circumstances of the event.

Alex just smiled. "What can I say? The man is a poor loser."

Delia pulled Margaret closer to her. "Don't worry about it. Devoy is just jealous that Alex is the new favorite. Men never like giving up their power to a rival."

The doors to the Opera House opened and ushers directed people to their seats. Margaret slipped her arm in Alex's and they climbed the stairs to their box seats above. Margaret wondered if Alex's troubles with Devoy were indeed over.

Chapter 24

"OH NOT ANOTHER bouquet." Margaret shook her head. "You must have bought out every flower vendor in Chicago." She inhaled the fragrance of the pink roses and her eyes met his.

Alex's smile widened. "I am glad it pleases you." He set his hat next to his gloves and slipped out of his mohair overcoat then handed it to Mrs. O'Brien.

"You are being too generous." She wondered why he was doing this.

"I want only the best for my wife." He pulled out a small box from his vest pocket and gave it to her.

When she opened it, two diamond earrings surrounded by emeralds glistened in the hall light.

"Do you like them?" he asked. "I picked them out myself."

Maybe she was being too harsh on him. Since their trip back from Dublin he had been trying hard to win her love and respect. Perhaps she should quit searching for alternative motives in everything he did.

Alex's new position as President of both the secret *Clan na Gael* and the public Irish National League of America left Margaret dizzy from so many dinner parties and social gatherings to attend. She found it surprising how easily she slipped into her role as Alex's wife. She had access to a variety of businessmen and aspiring politicians to fill the pages of the *Chicago Tribune* with news. Rumors were circulating that she had authored a book, and several organizations asked her to be on their board, including the Chicago Board of Education. Wives that had never spoken to her before were now sending Margaret invitations to join them for tea.

Her quick rise in social status had Margaret's closet brimming with new gowns and hats as Alex indulged her by taking her on shopping jaunts to the best dressmaker in town. Much to her dismay, she found their names mentioned in the society page of a rival Chicago newspaper.

In June, the 1884 National Republican Convention took place in Chicago and Blaine was chosen as their Presidential candidate. Margaret covered the event for the *Chicago Tribune* and Alex was a featured speaker. Surrounded by the excitement of rising politicians and influential businessmen, the struggles of the former Land League faded into a mere topic of discussion for Margaret and less of a pressing reality.

Then one day the parties stopped. Margaret was confused as to why Alex now turned down invitations to various high profile events when previously he relished in receiving them. Then he abruptly resigned as president of the Irish National League of America. When she inquired as to the reason for the sudden change, Alex told her he had more important things to do than hobnob with society.

A veil of secrecy fell upon their household. Margaret would arrive home to find the living room curtains drawn in the middle of the day. On the evenings Alex expected Clan members, a special male servant or guard, as Margaret called him, attended to the answering of the front door. This servant, who wouldn't give

Margaret his name, carefully checked the arriving men's numbers against a private list he always kept with him.

Curiosity and concern were driving Margaret crazy. Why had everything taken a sudden turn? She vacillated between enlisting Delany to help her uncover the secrets that Alex was involved with and turning a blind eye to the whole thing. Her instinct as a journalist was pushing her to find out more, and if she couldn't write about whatever Alex was up to, perhaps Delany could. But then again, merely mentioning the secret meetings taking place in her home might lead to unnecessary trouble for Delany. She would need more information before she could make a decision on which path to take.

Margaret constantly searched for evidence as to what was being discussed behind the door of the library. She tried listening but nothing made sense. Murmurs and laughter seeped through the cracks. Clues were peppered with mystery but the answer to the riddle stayed locked in the room. Odd number of knocks at the front door, ashes from burnt papers in the fireplace, numbers instead of names, what did all of this mean? Alex's answers were vague, leaving her to piece together fragments of lies in search of the truth.

Margaret had to ask Alex. She wanted to know the truth. The library door was unlocked for a change and open but a crack, so Margaret gave it shove. Behind his polished mahogany desk with its satinwood inlay border sat Alex with a cryptic message before him. Henri was leaning forward in a wooden chair, facing his leader. Both their surprised faces turned and their gaze met hers. She could smell their secrets like lingering cigar smoke in the room.

Margaret took a few confident steps forward as Alex slipped his mysterious composition into the drawer at his waist. She slapped the London edition of *The Times* in front of him.

"Did you have anything to do with this?" Margaret folded her arms across her chest, waiting. Seconds passed. "Well?" she demanded.

"Let me read it first before you accuse me of something I don't know anything about."

Henri got up and walked around to peer over Alex's shoulder.

"It says an American by the name of Gallagher was arrested along with five other men in London with 500 pounds of explosives," Margaret recited. She tapped her foot impatiently on the hardwood floor. "Did you send him there?"

"Of course not," Alex said, pushing away from the desk, as if repelling the accusation. "Apparently, this man is someone who took it upon himself to cause trouble."

"Are you telling me that he wasn't a member of the Clan?" Margaret leaned in trying to read his face for a telltale sign of deceit.

"Possibly he was. I can't keep tabs on everyone," he replied.

She could tell he was annoyed at her confrontation. "I thought it was your job to keep the radicals under control." If he knew about this, wasn't it his job to stop the lunatic?

"Margaret, if you don't mind, we can discuss this later." Alex placed his hand on her back and ushered her out then went back inside and closed the door behind him, but it failed to latch. Margaret gave it a nudge, and cupping her ear, she listened to their conversation.

"I think they are trying to figure out if the orders came from us or Rossa," Alex said in an angry voice.

"Personally, I think Mr. Gallagher made a deal with the bastard," Henri said. "Double- crossed us."

"Someone must have tipped off the authorities," said Alex. "Damn it."

"What do you suggest we do now?" Henri asked.

"Get Lomasney. I want to have a talk with him."

As quietly as she could, Margaret stepped down the hall and went into the parlor. Who was Lomasney? She paced back and forth. Maybe she could ask around. She bit her lip. If Alex found out he would be furious with her. Perhaps it would be best if she just waited to see what Alex did next.

Late that night Alex knocked on her bedroom door.

"Darling are you awake?" He opened the door and came in.

Margaret lit the lamp. Alex sat on the side of the bed next to her. He had his robe on. She suspected he hadn't come just for conversation.

"I would like you to write an article denying any connection between the activities of any Irish in America and this Gallagher fellow. Claim that he was some deranged man acting on his own. That I never met the man."

She could smell the alcohol on his breath.

"I don't want anyone thinking I had a hand in this," Alex said

"Did you?" Margaret asked. She folded her arms across her chest.

"No. I told you that earlier." Alex fingered the blanket, avoiding her eyes.

"Did he know someone else in the Clan? Perhaps another member was involved." Margaret yawned then pushed her hair out of her eyes. It was late.

"Hell, Margaret just write the damn article." Alex flipped the blanket back in frustration.

"Is there someone I can interview about this?" Margaret reached for the blanket but Alex grabbed her hand.

"I'm head of the *Clan na Gael*. My comments are all you need."

"But…"

"I'll expect the article in this week's paper." He released her hand.

She had no choice. "Alright, I'll write the article," she said. "Now, will you leave so I can go back to sleep?"

Alex glared at her. She wondered what he was thinking.

"You don't believe me. My own wife doesn't believe me." He dropped his head.

"Alex, I don't know what to believe, what with all these strangers coming and going. You refuse to tell me anything so I can't help but wonder." Margaret was frustrated with him.

"I don't want you snooping around. It would get us both into trouble."

Margaret hadn't considered the possibility that Alex would be held accountable for any bits of information she discovered. Perhaps it would be best for her to suppress her curiosity and avoid writing about any suspicious activity regarding the Irish in America.

"You just have to trust me." Alex patted the back of her hand.

"Good day, Mrs. Sullivan." The man lifted his hat.

He was slender in build and spoke with a lisp. She thought Lomasney looked more like the bookseller he was than a rebel.

"I've known Lomasney a long time," Henri leaned over and whispered to her. "We used to be neighbors. Don't worry. He wouldn't hurt a soul."

"We are glad you could come." Alex welcomed Lomasney. "You remember Henri, don't you?"

"Yes. Good to see you again, Henri. It has been a while since we last spoke, hasn't it?" Lomasney shook Henri's hand and turned to Alex. "Well, I am sure this isn't a social visit. What can I do for you fellas?" Lomasney asked.

"We would like for you to go to London and do some work for us." Alex patted the little man on the shoulder then led him into the library where several anxious Clan members were waiting to meet with him.

Alex shut the door in Margaret's face. She stood there for a moment, the young man standing guard smiled at her.

"Would you like some tea?" she asked him.

"Maybe later, mum." His look told her that she needed to move away. This was private business.

After the men left, she heard Alex knock on the door to her study and then step into the room.

"Sorry to bother you but I have a request." He stood next to the fireplace.

Margaret scooted her chair back and got up. "What kind of request?" There were a few things she wanted to ask him, too.

"Do you know of anyone from the old Land League who might be able to assist Lomasney when he arrives in London?" Alex asked sheepishly.

Margaret folded her arms across her chest. "Why are you asking me? Can't you find one of your henchmen to do it?" She was surprised that Alex would even consider her in any of his plans.

"To be honest, I would like to find someone outside our organization." He picked up a figurine of a woman off the fireplace mantle and studied it, turning it over and looking at its bottom as though he thought he would be able to see what was under the statue's dress.

"You're serious?" Margaret was puzzled.

"Of course I am. Why else would I ask?"

"First, tell me what you are up to with all these secret meetings?"

"Please, Margaret. You know that is private business. I told you when I took this job that I wouldn't be able to discuss what we do. You are a reporter, for God's sake."

"Why are you sending this man Lomasney to London?"

"We want him to find out who is causing trouble over there and getting us blamed for things we have no part in."

Perhaps Alex wanted to prevent a small group of rebels from acting on their own. Maybe she wasn't giving him enough credit. Alex could be secretly trying to round up the trouble makers.

"What would they be expected to do?" she asked.

"Nothing much, just help him find a place to stay." Alex set the figurine back down.

"Why? What exactly will Mr. Lomasney be doing in London?" She rubbed her temple.

"Just gathering information…"

"How will he do that?"

"You know I can't tell you." He leaned his arm on the mantel. "It's nothing dangerous."

Margaret was skeptical. "I wouldn't want to put anyone in harm's way."

"Of course not."

"You promise me they won't be expected to do anything dangerous?" Margaret asked.

"You have my word." Alex placed his hand on his heart then raised this other hand, palm outward. "I swear to you."

Emma's husband's name came to her mind. Emma had told her that Peter was a member of the IRB and she assumed him to be trustworthy. At least Emma had never shared any doubts about her husband's loyalty. "Perhaps I do know of someone," Margaret replied.

"Wonderful." Alex went to her and pulled her toward him. "I knew I could count on you to be a good little soldier."

She pushed on his chest. "I am not one of your Clan members." She hoped he wouldn't expect her to do other favors such as this for him in the future.

"No. You are an independent woman." He tried to kiss her lips but she turned her head away. "But, you are also my wife and I would appreciate it if you would act like it sometimes." He dropped his arms from her. "You want me to go out and find a whore? Is that what you wish?"

Margaret avoided his eyes. She wasn't in the mood for entertaining him tonight. He got what he asked for, he could leave now.

"Write to your friends and let them know that Lomasney will be contacting them when he arrives in London. He'll be traveling under the name of Waldeon." He walked to the door then stood there looking back at her. "Darling… Thank you."

Margaret went to her study, opened a bottle of ink, and set a blank page before her then composed a letter to Emma. She hoped she was doing the right thing.

When she finished, Margaret put down her pen and went to her window. She pulled the curtains back and looked up into the sky. The moon was full. A cloud drifted across its surface and loneliness blew in the open window. How long can you love someone you never see, she wondered? So far away; so long ago. Her memories of Michael were the only thing that kept her from going insane. Here in her house in Chicago with Alex she felt lost. She longed to see the green meadows and the stone walls of Ireland again, to watch the clouds in the sky change from darkness to light, to feel Michael's whiskers on her skin. She should be ashamed for having such thoughts, but she wasn't.

Was God punishing her? Was this secret misery she felt her penance for the sin of loving Michael? Forever tied to a man she detested. Certainly God didn't intend for her life to be like this? Margaret closed the curtains and sat down and cried.

Chapter 25

ON HER WAY to the dining room Margaret noticed that Alex had a guest in the library. However, on further investigation, she found the guest to be none other than Alex's confidant, Henri.

"Are you sure that it's wise?" Henri leaned against the door frame, twisting the point of his waxed mustache.

"I want Dr. Cronin as far away from me as possible. I don't care what you tell the other members. Just get rid of the bastard. Claim he is a spy. God knows there are plenty lurking around. And if that doesn't work I'll pay him a visit myself."

Alex came bursting out of the library. "And Rossa, too. He is nothing but trouble; dipped his hands too many times into the Skirmishing Funds. I don't want him going around me anymore." The veins on his neck stood out as he moved down the hall past her.

Margaret had heard about Rossa, a former Fenian and quite devious. He and Devoy were prison mates before the British shipped them to America.

"This will cause an uproar from Devoy's supporters," said Henri, trailing after Alex down the hall.

"I don't give a damn about Devoy and his supporters. I'm in charge now, not him." Alex slammed the front door behind him and climbed into a carriage, leaving Henri standing in the foyer with his mouth gaping open.

"I'm sorry, Mrs. Sullivan. You weren't supposed to hear that." Henri fiddled with the hat in his hand.

"Henri, is there something I should be concerned about?" She knew Alex could have quite a temper and she hoped it was nothing too serious.

"Dr. Cronin is making claims against Alex, but nothing you should worry about."

"What kind of claims?" Margaret asked. Alex was known to become angry, even violent, when anyone questioned his honor. She hoped he didn't do anything he might regret later.

"Sorry, you will have to take it up with him."

"Alex?" Margaret knocked on the door to the library. "Is everything all right?"

"Come in." He reached for the opened bottle of whiskey and poured himself a drink as she entered.

Maybe she could charm him into telling her something. "I know you aren't supposed to discuss any Clan business with me…"

"Come here." He threw his head back, gulped down the contents of his glass, and then wiped his mouth with the back of his hand. He motioned her over to him. She didn't know how many glasses he had consumed before she disturbed him. Hesitantly, she walked over.

"You don't think I'm an evil man, do you?"

Evil? She never thought of him as evil. Arrogant, controlling, forceful, and hot-tempered, but not evil. "Why would you ask that question?" She could tell that the alcohol was affecting him.

He ran his finger back and forth across the lace on her bodice.

"You know I want what's best for Ireland."

"Of course," she replied. She had no idea what was going on in his mind.

Alex stood up, wrapped his arms gently around Margaret, and laid his head on her shoulder. He had never done that to her before and she wasn't sure how to respond.

Hesitantly, Margaret wrapped hers around him. It was a strange moment. He obviously just wanted to be held by her.

After a few minutes, he let go and backed away then motioned for her to leave.

Something was definitely going on, she thought. That could be the only explanation.

It was Mrs. O'Brien's day off, and Alex had left earlier with Henri. Margaret had the house to herself. When she checked the library door, she found it locked so she gave it a shove, but it didn't open. When she tried her hat pin it was useless in the lock. Leaning up against the door, she pondered what she needed to do to get inside.

Margaret opened the back door to her house and looked around to see if anyone was watching. She crouched down then ran over and hid behind a hydrangea bush. From there she surveyed the distance between the ground and the window to the library. She remembered there was a ladder stored in the carriage house.

Margaret placed the ladder up against the frame to the window, climbed a few rungs, and pushed up on the glass, hoping it wasn't latched closed. The window moved slightly up so she leaned in and pushed harder. The glass cracked and splintered. A piece fell out onto the ground below her.

She wasn't about to give up. Putting her fingers under the gap at the bottom of the frame, Margaret shoved the window up as far as she could. Fighting the drapery, she found the opening, poked her body through, and climbed in, tearing the hem of her skirt in the process. She then closed the window and covered it back up with the heavy fabric.

She glanced around. A threatening-looking military saber lay across Alex's desk. Underneath it were papers written in code. When Margaret lifted the saber the edge sliced her hand. The wound didn't appear deep, just a surface cut. She took out her kerchief and wrapped her hand to stop the bleeding. Then Margaret pulled a tiny notebook from her pocket and took a pencil from the top drawer of Alex's desk. She carefully copied the coded message from both of the papers then returned Alex's pencil.

Not knowing what time Alex would return, Margaret decided to leave rather than risk being caught in there. She unlocked the library door. Once in the hall she relocked the door and yanked it closed. She ran out the back door and returned the ladder to the carriage house then she looked around for a rock. She hurled a fist-sized stone at the window but she hit the side of the house instead. She retrieved it and then threw it again. This time it hit its mark with a crash, sending broken glass tumbling to the ground. She licked her upper lip and then tossed the rock at the parlor window, hoping to make it look like the work of some mischievous juvenile. Then Margaret walked quickly down the street to avoid being home when Alex arrived.

Margaret returned home with a bag of sweets to find Officer Murphy in her parlor talking with Alex and Henri. She was about to ramble off the alibi she had practiced but Alex put his finger to his lip to shush her.

"Let me go over this again. When you got home the back door was unlatched and your library window was smashed? You are sure nothing was taken?" Murphy asked.

Margaret had met Murphy before and interviewed him for an article she had written about crime in Chicago. Margaret pondered the idea that Murphy could be a secret *Clan na Gael* member. Given the number of Irishmen amongst their ranks, there was a strong possibly that the Clan had infiltrated the law.

"No, but I want whoever threw that rock severely punished," Alex replied. "Margaret, darling, we have been the victim of what could have been a robbery. It doesn't make sense. Something must have frightened them off. I wonder if they were searching for something in the library."

"Perhaps it was a spy," said Henri. "That would explain why nothing of value was taken."

"Yes, that is no doubt the logical conclusion," said Officer Murphy. "I won't drag the department into this investigation. I will leave that to your men, Alex."

Margaret swallowed hard. "I bought some sweets if any of you gentlemen would like some?"

"Run upstairs, dear. We would like to continue this discussion in private."

"Of course." When she set the bag on the table, she noticed a small dark line of dried blood on the side where she had been holding it.

"I think I'll have a sweet," said Henri. He reached over and scooped up the bag. Holding it in his palm he foraged the contents inside.

"Margaret," Alex said in a stern voice. He motioned with his hand for her to leave.

Margaret's heart beat wildly. Grabbing the bag from Henri would not be wise, but she didn't want to leave it.

Alex glared at Margaret until she left the room.

Margaret decided that she was going to figure out for herself what was going on. She had already come to the conclusion that each member of the Clan had been assigned a number in order to hide their true identity. The different branches also went by numbers, with the leadership of each consisting of a Commander, Senior Guard, and Junior Guard.

She took out the notebook in which she had copied the coded message from Alex's office and a sheet of paper. Arranging and rearranging the letters, she discovered that by moving the alphabet one letter she was able to decipher one of the pages on Alex's desk. It appeared to be an oath for the swearing in ceremony of new members of the *Clan na Gael.*

> *…The object of the Clan na Gael, also known as the Irish Republican Brotherhood, is to aid the Irish people in attainment of complete and absolute independence of Ireland and the overthrow of British domination…… under penalty of death the signer swears to keep secret the names and everything connected with the C's from all not entitled to know such secrets.*

She had hoped to find evidence of what Alex was up to, not this. There was nothing out of the ordinary here. Other than swearing to free Ireland, these were the same words that could be heard at most initiations into men's clubs around the country.

A knock on the door startled Margaret. She shoved her notebook down in her pocket and slid her deciphered note into a file amongst the papers for an article she had been working on. Then she placed the file under several others sitting on her desk.

"Who is it?" Margaret asked, folding her hands in front of her on top of a blank sheet of paper.

Alex stepped in with a bottle of opened wine and two glasses.

"Darling, I thought we could spend some time together. I know I have been neglecting you lately and I'm…" He looked at her sheepishly, "How do I say it without sounding vulgar? I'm… missing you."

Margaret knew refusing him would not be a good idea. She got up from her desk and walked into her bedroom. She removed her hair pins and shook her head, letting her hair fall onto her shoulders. Alex held out a drink for her. When she reached for it, he took her hand and turned over her palm.

"Did you cut yourself?" he asked, studying her hand.

She pulled her hand away. "It happened at work. Foolish me, I grabbed the wrong end of a pair of scissors."

"Hmm." He looked at her for a moment then smiled. "You didn't happen to go into the library recently, did you?" He handed her the wine glass.

"Of course not. I know you wouldn't approve." She took a gulp of wine.

He looked over at her study. "How is the bird doing?" Alex went into the room.

"It seems to being doing quite well. It sings to me every morning." Margaret slipped the notebook from her pocket into a drawer beneath her jewelry box. She quickly unbuttoned her dress. He was in there a long time, she thought. What could he be doing? Margaret hung her dress in the wardrobe along with her crinoline. She needed to hurry up and distract him from going through her files. She gulped down the wine, poured another, and gulped that glass too. Margaret poured a third to sip on, then took her glass and went to the entry to her study in her lacy camisole and drawers. She hoped he hadn't found her paper.

"What are you doing in here?" She tried to keep her voice soft and alluring.

Alex leaned back in her chair. He patted his lap. "I thought we would try something different tonight."

The next day after Mass, Margaret went through her files looking for the paper on which she deciphered the membership oath for the *Clan na Gael*. She could have sworn she put it in with the article on Blaine. She dumped the papers onto her desk and went through each, flipping them over as she did. It wasn't there. She tapped her pencil on her desk nervously. Where else could it be? She paced back and forth.

Beatrice fluttered her wings. Margaret went over and poked her finger in the cage and rubbed the bird's head. Margaret crouched down and unlatched the door. She put her finger out and Beatrice hopped on. Margaret held the bird up. "Pretty bird," she said. Beatrice just cocked her head and stared back. "Do you know where my paper went?" Margaret asked. "If you could only talk." Margaret put the bird back in its cage and retrieved a cracker to give to Beatrice. When she poked it through the bars, it fell to the bottom. Margaret opened the door and reached in, scooping up some torn paper along with the cracker. She set the cracker in the dish with Beatrice's bird seed. She carried the paper with her to toss in the basket she kept by her desk for garbage. When she dropped it in, something caught her eye. It was her handwriting. Margaret pulled out the scraps. She went to Beatrice's cage and scooped up a handful of the pieces and placed them on her desk. Moving and turning them like a puzzle, she was able to identify some of the words: *kept secret under penalty of death.* She bit her lip. Would that include her? Maybe she should curtail her quest to know what Alex was doing for a while.

Chapter 26

MARGARET'S OFFICE AT the *Chicago Tribune* was buzzing with talk of the recent events in London.

"Are you certain you don't have any information about this?" Delany looked worried. "I would think your husband, with his connections, might know something about these rebel activities."

"As I told you, Alex is just as concerned as everyone else is about the bombings," Margaret replied.

"There was even an explosion at the *London Times*." Edwards tapped his pencil nervously on the corner of her desk. "Now they are going after the press."

"Apparently, seventy-two people were injured in the Praed Street railway explosion. They found dynamite at the Paddington Praed Street, Charing Cross, and Blackfriars underground stations," Delany said. "One explosion even took place in the Parliament building."

"I can't believe that anyone would do such a thing." Margaret thought about the poor families of those injured.

"What surprised me are the celebrations going on in the saloons. You would think it was a boxing match with all the cheers following each bomb report," Delany stated.

The pressure of defending her husband was wearing Margaret down. Certainly it was this man Rossa's fault, she thought.

"Another telegram just came in." The front desk boy handed a slip of paper to Margaret.

Her eyes scanned the message. "Oh my God." She put a hand to her mouth and reached behind her with the other for the chair before she collapsed into it.

"What is it?" Edwards asked.

Delany took the paper from her.

"It says someone by the name of Lomasney was killed while setting off a bomb under London Bridge. He and two other men were blown to bits. Authorities had been trailing him. There were several witnesses, including the wife of one of the deceased."

Margaret ran up the stairs to Alex's law office. She burst past Mr. Donovan, Alex's stenographer and secretary, who jumped to his feet. "Wait! Mrs. Sullivan, you can't go in there. He is with someone."

"I don't particularly care." She pushed open the door. Alex looked surprised to see her. So did the little man in the walrus mustache sitting across from him.

"Excuse me," Alex said, scrambling from his chair. He took Margaret by the arm and ushered her out into the hall.

"I know. I just heard the news myself," Alex whispered. His face showed genuine concern. "However, this is neither the time nor place to discuss this." He rapidly led her to the top of the stairs.

"Did you know?" Margaret's throat tightened. Her composure was giving way and anxiety was starting to consume her.

"Go home." He pushed her toward the stairs. "We'll discuss this later." He ran his fingers across the top of his hair then stood there like he wasn't sure what to do. He started to walk away but then turned back around.

"I will be home shortly. Please, just go." He reached out to embrace her then let his arms drop back down. "I'm sorry… Margaret."

She watched as he disappeared back into his office and closed the door.

While she was inside, a light snow had begun to fall and now the streets were dusted with white. She felt her heart beating rapidly. Rather than take a cab, she decided to walk home. Her pace remained steady while her mind raced from one thought to another, chastising herself for turning a blind eye to Alex's mischief, and soon she was climbing the stairs to her front door.

Inside, she shed her snow-covered hat and coat, removed her shoes, and then went into the parlor and stood by the fire. She shivered from the cold.

"Would you care from some hot tea, mum?" Mrs. O'Brien asked.

"Please," Margaret replied.

Mrs. O'Brien fetched a pot of tea and a cup, brought them in on a tray, and then set the tray on a table. When Margaret picked up the delicate cup, her hands were trembling so hard she had to put it down again. She sat in a chair but was too restless to remain and got up.

Margaret impatiently looked through the sheer curtains for signs of Alex's arrival. Ice ferns were forming on her parlor window while roots of resentment were spreading in her mind. A carriage trotted by and stopped in front of her neighbor's house. A man got out holding a large package, then disappeared inside. A steady snow had fallen, covering the tracks of other earlier travelers, and now the neighborhood sat quiet in a hard blue glow. Margaret remembered that in a week people would be celebrating the birth of the son of God while Emma and James would be mourning the death of a man.

She had been pacing in the parlor for at least an hour by the time Alex arrived home. Her anger had now worked itself into a fury.

"You told me he was just going to gather information. Did you know he was a dynamiter?" Margaret rubbed her hands back and forth, pressing her thumb into her palms.

"I knew you wouldn't cooperate if I told you."

"I trusted you," she said. Her body was tense with anger. "How could you lie to me?"

"You said you wanted me to be the leader of the Clan," he said sarcastically as he placed his knuckles on his hip. "What did you expect?" He threw his other hand in the air as if flinging the guilt on to her.

"Don't you dare blame me for this." She was furious. How could he even suggest she was responsible? Bitterness and anger tore away her cloak of self-control. Knotting her hands into fists, she let the rage overcome her, hitting him full force, pounding on his chest.

"Please, calm down." He quickly seized her arms and pulled them down to her sides.

She thought he might break her arms he held them so tightly. He must have realized he was hurting her because he suddenly released his grip and backed away.

"How could you do this? People died. Emma's husband died because of you. I told her she could trust Lomasney. Oh, my God! It's my fault her husband is dead." Her voice cracked, she felt sucked in by the undertow of emotions.

"We did it for Ireland," Alex said, with righteous indignation.

The words struck her like a sword straight to her heart. Did he think he had the right to do such a thing?

"Were you trying to start a war? Who was going to fight in this war? The defenseless peasants in Ireland? They would have been slaughtered."

"Don't be ridiculous. We have been shipping arms to them for years."

"I don't believe this. What were you thinking? A war, for God's sake!"

"You think setting off a few dozen bombs is a war? We only wanted to get Britain's attention so the authorities would listen to us."

Now he was trying to downplay the impact of his actions, she screamed in her mind. This was ludicrous!

"I'm sick, sick of you and your lies!" She slapped him as hard as she could across the face. He threw his head back and his hand reached for her neck, but she stepped back, causing him to miss. His veins stood out and his eyes were murderous. She would pay for this later, no doubt, but right now she didn't care. She ran up the stairs to her room and slammed the door, locking it behind her.

He followed and rattled the knob. "Margaret, unlock the door!" Alex demanded.

"Leave me alone!"

She hurled the vase filled with his thorny roses to the wall. Pink petals lay scattered on the carpet with all their beauty knocked out of them. She pounded her pillow until broken goose feathers rained like lies around her.

After a while she heard voices downstairs. Henri and Alex were talking in muffled tones. She didn't want to know what they were discussing. She didn't want to know anything at the moment.

Feeling around in her satchel for the little velvet pouch that contained her rosary, she came across the drawing James had made for her. His burned arms of sorrow wrapped around her regret. No confession could pardon the loss from the hideous crime that took this child's father.

Nervously, she rubbed the beads between her fingers, reciting the appropriate prayer for each one, hoping to wear away the guilt. She prayed to the Virgin Mother to comfort not only her, but Emma as well. In the silence, her tightness gave way to numbness; serenity had lit a candle in the chapel of her mind.

It was now dark in her room. She struck a match and soon her lamp glowed. In the silence, she got undressed and crawled into bed.

There was a tap on her door. "Mrs. Sullivan, you need to eat something. I brewed you a fresh pot of tea."

Margaret unlocked the only barrier between her and the world. Mrs. O'Brien entered with her face bunched up in a nervous frown. The tray was placed on the table next to Margaret's bed. Mrs. O'Brien left without a word. Obviously, the woman had heard the tirade earlier.

Margaret curled her legs under her as she sat nibbling on her dinner of fowl and gravy. She retrieved her book of poems from her bedside table, hoping for something that would bring her comfort. When she opened the book, the tome revealed the poem Michael had read to her on the trip to Ireland.

"Oh, my dear Michael." She touched the words:

> *Come o'er the sea,*
> *Maiden with me,*
> *Mine through sunshine, storm, and snows. . .*

"For the love of Ireland." Her lips trembled. "We have all sacrificed so much. Will we ever be free of the curse of this struggle?"

After drinking her tea, Margaret became quite drowsy.

The next few days were a blur. Margaret didn't remember leaving her room. She thought she recalled Alex coming to visit her—the smell of whiskey, him touching her. It might have been a dream. Something awful had happened but she couldn't remember what it was.

"Good morning, mum." Mrs. O'Brien brought her tea in on a tray. Next to the tea was a small thin brown bottle. Mrs. O'Brien opened the stopper and stirred some of its contents into the teapot.

"What is that?" Margaret's mind was still fuzzy from sleep.

"Something to help you feel better, mum.

"Was I sick? I don't remember."

"Exhaustion, Mr. Sullivan thought you needed a rest."

"I have to go to work." Margaret pulled back the covers but dizziness made her unsure of her ability to stand and she laid back down again.

"Mr. Sullivan told the paper you wouldn't be in for a while, not until you were better."

Her body felt strange. She wasn't going to be able to walk just yet.

Margaret drank her tea and went back to sleep.

Limpid images and shadows dipped and swayed on the floor of her imagination. Myths and facts, opulence and poverty, enemies and friends all danced together in a great waltz she did not comprehend. Michael made love to her… or was it Alex? Occasionally her dreaming gave way to half-awake times in which she had visitors. She thought that she heard Henri's voice but she could have been mistaken. She had heard Michael's, too… but that was in Ireland, not here in her prison.

When she awoke, Alex was sitting on the side of her bed stroking her hair. He leaned over and kissed her on the mouth. This startled her. She turned her head to the side, away from him.

"How are you feeling?" His voice sounded flat and despondent.

"I don't know. My mind is empty and I feel strange." Her mouth was dry.

His fingers touched the side of her cheek then traveled down her neck to the space above her breasts where he made a little circle with his forefinger. He stared at his hand, as though she wasn't aware of what he was doing.

"Alex, why am I here?" Her words echoed in her head.

He dropped his hand and his eyes met hers. "You live here."

"No. Why am I in bed?" She pushed herself up into a sitting position and crossed her arms to hide the opening in her nightdress.

"You had a nervous disorder brought on by exhaustion." He got up and stood next to her.

"I don't remember seeing a doctor." She yawned and then wiped the clusters from her eyes with her fingers.

"You were asleep when he came." His look was one of concern.

"I want to get up." She threw back the embroidered coverlet.

"No, darling, I think you need to rest." He put the covers back, tucking them in around her.

Margaret tried lifting her body but it was heavy and didn't respond the way it should.

"See. You are still too weak to get out of bed. You stay here. I am going to the office and I will come see you again when I get home." He patted her on the head and left.

Trying to shake off the dizziness that had rendered her slow and dull, she reached for the glass of water on her night stand. Next to it she noticed a brown bottle. The label had been peeled off, leaving behind the residue of gum and torn paper. Holding up the glass, she carefully inspected the water. It appeared clear so she took a sip. She suspected her condition might be the result of what was in the bottle. Laudanum, perhaps?

After a few hours, her thoughts slowly began to come back into focus, confirming the idea that she had been drugged. If Alex was capable of this, what else might he do to her in the future? Apparently lying to her didn't seem to bother him. Damn him. She would never trust him again.

Once she felt certain that she wouldn't be disturbed, Margaret went to her study. She sat at her desk and wrote to Emma, begging for forgiveness. Sadly, she realized that Emma would never understand. How many times had she written and promised Emma that things would get better, as if she could make it happen? Perhaps Emma believed her and that was why she let her husband get involved in Lomasney's plan. Margaret felt ashamed. She had no right to be forgiven. It was her fault that Emma's husband had died. Margaret crumpled up the letter and threw it in the waste basket.

Over the next two days, Margaret pretended to be in a somnolent state whenever Alex or Mrs. O'Brien came into her room. Having witnessed them both adding drops from the brown bottle into her tea, she dumped the contents into the chamber pot under her bed. She wanted to be fully alert when she confronted Alex.

Margaret waited for Alex in the parlor. There was a foot of snow outside but she expected him to arrive home any minute, just the same. The fire crackled and the orange flames ate at the wood. Shadows danced around the room. What would his excuse be? Would he just tell her another lie? Her palms were warm from constant rubbing. She adjusted her sitting position in the chair. The sound of stomping on the porch alerted her to his return. She took a deep breath then exhaled. The front door opened, Alex walked in and set down his hat on the hall table then he took off his overcoat and handed it to Mrs. O'Brien.

Margaret folded her hands on top of the book to keep herself from nervously fiddling with her fingers. Alex stood at the parlor doorway looking at her. His face showed concern. "Darling, do you think it is wise to be down here?"

Margaret set the book down that she had attempted to read but couldn't. "I'm feeling much better now that I have given up drinking tea," Margaret said coldly.

"So, you know." He shifted his weight and looked down at the floor.

"Why did you feel the need to drug me?" Clenching her hands into fists, she rose from her chair to confront him. "Were you afraid that I would write an article telling the world my husband is responsible for the recent deaths in England?"

He looked at her. "No, I thought you had more sense than to do something that stupid."

"Then why?" She took a couple of steps toward him.

"Your sensitivity worried me." He folded his arms in front of his vest. "You left me no other choice."

"I'm not a child; I'm quite capable of dealing with bad news."

"I'm terribly sorry about your friend's husband." He could sound so sincere.

"It was an unfortunate accident." Alex raised his hands like he wanted to hand her his guilt.

Apparently, this was his apology, Margaret thought. She wanted to blame him. Normally he would be throwing excuses at her, but he just stood there silent. She was prepared to criticize, to argue, to yell, but now she was having second thoughts. He looked sincerely sad. Was she being unreasonable? Perhaps she had accused him unfairly. Maybe he really was concerned about how hard she took the news. This may have been an isolated incident, an accident. Didn't Henri tell her Lomasney wouldn't hurt anyone? After all, Alex had led her to believe that he was trying to be a good leader. Maybe he had no other choice in the matter. Or perhaps he had been tricked. Her mind was tired of trying to figure out reasons for his behavior. Alex didn't make the best choices sometimes and this had been one of them.

Margaret let out a breath. "The whole situation in Ireland is unfortunate. I wish there was a better way."

"Can you forgive me?" he asked.

Margaret couldn't bring herself to dress a lie. "I don't know." She needed more time to decide. Right now, she was confused and didn't want to forgive him.

"You may think I am a monster, and at times I probably don't deserve more than your tolerance, but I do love you."

Margaret looked away. What was she to tell him? That sometimes she could barely stand to live under the same roof with him? That it took all of her will power to suppress any feelings she had? Her life with him was a charade. It was a paradox: the price she paid for independence was her freedom.

When she looked back, he was gone. The door to the library slammed.

The Christmas Eve's midnight Mass did little to restore Margaret's faith in God's commandments. Instead of returning home filled with notions of rewards in heaven for earthly acts and unwavering faith while tolerating unbearable pain, she felt burdened by her own sins and those of others. Her heart was empty of virtues like honesty, compassion, loyalty, tolerance, forgiveness, and love.

What is love, she asked herself? Is it some fantasy feeling that is manifested from one's own mind or is it a gift from God? She lost count of how many times Alex had told her that he loved her, but wasn't he confusing lust with love? She had heard about a parent's love for a child but she didn't have any of her own. Only James, and now he may hate her for her part in his father's death. Then there was Michael—a man she longed to be with but couldn't because their lives were too far apart. Is it enough to just respect each other and call that love? She did not know the answer to the question regarding the meaning of love, but, she did know that things had to change or she would sink further into her own hell.

Chapter 27

T HE HOLIDAYS WERE over and the snow had melted. Things appeared to go back to the way they had been before she learned about the bombings. That is, except for the way she felt toward Alex, which would never be the same. After thinking about it, she came to the conclusion that Alex was, without doubt, guilty of lying to her in order to solicit her participation in his evil plans. She could never forgive him for that.

Flowers and chocolates arrived—tokens meant to win back her respect, if not her forgiveness. He even gave her a gift of expensive French perfume and a silk nightgown, which she had no intention of ever wearing. What went through his mind was a mystery to her. These bribes did not impress her and she wasn't about to have a change of heart. He was clever at manipulating her but she could be just as clever at avoiding his control.

Henri arrived to accompany Alex to a meeting that night. "Are you feeling better?" Henri asked. "I can give you something if you need it." He set his hat down on a table in the parlor and opened his valise and foraged through its contents.

"Thank you. Unfortunately, a drug will not cure my guilt." Margaret gazed at the painted vase on the fireplace mantel with its idyllic scene of a happy maiden.

"We all deeply regret the circumstances of the London Bridge affair." Henri snapped his valise closed then set it on the carpet next to a chair.

"It was because of me an innocent man died," Margaret said. She had come to terms with what happened in her mind but the weight of it still felt like a cold stone in her heart.

"Pardon me for saying this." Henri went to the window and looked out through the sheer curtains at the street beyond. "He couldn't have been as innocent as you may think. Don't forget, he made that choice to get in the boat with Lomasney, not you."

"Perhaps you are right, and I am being too hard on myself." Margaret brought her hands together in front of her dress and twiddled her thumbs nervously.

"And Alex?" Henri turned and faced Margaret.

In the light of the room, Margaret thought Henri looked even more like a weasel than usual, with his little eyes and waxed mustache. He had played a part in this, too, by providing the drug to keep her sedated.

"Alex…" She forced a smile. "The poor dear, I am a terrible wife. I expect so much of him and yet I offer so little in return in the way of support." The lying words burned in her mouth. Just the same, she hoped Henri would pass her obligatory sympathy onto her husband. They would discuss, no doubt, how drugging her had been a good idea for her mental health. After all, the weasel was nothing more than Alex's puppet.

"He cares a great deal for you." Henri sounded sincere.

That was hard to believe at the moment. Alex may tell her he loved her, but she was no more than bric-a-brac that decorated Alex's life, something to take off the shelf and fondle.

"He can be a difficult man at times, however." Henri smiled.

"Thank you, Henri, for your understanding." She nodded at Henri.

"It's a pleasure, Mrs. Sullivan." He gave her a slight bow.

"Are you ready?" Alex entered with his hat and coat. "We don't want to be late for the meeting."

Margaret donned her coat and hat and scurried off to work. A month at home was enough for her. Now that she was alert and with the holidays behind her she could no longer stand being trapped inside the house with nothing to do. Besides, she wanted to know what was going on in the world. Alex had hidden all of the newspapers in the library and their only visitor had been Henri, who was tight lipped about most everything. At least she would have someone interesting to talk to at the office.

She climbed the familiar stairs, checked her cubbyhole for mail and messages, and then headed back toward her office.

"Mrs. Sullivan! We didn't expect to see you back so soon." Delany craned his neck as Margaret walked past his office. "How are you feeling?"

She backtracked and poked her head in the door. "Thank you for your concern. However, I'm much better now."

Delany pushed his chair back and stood up, and then followed her down the hall to her office.

Margaret removed her gloves and untied her hat. "Anything interesting going on while I was away?" She slipped her coat off and hung it on the coat rack.

"*The Times* in London has been running articles accusing Charles Parnell of being involved with rebels and the bombings." He looped his thumbs in his suspenders and leaned back. "Parnell? That is interesting." She went to the window and looked out but there was nothing to see, only the hard wall of dirty red bricks on the building next door.

"They published a letter that he supposedly wrote supporting the Phoenix Park murders," Delany continued. "They claim the Land League was involved."

"That is ridiculous." Margaret sat down and shuffled through the pile of papers in her inbox.

"Parnell had requested an inquest to clear his name, and apparently the government is looking into the allegations. They have scheduled a trial. Should be quite a story."

Margaret looked up. "I want to go to London."

"Do you think that is wise?" Delany eyed her. "After all, you've been ill."

"My health has greatly improved and I see no reason it should prevent me from doing my job. Besides, I have to go. I know about Parnell and the Land League. I was involved with the organization, or have you forgotten?"

"Is that the only reason you want to go?" Delany walked over and sat on the corner of her desk and looked at her. "I'm worried about you, Margaret. It is not like you to have a nervous disorder."

She tapped her pencil on the desk. Should she say anything? If she did, she would regret it later. It was too big of a scandal. She couldn't even hint at what happened. No, Alex's involvement with the bombings had to remain a secret, and she hoped to God Delany didn't piece anything together, either. Their lives would both be in danger if he did.

"Is it Alex?"

Did he suspect something? Delany was an expert at spotting the truth.

"I've heard from some of my sources that he has quite a temper. He didn't hurt you did he?"

"No, of course not," she replied. Alex had never struck *her*, though he wasn't above using physical force to make his point. "I would like to go to London. This is an important story and that is all." Margaret wanted to get away and clear her head so that she could figure things out. Perhaps she could travel to Ireland for a few days.

"Do you want me to go with you?" Delany looked intensely at her.

She didn't need a chaperone. "No. I want to go by myself," she replied. He was such a sweet man. It was obvious that he was concerned about her; however, this she would do alone.

"Well, I am sure you are the best person we have to cover the story."

"Wish me luck. I still need to convince Mr. White."

"I'll put in a good word for you."

She had made her decision. "Oh, and Delany, I may be gone for a while."

He looked back at her from the doorway. "Just send me whatever you want printed and let me know where to wire your money."

"Mr. Sullivan is upstairs preparing to leave on a trip. He is in one of his moods, mum," Mrs. O'Brien warned her.

"Thank you for letting me know." It is going to be all right. Margaret told herself. She planned to announce to him that she was going to London. Of course, she might have to lie to him to get him to agree and if he objected she planned to go regardless. His bullying and intimidation were not going to stop her. It was her good fortune that he would be gone on a trip. He wouldn't be around to drug her or lock her in her room or whatever other sinister idea he might come up with to keep her home.

Margaret climbed the stairs, walked past her bedroom, and then proceeded down the hall to Alex's bedroom. She stopped outside and took a deep breath. She hadn't been in his room in years. His conjugal visits always took place in her room. She knocked on the open door and peeked in. On the wall next to the window was a framed Pinkerton Detective Agency poster offering $1,000 reward for the James Gang for train robbery. A dozen rifles hung on a gun rack on a side wall. But what bothered her most was hanging on the wall next to his bed: a gilded frame surrounded a painting, the kind that was found in a western saloon, of a naked woman. It was a large painting, very life-like, and the woman had her body arranged in a very inviting position. How disgusting and vulgar, she thought. Margaret swallowed hard then turned away. She knew Alex considered himself an expert in carnal knowledge, but she had no idea when or where he had acquired it. There were things about her husband she would rather not know.

The drawers were open in his dresser and several white shirts were laid over the back of a wooden chair.

"I'm surprised to see you in here." Alex gave her a sideways glance then went back to his packing.

"Are you going somewhere?" she asked, keeping her vision diverted from the painting.

Alex looked over at her again. "Yes. Buffalo, New York."

To Margaret, that seemed like an odd place for anyone to go, much less Alex.

"Why Buffalo?"

"It's that arrogant bastard Dr. Cronin's fault." Alex swung his arm in the air. "He is causing trouble because I tossed him out of the Clan. Spreading lies. He and Devoy are both out to get me."

Margaret was surprised. When Dr. Cronin moved to Chicago wasn't it Alex who secured a job for him and introduced him around town? Something must have happened. Devoy was another matter. Margaret remembered the night at the Opera House right after Alex was elected President of the Irish National League of America and Devoy had confronted him. She thought they had worked things out, but obviously not if they were still feuding.

"What are you talking about?" Margaret was confused. "What lies have they been spreading?"

"The Clan is putting me on trial for mishandling funds. I've been accused of embezzlement." He slammed his fist down on the dresser. "Me, of all people."

"Embezzlement? That is quite serious." Margaret reflected on the charge. They were not one of the wealthiest couples in Chicago by any means, but they lived well. Alex had many successful clients he represented and had won several big cases including one against the railroad. It was true that after being elected president of the Clan he had loosened the purse strings and indulged in a few luxuries. Alex might be guilty of being too generous at times. Just the same, he would never do anything to tarnish his reputation in the eyes of the Clan. It was too important to him.

"It's just a ploy to discredit me. He will pay for this, I assure you. No one makes a fool out of me and gets away with it."

He pulled out his revolver from the top drawer of his dresser, flipped open the cylinder, shoved bullets into the chambers, and snapped it closed. He put the gun into his waistband, and then he threw several boxes of shells into his satchel. Margaret wondered why he felt the need to arm himself if the charge was only a ploy.

"Who else is going?" Maybe, if he had an ally he wouldn't feel so threatened. "Do you know who will be on the jury?"

"Henri will back me up."

"I'm sure this is just a misunderstanding. You'll be able to prove that you're innocent, of course?" The words slipped from her mouth.

Alex stared at her. "Why do you ask?"

"Forgive me for mentioning it. I… I only want to make sure that you are prepared to present your case; but of course, you would know better than I. You're the attorney."

"I shouldn't have to present receipts, for God's sake. What we spend our money on isn't for public record. Besides, everyone knows me. I've spent years honing my reputation. If it wasn't for that goddamn Dr. Cronin and Devoy, there would be no question."

She bit her lip. "I'm sure you will be able to straighten everything out," Margaret said. Here was her opportunity. She should just come out and say it, she told herself. "Considering the fact that you will be away for a while…"

"Yes?" He looked up from folding his socks.

"I'm going to London to cover the Parnell trial." There she said it.

"Are you?" He opened his wardrobe, took several suits out, and hung them neatly in the portmanteau. "Amusing don't you think? Parnell accused of being in partnership with us? He is the most useless man the Irish ever came up with."

"I know you have never liked Charles, and I don't have much respect for the man. However, someone needs to print the truth."

"The truth?" Alex slammed the top drawer of his dresser closed. "For God's sake, Margaret, don't act so righteous." He slammed another drawer closed. "The world is full of lies. No one wants to hear the goddamn truth, much less read about it."

She could feel the blood rush through her. "I always try to give a fair opinion of the people and events I write about," Margaret snapped.

Alex smiled his wicked smile.

"Come here." He motioned her over to him. "I'm glad you are feeling better."

Not now, she thought. Reluctantly, she went to him and he put his arms around her. There was no way to get out of it without upsetting him. She felt the hardness of his loaded revolver against her side. He reached up, put his hand behind her head, and forced his tongue in her mouth when he kissed her. She wanted to gag, but didn't.

He pulled back, kissed her nose, and said, "Promise me you will stay away from that Davitt fellow when you get to London."

Margaret stiffened. "I have no intention of seeing him," she lied. "I'm going to cover the Parnell trial, that's all."

"You better not be lying to me." He took his gun from his waistband and set it on the table. Then he pushed his clothes to the side of his bed, reached around, scooped her up, and put her on top.

Margaret stared up at the naked lady. She didn't want him to do this. "No." Margaret rolled away and climbed back down. She wouldn't be his whore tonight.

"You selfish…" Alex gripped her forearm tightly.

"Let go of me," Margaret demanded.

Alex glared at her. "I'll respect your wishes for now." He grabbed her other forearm so that she stood in front of him. "But there will be no resistance when I return."

Margaret turned her eyes to the wanted poster on the wall. Perhaps he was expecting her to agree with him. However, Margaret was cool and wouldn't respond.

He shook her, trying to get her attention. When she looked at him there was anger in his eyes. He raised his voice, and this time he shook her harder. "You don't have a choice. You're my wife, goddamn it. It's your obligation. You understand?" His eyes bore into her. "Do you?"

"Yes," she said, detesting everything about him. If she could, she'd slit his throat and not regret it. He was a monster.

As quickly as his anger surfaced, it receded, as if she had imagined the whole incident that just took place. Margaret would not soon forget his actions, however.

Now, Alex had other things on his mind and had gone back to packing his belongings. As Margaret passed through the doorway and out into the hall, she heard him call out to her. "Oh, by the way, give Delia Parnell my best when you see her. I'm sure she will be there for the entertainment."

In the privacy of her study, Margaret pulled out her journal. Dunking her pen in the ink, she hesitated. What was she going to write? Only thoughts of anger came to her mind. She scratched a dark line of blue back and forth across the page, scribbling faster and faster until the pen ran dry and she was ripping the page with the point. She hated Alex for the way he treated her. She threw the journal across the room, spilling ink onto her table. He seemed to delight in tormenting her, like some animal needing to prove its dominance. Did other women suffer at the hands of their husbands like she did? She hated life with him and she hated his involvement with the Clan. She doubted that anything he did was for the good of Ireland.

Margaret went to her room and opened a drawer in her dresser. She pulled out the silk nightgown Alex had bought her. She went back to her table and sopped up the ink, staining the garment, and then tossed it in the wastebasket.

Beatrice stirred in her cage. Margaret poked her finger in and scratched the bird's head. She opened the little door and the canary hopped on her finger. She brought the bird out.

"Oh, Beatrice, what am I going to do?" She set the bird on top of its cage, pulled the drapes back, and opened the window to let in some fresh air. Margaret looked out at the street below. The sun was just starting to set. A young couple walked by. Why had she married Alex? Why had she married at all? It wasn't for money or prestige, for those things never mattered to her. It was for her career, a career as the unknown journalist. She had always envied powerful men. They possessed what she could never have. Now look where that envy had gotten her, under the thumb of Alex, writing lies and not reporting the truth. What happened to her principles and high standards? She once believed that her articles would educate and inform people, but did they? Has anyone taken the time to read the book she worked so hard to write? Some of the articles she had written she was proud of, especially those about the Land League. But, now she wasn't proud of anything in her life.

Margaret turned away from the window and left the room. Downstairs, she slipped her coat on and grabbed her hat and gloves.

"Will you be gone long, mum?" Mrs. O'Brien asked as she emerged through kitchen the door.

"I don't know." Margaret went out into the street. When she looked back at the house she saw the shadow of Alex standing in the upstairs window peering out. Margaret swiftly walked down the street to the corner and waved down a cab.

"Where to, mum?" the cabbie asked, opening the carriage door for her.

"Holy Name Cathedral."

Margaret lit a candle in front of the statue of Mary. The flame cast a surreal shadow on Margaret's empty soul. She was raw and exposed, her weeping heart cried out. Her tearful eyes gazed at the outline of the statue. Mary stood before Margaret with outstretched arms open to receive her frightened human soul, offering tenderness to soothe her earthly pain. From the statue's shoulders hung a mantle washed in a coalescing blue of the sky and ocean. Beneath her feet, the enemy of salvation, a serpent lay crushed. Margaret pulled out her rosary and knelt.

"Blessed Mary, I need your help." Tears dropped onto the front of her dress. "I have tried to follow God's commandments, and I have failed. I have tried to be a good wife, but have failed. And my attempts to help the less fortunate have failed. Now, I am at a loss of what to do. My heart is numb, frustration has replaced my hope. I am full of anger and hate. I don't know who I am anymore or who I want to be. Forgive me for wanting to break my marriage vows, but I can't go on living like this."

She sat in silence for what have must have been an hour before Father Leary tapped her on the shoulder. "Margaret, is there something I can do for you?"

"Oh, no, Father. Thank you." She got up to leave.

"I read your book. I think you did a fine job of describing the situation in Ireland."

"Thank you."

"I hope you are going to continue to write."

Margaret had no idea what she would be writing about after the Parnell trial.

Margaret could see that the lights were out in Alex's room as she paid the driver and climbed the steps to her home.

"Would you like me to fix a plate of food, mum? Mr. Sullivan has gone out to dinner. He said he would be back later," Mrs. O'Brien said while tying her apron behind her back.

"Yes, that would be fine. Could you bring it to my room? Thank you."

Margaret went into her study then over to Beatrice's cage. The door hung open. Panicked, Margaret looked around but didn't see the bird anywhere. Then she noticed a breeze blowing the curtains. She had forgotten to close the window.

Margaret sat in her chair and stared at the cage. It was an expensive, ornate cage, grander than a little canary really needed. There were many wooden dowels for Beatrice to sit on; however, she chose the one at the top. Mrs. O'Brien always made sure that there was plenty of food and water, and occasionally Margaret gave her a cracker to nibble on. Now and then she was even let out to stretch her wings. Perhaps that wasn't enough to keep Beatrice from flying away.

Margaret left the room and closed the door, and then walked over and stood next to the fireplace in her bedroom. She picked up the delicate figurine of the frozen woman off of the mantel and hurtled it against the wall, smashing it into pieces. She glanced around her room at the things she had decorated her life with: books, trinkets, the fancy gowns that hung in her closet. Her jewelry box was full of expensive items Alex had given her over the years.

Could she give this up? Could she give up her job at the *Chicago Tribune*? If she left Alex for good, she would never be able to return to Chicago. What would she write about? Alex was her access to politicians and powerful businessmen. No man of any importance would discuss politics with a woman not accompanied by a man especially if they knew she was a journalist. How would she earn a living? Well, she still had time to figure it all out.

Chapter 28

A S SOON AS Alex and Henri left for the train station Margaret went to work on her plan. She retrieved the bag containing the money she had been saving over the years that was tied under her bed. She counted it and then divided it up. Some of the money she put into a coin purse in her satchel, the rest she put into an envelope. She had a few errands to do on her way to the office.

With boxes piled high in her arms, she climbed the stairs to the lobby of the *Chicago Tribune*. She walked past Delany's open door but didn't say hello. Once in her office, she closed the door behind her. She opened one of the boxes and took out the black mourning dress, which seemed appropriate for the occasion. It wasn't a custom gown; instead it was ready-made and lacked normal adornments of ruffles and lace. It was easy to get in and out of, and that was all she cared about. Then she slipped on the dark-haired wig she had just bought, making sure none of her red locks poked out. Next she put on the hat, shoved a few pins in here and there, and she was ready.

Margaret unlocked her desk and took out the metal box containing the new identification she had made. Slowly she opened her office door and peeked out into the hall. It was empty. Quickly she scurried out the door past Delany's office.

"Madam?" Delany got up from his desk and walked out in the hall. "Can I help you?"

She held her fingers to her lips. "It's me, Margaret."

"You never cease to surprise me, madam." He gave her a bow and she quickly left.

When she entered the First National Bank, Margaret glanced around; this would be a good place to test her disguise. After she had filled out the necessary forms, she threw her shoulders back and confidently got in line at the teller's cage. The man standing behind her turned and looked across the room to someone he obviously knew. Moments later, a tall man with a handlebar mustache came over and joined him.

"Good day, Walter. Have you heard the news about Charles Parnell?"

"Yes, I just read in the *London Times* that he and Michael Davitt are guilty of all sorts of crimes. I guess the Land League was a cover for an Irish militia," the one named Walter replied.

"I wouldn't trust the *London Times* to print the truth."

"I met Mr. Davitt years ago. He seemed like a nice enough individual, but, then again, so did Alex Sullivan."

"Yes, I understand. I ran up against Sullivan in court once. He greased the palms of more than one jury member on my case, and the main witness never showed. He turned up dead several days later. Need I say more?"

Margaret shifted her satchel to her other arm. Was she doing the right thing? She could always change her mind in London. Alex would never know.

The line moved forward and Margaret went to the available teller's cage and opened up her satchel then handed the man several stacks of bills. Some of the money had come from the sale of her book. Alex had let her keep it to "buy gifts for herself." She could not think of a more appropriate gift for herself than a new identity and a trip to London.

"Will this be going into your husband's account?" the beady eyed teller asked.

"No. I happen to be a widow. My late husband kept his money stuffed under the bed and now that he's gone, I thought it would be safer in the bank," Margaret replied.

"That is very smart of you, madam."

"I plan on traveling abroad. I won't have any problem transferring funds, will I?"

"No. No, of course not," he said while counting out her bills.

Margaret handed the teller the appropriate paperwork. She glanced over at the next cage and noticed Alex's stenographer, Mr. Donovan. He was looking intently at her.

He tipped his hat. "Excuse me madam, for staring. I don't want to appear rude, but your name has slipped my mind."

"It is most likely because we have never met before," she replied, putting her gloved hand to the side of her cheek.

"I'm Mr. Donovan." He tipped his hat. "You are?"

"I don't wish to give my name to strangers."

"I am sure I know you. Your face looks familiar." He smiled, studying her. "Perchance you know Mr. Alexander Sullivan?"

"Why would you ask?" Margaret could feel her pulse quicken. *God, please don't let him recognize me.*

"He is a prominent attorney. I work for him. I thought I might have seen you in his office before."

"No, I don't know the man. Now, if you will excuse me, I will get on with my day." Margaret took her paperwork and quickly headed for the door. Outside, she hailed a cab. Maybe Mr. Donovan didn't recognize her, after all. She wasn't so sure she would be able to fool Alex, though. Perhaps she was only fooling herself.

Margaret returned to her office, pulled off her wig, and then changed back into her regular clothes. She neatly put her disguise back in their containers and tied a string around the outside of the boxes. The key was retrieved from its hiding place under her drawer; she unlocked the file cabinet and took out her scrapbook. She flipped through the pages until she found what she was looking for: Michael's face captured in ink on an old sheet of newsprint. She could hardly believe that after all these years she would finally see him in the flesh again.

With some brown paper she carefully wrapped the book, placed it in a box, and then wrapped the box. She would give it to Delany to send to her after she got settled.

When Margaret returned to her house she went through all her possessions in both her study and bedroom.

"Mrs. O'Brien, I think I will need two more trunks." Margaret called from the top of the second floor landing.

"How long do you plan to be gone, mum?" Mrs. O'Brien looked up at her from the bottom of the stairs.

"These trials can go on for quite some time. I expect to be gone for several months."

"Does Mr. Sullivan know you are going to be gone that long? I don't think he would approve." Mrs. O'Brien shook her head.

"I'll send him a telegram once I get to London." Margaret tried to sound light and not concerned.

"Will he be joining you there?" Mrs. O'Brien put her hands on her hips.

"No, I'm afraid not," Margaret replied. "He has business here to take care of." Margaret had no idea if he had pending business or not. Certainly he couldn't just pack up and sail over to London because she was covering the trial.

"Do you happen to know when Mr. Sullivan will be returning, mum?"

Margaret hadn't really given Alex's trial much thought. It would take him a while to travel to Buffalo and back, and the trial would last at least a week, maybe two. She would be in London before he returned.

"I suspect that he will wire you and let you know his schedule." Margaret turned to go to her room, but then went back to the railing and called out, "Could you be a dear and get me a piece of currant cake?" She needed something to occupy Mrs. O'Brien.

"But, mum, we are out of cake. Do you want me to go out and buy some or would you prefer I make it from scratch?"

"Please, bake one for me."

"Whatever you wish. Will that be all for now?"

"Yes. That will be all."

With Mrs. O'Brien occupied, Margaret could tend to her other tasks. She would have to create the illusion that she would be returning, and so a few things would need to be left behind. She would leave the inexpensive jewels, some of her gowns, and maybe a hat or two.

Margaret went to her bureau and pulled out her box of buttons. They would be going with her. She carried the box to her desk and removed its lid. She took out the pouch containing her special buttons, her keepsakes from Ireland. Each button had its own story of someone she had met and places she had been. There were buttons from O'Doul, James, Anna, and the dressmaker, the one she found on the ship over to Ireland, a button from the IRB member, and another from Michael. A few of the buttons were fancy, the rest were not. Margaret rolled each one of them between her thumb and forefinger and said a prayer for the souls they represented then laid them out in a row in front of her. From her sewing box she chose a long needle and a ribbon. Carefully, Margaret pushed the thread through the holes of the buttons and attached each button to the ribbon. Once they were all secure, she admired her series of memories, and then put the ribbon into her velvet pouch next to her rosary.

Margaret opened her satchel and pulled out her small ladies revolver. It was a good thing she was able to have it cleaned this morning. She lifted her skirt and slid the gun into her new thigh garter holster. She wanted to get used to the feel of wearing it before she left.

On her desk sat the pearl-handled letter opener which she put in her satchel along with a box of bullets.

Once she was satisfied that she had packed only items that were important to her, she went downstairs for one last dinner. On her way to the dining room she tried the handle of the library door. It wouldn't turn. She leaned into the door and shoved. It opened and so she went inside and quietly closed it behind her. Alex's desk was clear of any papers. She tried the drawers which were locked. She removed a pin from her hair and poked it in the lock. The top drawer opened. As far as she could tell it contained mostly writing paraphernalia. She felt around and discovered that one of the cubby holes containing a pot of glue moved. She wiggled it and it lifted out. Underneath was a key. She unlocked the other drawers, and going from one to the next, she pulled out papers and quickly leafed through his files. Everything was written in code. There wasn't time to decipher their meaning. Besides, what good would it do her? She was leaving, and if she did discover something that had been kept secret, she wouldn't be able to write about it.

In one file she found an envelope. Inside the envelope there was a stock exchange receipt for $100,000 with Alex's law firm listed as the purchaser. That seemed rather odd. How did his firm come up with that much money? She shoved the receipt back and returned all the papers to the files where she found them. Disappointed there were no clues about his Clan business, Margaret locked the desk drawers.

As Margaret was about to leave she noticed a cigar box on top of a bookshelf. It probably contained cigars, she thought. She would check it just the same. Taking it down, she set it on his desk. When she lifted the lid, she screamed.

Mrs. O'Brien came running in.

"What is it, mum?"

Margaret held her hand to her mouth. "It's Beatrice. She's dead."

PART 3

London

1889

Chapter 29

MARGARET STOOD OUTSIDE in the cold and looked up at the light in the window. She prayed for the right words, hoping they would come to her. When she opened her mouth and exhaled, her breath turned into a little puff of gray then dissipated in the air. She had come this far, and yet she was afraid to go the rest of the way. She didn't know how Emma would react to seeing her, but whatever the response, Margaret was ready to face it. The guilt she carried within had to be worse than anything Emma could say to her.

Margaret went inside the building and climbed the stairs to the second floor. She stood in front of the door and knocked. There was no response. She knocked again. Margaret put her ear to the door and listened. She thought she heard a sound, so she pounded on the door.

"Who's there?" a voice asked.

"Margaret Sullivan." Her hands trembled.

The door opened a crack. James stood looking at her. He wasn't a child anymore, but a grown boy in his early teens. His long dark shaggy hair was thick and wavy like his mother's. His jaw and nose now resembled his departed father, she assumed. Margaret regretted the fact that she had never met Peter while he was alive.

"Is your mother here?"

James pointed to a pile of bedding on the floor. Huddled beneath a blanket lay Emma. Margaret walked over, bent down, and touched Emma's shoulder. "Are you all right?" she asked.

Emma didn't move. Margaret pulled the blanket back, and when she did, Emma's spittle flew onto her face. Margaret didn't wince, but instead wiped her cheek with a handkerchief she had stuffed in her sleeve. She knelt on the floor next to Emma.

"Hit me if you want. I deserve it."

Emma just looked away.

"Yell at me. Please." Margaret heard her own voice crack. She wanted to be punished for her role in Alex's wicked plan.

Emma was silent.

"Since Father died, she won't talk to anyone but me, and barely says a word when she does," James said. "She stays cooped up in here all day. I go to the market for food after school. I'm looking for a job… I don't know what else to do."

Margaret stood up and put her arm around James. When she felt his stiff body, her emotions sprung to the surface and a tear rolled down her cheek. Her pain tasted bitter in her mouth. No words could change the past.

After a moment, she released James from her arm. She tried to slip on her mask of composure, but the truth wouldn't let her. She could not pretend everything was all right, because it wasn't. There was nothing right about what had happened, and there was nothing she could do to make Emma's pain go away.

Feeling helpless, and not knowing what else to do, Margaret put a brick of sod on the fire and searched around for a pot to make some tea. The room appeared cluttered and in need of a good scrubbing. When she reached down to gather up a crumpled British newspaper littering the floor, a mouse scurried by. It startled her and she brought her hands to her mouth and gasped.

"Are you still going to send us money?" James asked. He folded his arms across his chest.

"Why wouldn't I?" Margaret replied. In truth, she had no idea if she would be able to or not. Now that she had decided to leave Alex her future was unclear. The thought that she, too, may end up living in a place like this sent shivers through her.

"Mother thought you only sent us money because you wanted Father to…"

"No. That is not true." Margaret interrupted. "I sent the money because I…I wanted you both to have a better life." Margaret felt heavy with guilt again. "And now I have ruined it." She sniffed back a sob and realized this was not going the way she had expected. The relief she had been desperately seeking was not to be found here, only the reality of the consequences of her Irish nationalist behavior. She had promised Emma she would make things better and all she did was make things worse. How arrogant of her to think she could change the life of anyone else when she barely had the courage to change her own? She was a fool and it was a mistake to come here.

Margaret went to the door to leave. With her back to James she said, "I'm sorry. I don't deserve to be forgiven for what I've done. But please know you won't be suffering alone. I will live with the guilt of your father's death for the rest of my life."

When she placed her hand on the doorknob Margaret heard Emma pushing herself up from the floor.

"Don't go," Emma said, stumbling over to Margaret. "It wasn't your fault. He went willingly. I tried to stop him but he wouldn't listen to me."

Margaret's lip trembled.

Emma wrapped her arms around Margaret and then whispered in her ear, "Thank you for coming to see me."

"No, thank *you* for seeing me," Margaret uttered out loud, then she silently thanked God for granting her this moment.

<h1 style="text-align:center">Chapter 30</h1>

SPYING ONE EMPTY chair in the middle of the women's viewing section of the House of Commons, Margaret weaved her way around several curious spectators, reaching the chair before someone else got to it first. She sat down and proceeded to get comfortable. Pulling out a sharp pencil and her writing pad from her satchel, she reflected on how nice it was to be in London and away from Alex. She was proud of herself and excited about her future.

While she waited for the trial to begin, Margaret looked around at the ornate wood paneled walls and the ladies leaning against the detailed brass railing in their stylish hats and leg-of- mutton sleeved dresses. Some were most likely wives of those there to testify, others just curious onlookers. Below, rows of seats rapidly filled with men in dark suits, many of them Irish Members of Parliament. She adjusted her skirt and sat back and waited. It had all the excitement of the opening night at the symphony. Off to her left Margaret caught a glimpse of the granddame, Delia Parnell, in one of her famous large hats, making her way over to join her. She was coming to hear what everyone had to say about her son, no doubt.

"Pardon me, but could you move, please?" Delia said while motioning with her wrist to the woman next to Margaret. "I'm an old woman and my eyes don't see as well as they used to."

Annoyed, the woman gathered her belongings then trotted off to another seat without uttering a single word. Margaret suspected the fleeing woman was the wife of one of the MPs.

"That's much better." Delia settled into her chair like a mother hen on a nest. "How could anyone believe such nonsense about poor Charles?"

Delia had aged since Margaret last saw her. Wrinkles were now more pronounced around her eyes and her mouth, and gray had replaced much of her raven hair. Margaret couldn't remember when they last spoke. They would, no doubt, share stories over a glass of Madeira later.

"They have made some pretty strong accusations," Margaret said, tapping her pencil on the paper in her lap. "We shall see if they can prove any of them."

"We both know they won't, don't we, dear?" Delia sat up straight in her chair with the grandness of a woman of means. "If Charles had been guilty of half their charges, Ireland would be free by now. But that is more than a mother could hope for." Delia tilted her head slightly toward Margaret. "Unfortunately, instead we have this ridiculous inquest."

Margaret smiled. In the midst of all the uproar around the rumors that her son was guilty of treason, Delia still hadn't given up on her radical ideas. Margaret set down her pencil and pulled out her brass and bone opera glasses from their case in her satchel. Adjusting the wheel, she scanned the men below.

The commissioners filed in and sat down. Sir Russell took out a file from his satchel, opened it, and started looking through an assortment of documents. Margaret had learned that Sir Russell would be representing Charles Parnell and the Land League during the trial and she hoped he would present enough evidence to prove their innocence.

Michael walked in and took a seat on the bench behind Sir Russell. Margaret's heart fluttered with excitement. Her gaze lingered on his face for a moment. Though it had been many years since she had last seen him, he was still the handsome man she remembered. Realizing she was staring, Margaret set the glasses in her lap.

"Did you know Michael has been studying to be a Barrister?" Delia turned toward Margaret. "Of course not. How silly of me to assume you would take an interest in Michael's pursuits."

Margaret smiled. She had a scrapbook full of information about Michael. Keeping up on his activities had been a challenge. It wasn't easy to know what he was doing from so far away. She hoped he hadn't found a wife yet. If Michael had, then she wished them the best.

For several weeks Delia sat next to Margaret as the trial dragged on. They listened as men from all over Ireland stood in the box telling stories of their affiliation with the Land League.

"It just boils my blood to listen to this," Delia complained. "The British think it is their God-given right to dominate Ireland and that it is a crime to want to be free." Delia put down her opera glasses. "Any intelligent person could see why these men were driven to take up arms, and yet the British go on and on about how ungrateful the Irish have been instead of looking at the real problem."

When Michael was called to testify, Margaret peered through her opera glasses and focused on him. She had hoped earlier that they could spend time together while the trial was going on. That secret place where her love laid hidden all these years was begging for acknowledgement. Unfortunately, the opportunity hadn't presented itself for them to reconnect, and she didn't want to bother him while he had so much on his mind. Later, during a lull in the trial, she would send him a note and invite him for tea.

Margaret's heart ached with pride as she watched Michael present his testimony.

"The Land League was created because no one cared about the people of Ireland. You brought this disgrace upon yourselves by your cruelty and complete disregard for the Irish. We did not bear arms against those that turned us out into the streets, and yet you still sought to persecute us anyway. Britain should be on trial. The British authorities are the ones guilty of horrific crimes, not the Land League," Michael told the court.

"Well, Mr. Davitt, Britain is not on trial," Sir Henry James said while waddling back and forth like a penguin. "Mr. Charles Stewart Parnell apparently wasn't satisfied with his position as Member of Parliament and so he formed the Land League, an organization of militant rebels, to take up arms against the Crown."

"Not true," Michael objected. "The Land League was not only my idea, but that of several fed up Irishmen who favor land rights. I was the one who convinced Charles Parnell to be president. He is not, and has never been, a member of a rebel organization."

Delia let out a sigh. "I can't stand listening to this anymore. Let me know if anything interesting happens." Delia gathered up her skirt and departed. Margaret watched her disappear behind a long row of hats with bows and feathers bobbing and swaying as ladies leaned in to gossip about the trial.

Once Margaret had dreamt of covering such a trial, but after weeks of listening, she had grown tired of watching powerful men manipulate others and tired of men dictating how things should be. Amidst all of the accusations being hurled at the Land League, a woman's name was never mentioned once. What about Anna and all of the other women of the Ladies Land League who traveled the muddy roads, working diligently to help the poor? Certainly they were equally guilty in the conspiracy to make life better for the poor in Ireland. Why hadn't the British called them to testify? All of the good they did had been swept like dirt under the rug of propriety.

It was such a pity. Up here in the gallery, sprinkled amongst ladies of society, were the unknown faces of former Ladies Land League members watching through the brass railing as the men below made decisions about what was right and wrong for their country

Margaret put her papers into her satchel and closed it. She made her way to the hall past the frescos and ornately decorated walls. She remembered thinking that the interior looked like a church the first time she visited the building. Now it seemed more like purgatory with souls waiting to be released.

Margaret was grateful that she had rented a suite at the Westminster Hotel instead of a little bedroom. A smaller size would have felt cramped after the first week of the trial. This room was large but not too big, and it was tastefully decorated in comfortable, yet functional furniture. It was going to be her home for a while, at least until she found another place to live. Her bed sat tucked behind the settee so that she could sit facing away from it and look at the picture on the wall while drinking her tea.

The trial was long and tedious, as she knew it would be. Margaret walked over to the overstuffed, high back chair and sat down, removed her shoes and then wiggled her toes. No doubt Alex would follow the Parnell trial in the newspaper. A letter now and then on hotel stationary would ease his mind while she was away. She would definitely need to start looking for a place to live, however. Perhaps she would take a place in Dublin if the trial didn't go on too long. Delia might have a suggestion or two. Tomorrow, on her way to the trial, she would stop by the front desk and leave a message for Delia to join her for afternoon tea. They could discuss her plans then.

In the morning when Margaret arrived at the House of Commons she heard whispers that today there would be a special witness. She took her usual seat overlooking the witness box and prepared to take notes. When the mysterious witness entered, several ladies stood up, blocking her view. Margaret thought it might be an acquaintance of Charles or some British Lord. She would know who it was soon enough.

"Could you please sit down?" Margaret finally asked in a hushed voice to a couple of nearby women. Their skirts filled the open space between the brass rails. When they obliged her request she noticed a man in a black suit weaving his way down the aisle to the witness box below. From her vantage point above the center she couldn't tell who the man was but he did have a familiar way of carrying himself.

Sir James, one of the attorneys for the opposition, stepped forward and asked the mysterious new witness, "Your name?"

"Thomas Philip Beach, however, I went by the name of Henri Le Caron in America," the man replied.

Did she hear him correctly? Margaret leaned forward and raised her opera glasses.

Sir James continued his questioning, "Is it true that you are here to provide information regarding your association with the Fenians in America, and that you claim to be in the employment of the British government?"

"Yes. However, I don't consider myself to be an informer, nor a traitor. I am only a military spy who has been serving amongst the enemies of my country."

It was indeed Henri. Margaret tapped her foot nervously.

"Have you ever seen Mr. Parnell and members of a Fenian group together?"

"When Mr. Parnell and Mr. Davitt visited America I know for a fact that they were taken in hand exclusively by a revolutionary group known as the *Clan na Gael*," Henri replied.

"Did this American *Clan na Gael* or Republican Irish Brotherhood have a leader?" Sir James asked.

"Yes, there were several over the years," Henri replied. "However, the most prominent was a man by the name of Alexander Sullivan."

Margaret knocked over her satchel, making a loud noise as papers spilled and pencils rolled across the floor. Eyes from below looked up at her. "Sorry. Forgive me," she whispered. Margaret crouched down and scooped everything up, shoving paper and her opera glasses back in the satchel.

"Excuse me." Margaret reached down to retrieve a pencil, but it was out of sight. She nervously rummaged in her satchel for another. Once she was prepared again, she sat back and sighed nervously.

"How many members are in this organization, would you say?" Sir James cupped his hand to his ear as if to indicate to Henri to respond in a louder voice.

"Six years ago, the *Clan na Gael* contained thirty-two thousand members," Henri said, almost shouting. "It has grown since then, but I do not have exact numbers."

"And is the *Clan na Gael* a Fenian organization?" Sir James put his fists on his waist and leaned back.

Margaret rubbed her hands together nervously. Alex would be furious when he learned of this.

"Most definitely," Henri replied.

"Is it true, that these Fenians were engaged in violent activity against Britain?"

"Correct." Henri nodded his head.

"Were they engaged in raising money for the Land League?"

Why did they keep using the word "Fenian" in connection with the Land League? Did they think that the Land League was the devil's army sent to earth to cut the throats of every British citizen? She was tired of the continued allegations that the Land League was somehow connected to this mysterious militia.

"Well, that's what they told people," Henri replied.

"Did they ever raise money for humanitarian efforts?"

"Yes, but I was told in 1881 that the Land League in Ireland had already received money enough for its charity work and that the time had come for secret revolutionary activities."

That was the year Alex became president of the *Clan na Gael*, thought Margaret, and the same year Henri started coming around. Margaret shook her head. This was all too much to believe.

"I don't see how all of this relates to Mr. Parnell," Sir Russell objected.

Thank God. Maybe, Sir Russell can stop Henri from saying anything more, Margaret thought.

"It is easy to see that this presentation of American evidence is necessary in establishing an intimate relationship between the *Clan na Gael*, the Irish Republican Brotherhood, and the Land League, which the examination of Mr. Beach is meant to establish."

Shortly after midday there was an inrush of visitors. A buzz of excitement passed through the room as Charles Parnell entered. The collar of his light brown overcoat was raised up to his ears and he carried a bundle of papers and a black bag. Charles glanced at Henri as the spy went on with his testimony.

"They had set money, called Skirmishing Funds, aside for covert activity." Margaret thought Henri almost sounded like he was bragging. She was angry and disgusted with the man. What did he hope to gain by revealing this information?

"What were these Skirmishing Funds used for specifically?"

"Building submarine vessels, for one."

"What are submarine vessels?"

"A kind of torpedo. They intended to attack the British coast with them," Henri replied.

"This sounds like something out of a Jules Verne novel. This man's imagination is conjuring up conspiracies from fairytales. Again, I ask what Mr. Beach's testimony has to do with Mr. Parnell and the Land League?" Sir Russell asked. "Did Land League money pay for these bizarre schemes?"

Margaret remembered seeing the balance sheet in Alex's office with the cost of the submarine listed. What were those other expenses for?

"Yes. The money that financed the submarine came from the Clan's treasury." Henri smiled.

"And the Clan's money came from the Irish in America?"

Margaret was concerned. All of the money couldn't have gone for weapons. Women in all of the major cities in America had solicited funds to feed the poor in Ireland, money sent to the Land League office in New York. Those funds didn't pay for dynamite, did they? Michael would never approve of such a scheme. No, she knew some of the money went for a good cause. The Land League paid for rents and for places for people to live.

"Correct, but after Mr. Parnell's release from prison, all money collected for Ireland's Land League was turned over to the Clan by the League's treasurer, Mr. Egan. He had been keeping it safe in Paris. When Mr. Sullivan became President of the new Irish National League in America Egan turned over all the funds to him. Then, when Sullivan resigned, Mr. Egan took over the position. But everyone knows Sullivan was the one that ran things." Henri's longish, thin face wrinkled into a smile.

Alex was in charge of all of the money? Her husband was in charge of spending the money they worked so hard to raise? The Clan's treasurer allowed this? Margaret's mind raced to the night Alex was elected. Alex had been flush with money to spend and she remembered the jewelry, the gowns, and the flowers. After that, he no longer asked her for the money that she had earned from her book sales or her job at the paper. How could she not have figured it out?

"Was this money used for anything else?"

"Arms, of course, and dynamite." Henri changed position in his seat.

"This is secondhand information and cannot be regarded as evidence," Sir Charles Russell objected.

The lordships whispered to one another, and then the presiding judge announced, "Objection overruled."

Henri continued, "They paid men to come to London and set off bombs. W. M. Lomasney was one of the dynamiters. I provided information to Scotland Yard about his location and activity in advance. As a result, infiltrators were able to foul the nitroglycerin he and his co-conspirators used. You should have a record of that. As you will note, Mr. Lomasney and his assistants were blown up while attempting to destroy London Bridge."

Margaret felt a pain go through her. How could Henri orchestrate the murder of his friend and that of Emma's husband? The man was without a soul. The guilt for her involvement in this awful event weighed heavily on her. Both Alex and Henri were deceitful snakes, and she hoped they rotted in hell. Having heard enough for the day, Margaret gathered up her belongs and headed for the exit.

In the hall, hordes of people milled around, waiting for the latest bit of gossip about the evil doings of the Irish in America. Shoving past the smiling faces of people she did not care to know, she made her way through the crowd.

"What do you know about this Sullivan man?" she heard a reporter yell as she rushed past him.

"Nothing. Leave me alone," Margaret replied, hoping no one figured out she was his wife. She was so ashamed. Why had she stayed with Alex so long? She sighed. It wasn't just for the love of Ireland; it was because she was afraid of living in obscurity and poverty. Now, she decided as she walked, she would make a new future for herself. If she was to be poor, then so be it, but she would never, ever go back to Alex.

Chapter 31

ONCE INSIDE THE confines of her room at the hotel, Margaret unbuttoned her suit jacket and slipped it off, exposing the blouse she wore underneath. At the wash basin, she splashed water on her face and chest. So much terrible information had been revealed today, it was exhausting. By tomorrow, newsboys would be peddling papers with headlines about Alex and the *Clan na Gael* on every street corner. His reputation would be ruined, all of his secrets laid out in the open. It was a good thing that she was miles away from him, for Alex would be furious when he found out. Perhaps, though, this would give her a little more time. When the news reached Alex in Chicago, he would most likely be asked to give a statement. He would deny everything, of course, but traveling to London would be out of the question, at least until things died down.

There was a knock at the door.

"Telegram," she heard a voice call.

An envelope slipped under her door. Patting her face with the towel, Margaret walked over, picked it up, and read its contents.

Mrs. Sullivan,

I thought you would like to know they found Dr. Cronin's dead body jammed in a sewer. There is a warrant out for Alex's arrest for his murder. Delany

Margaret let the towel fall to the floor. Staring at the telegram, she paced back and forth. How many days had she been here? It had to be more than six weeks. When did Alex's trial end? What day had Dr. Cronin been murdered? How long ago did the police issue the warrant? She thought there would be more time. Alex wouldn't come here, would he? With all that Henri was revealing, Alex would certainly be arrested if he came to London. No, he would not risk it. Just the same, she would need to be careful. She pulled up her skirt and checked her gun to make sure that it was loaded then she went over and locked the door. Should she switch rooms or go to another hotel? What about her disguise? She would need to start wearing her wig. She crumpled up the telegram and threw it in the trash basket.

Margaret dumped the contents of her satchel onto the table next to her bed. The letter opener fell out onto the pile. She sat down and went through her various aliases. Her hand quivered. Seeing her velvet rosary bag, she picked it up and fished out her rosary and ribbon with the buttons.

There was a knock at the door. She set them on the table next to the settee.

"Who is it?" she asked.

There was no answer. She heard the sound of someone trying to open the door and then the sound of a key in the lock. The door opened.

"Hello, darling," the all too familiar voice greeted her.

"What are you doing here?" Margaret took a step back as her mind raced through various scenarios. Alex probably didn't know she was aware of the warrant. He also might not know she was planning to leave him. If she played along, it would give her time to figure out her escape.

"What kind of question is that? I came to see you, my darling." Alex replied, setting his travel case and bag down and closing the door. "I assumed you would be staying close to Parliament. You made it easy, checking in under your real name. When I told the front desk that my wife was staying here and that I had misplaced my key, they gave me a new one." He held it up.

Nervous, she asked, "How was your trial with the Clan?"

"I was found innocent, of course." He walked toward her to kiss her. She turned to the side to avoid him. He must have used an alias to book passage on the boat over. How else could he have gotten away?

"You could at least act happy to see me." Alex looked around the room, went to the window, pulled the curtain back, and peeked out. "I would have chosen a bigger room, myself." He let go of the curtain. "We'll find a different hotel tomorrow." He slipped off his mohair overcoat and tossed it on the settee.

"But I need to be close to Parliament, to cover the trial," Margaret said.

"Ah, the trial." He looked over at the bed. "I was thinking you needed a holiday from poor Mr. Parnell's troubles. Perhaps it is time to leave the writing of the news to men."

"Are you suggesting I discontinue my articles? This is an important story. I can't quit in the middle of the trial."

"Of course you can. I thought we might do some traveling, visit other countries."

He was planning to run away and take her with him. This couldn't happen. She would not be his accomplice. She had decided to leave him.

"What about my career?"

"I have come to liberate you from that profession. Your new career can be pleasing me." Alex laughed.

"But, you know how important writing is to me."

"Write a book of fiction, or a dime novel."

"But I am a journalist."

"My dear, you overestimate your importance. Let someone else cover these events."

Margaret didn't know how to respond. Alex was telling her that if she stayed with him, her career was over.

Alex picked up the ribbon with the buttons from the table. "What is this?" He inspected the odd assortment she had sewn to the ribbon.

"You know I collect buttons," Margaret replied. Must he have his fingerprints on everything she held precious?

He studied them. "These don't look to be fancy buttons, more like old discards."

"They have sentimental value," Margaret replied. How was she going to get rid of him?

"Sentimental?" He stretched the ribbon out. "Is this intended to be a necklace?" He looked over at Margaret and grinned. Alex then came toward her holding it out. "Here, let me put it around your neck for you."

Stay calm, she told herself. Cooperate. It is what he expects.

Alex stood behind her and put the ribbon round her neck, but did not tie it. The satin moved slowly back and forth, teasing her neck. He laid his fingers over the buttons stroking her throat with his forefinger then flipped the ribbon over so the buttons grazed her skin. He loosened it so that it rested on the top of her bosom. He jiggled the ribbon and the buttons bounced. Then he let go of one end and slid it up the side of her neck. His wet lips touched just below her hairline.

"I've missed you," he murmured in her ear. "You've missed me too, haven't you?" He took a deep breath, inhaling her perfume.

Margaret didn't answer. She stood stiffly while he played his game of seduction.

His breathing deepened as he dragged his lips around her neck and shoulders. The fingers of his hand slid down her chest and into her camisole. She couldn't stand it anymore. "Alex, must you?" Margaret raised her hand trying to brush his arm away.

"No," he said firmly. "You are my wife and I can touch you if I want."

"Please, I've been busy with the trial. Perhaps another time." She wasn't about to let him have free reign over her body.

"Another time. Another time. Well, the time has come, my dear." He pulled the ribbon around her neck.

Margaret reached up toward her neck but Alex grabbed her hand and held it down. He kissed her shoulder. "Ah, my independent wife."

The clock chimed four times in the background. The trial was over for the day, Margaret thought.

"Mrs. O'Brien told me that you were planning on being away for a long time," he said into her ear.

She swallowed hard. "The trial could go on for months."

The ribbon tightened around her throat. "You know how I don't like it when you don't tell me things." His snake-like tongue flicked her neck.

"Please, Alex, stop it," Margaret demanded.

"You weren't planning on leaving me, were you?" He yanked on the ribbon, digging the buttons into her skin.

"Of course not," she said, struggling with him to let her go.

"You would rather die than leave me." He pulled the ribbon tighter. "Wouldn't you?"

Margaret nodded her head.

"Good." He gave the ribbon another jerk and Margaret gasped for air. Suddenly, he released his tight hold and slid the ribbon off. Air flowed into her lungs. She reached up and touched her neck which burned where the buttons had scratched the skin. She hated him.

Alex leaned over and set the ribbon on the table.

Seeing the letter opener on the end table, Margaret quickly picked it up.

"I want you to leave me alone. Do you understand?" She held the blade out in front of her. "Now, get out." Margaret took a step backward.

"Darling, you don't really mean that," Alex said through clenched teeth. He took a step toward her and she moved away. Her heart raced. She glanced around the room. Could she make it to the door? It was unlocked.

She felt instant pain from the whack of his hand across her face and the letter opener dropped to the floor.

"See, it was foolish of you to do that." He reached down and picked it up.

How dare he slap her? She spit in his face. His hand flew up again, slapping her harder. He grabbed the back of her hair, pulled her around, and held the letter opener to her neck.

"You don't want me to cut you, do you?"

She shook her head.

"I didn't think so." He dropped the letter opener on to the floor and kicked it under the bed. He unbuttoned his jacket and slipped it off, revealing the gun he had tucked in a shoulder holster. He sat on the edge of the bed and yanked at his cowboy boot.

Margaret looked over to the door. She started to move toward it. Alex grabbed the back of her skirt. "Where do you think you are going?" He pulled her back.

"You hit me."

"Yes, you needed to be reminded of your place."

"I am not your property."

"Oh? That's right. You are an independent woman."

"You can't treat me like this."

"I will do whatever the hell I want. Now pull up your goddamn dress and spread your legs," Alex said while struggling with his boot. "Because I intend to give your quim a fucking, and I don't want you telling me no." Alex went back to yanking on his boot.

With her back to him, she leaned over and lifted her skirt. "I am not your whore!" Margaret pulled out her revolver. "Get out," Margaret demanded, pointing the gun at him. "Get out!" she yelled

"Now, what do you think you are going to do with that little gun?" Alex got up and walked toward her. "You surprise me, Margaret. I thought you didn't like violence." He laughed. "Are you going to shoot me?"

There was a knock at the door.

"Margaret, darling, may I come in?" The door swung open and Delia stepped into the room. "I know this must have been hard for you, listening to all that dreadful stuff about Alex."

Delia stood there for a moment looking at the gun Margaret was pointing at Alex. "Is this a bad time?" Delia asked sarcastically.

"Hello, Delia," Alex replied. "No. Come in."

"Delia," Margaret's voice cracked with panic. "I need help."

Delia acted as if nothing out of the ordinary were going on. "Calm down, dear. I'm sorry if I interrupted one of your marital spats. I'm sure you will be able sort these things out later, after I'm gone."

Margaret was puzzled. "But Alex struck me."

"Well, that is unfortunate, dear," Delia replied. "However, you are his wife and he has the right to do that."

Margaret knew what she said was true but she thought Delia would have shown more sympathy.

The door stood partially open. Margaret's hands trembled. Calm down. Think. She looked over at Alex. Would he shoot her in the back if she ran to the door? Before today, Margaret never thought he would hit her, but he did. God only knew what he plans to do to her after Delia leaves. If she only had the courage to just shoot him and run away, but her feet were heavy, her jaw ached, and she was confused. Dear God, I am such a coward. Show me what to do.

"What dreadful stuff are you referring to?" Alex asked, shoving his heel down into his boot, stomping on it. He turned to Margaret and motioned her over like nothing had taken place between them. "Come over here, darling."

She did not want to go to him but she knew she should. Things would only get worse if she refused. Nauseous, Margaret took a step closer.

"I'm sorry, dear, but your Mr. Henri Le Caron just announced to the world that you were behind the bombings in London," Delia said.

Alex's face flushed with anger, the veins stood out on his neck. "Henri? Henri Le Caron? He is a spy?" he yelled. "I'll kill the bastard." He kicked over the table; the lamp crashed on to the floor. Margaret's ribbon disappeared under the settee.

"Well, doing that isn't going to help Ireland, I'm afraid," Delia replied calmly. "If you are going to kill someone, pick someone important, like the Queen."

Margaret took another step closer to Alex and dropped the gun to her side.

Delia walked over to the high back chair and was just about to sit down on its cushion when she hesitated. Margaret looked over to see what Delia was looking at. Michael stood in the open doorway.

"Michael," Margaret gasped.

Alex grabbed Margaret's arm and yanked the gun from her. He fired. A shot hit the doorframe.

"Alex! No!" Margaret screamed. "Not Michael, please!" She choked back her tears.

Michael flew into the room toward Alex. Margaret's heart raced. Please, God, don't let Alex kill Michael.

"So, it's Ireland's former hero, Mr. Davitt. I'm not surprised to see you here." Alex pointed the gun at Michael, then back at Margaret. "I don't know which of you to kill first."

Margaret picked up her rosary which hung from the corner of the overturned table. Nervously, she rubbed one bead, then the next. She needed something to hold onto.

"I have not come to take her away from you, Alex." Michael spoke in a slow, deep, calming tone.

Alex threw Margaret's revolver onto the bed and pulled out the one he had in his holster, aiming it at Michael.

"Close the damn door, Delia!" Alex yelled. His full attention was on Michael.

Holding her rosary, Margaret brought her hands together at her waist. Alex wrapped his free arm around her chest tightly.

Delia shut the door then stood behind the high back overstuffed chair. "Darling, if there is going to be any gun fire I plan on ducking. So, please, don't shoot over here."

"So, Mr. Davitt has come to pay my wife a visit," Alex said slowly "And what else?" Alex inhaled deeply at Margaret's neck. "Perhaps smell her perfume?" He dragged his fingers across her throat. "Perhaps touch her skin?" Margaret froze. "And then maybe taste her moist… what? Lips?" Alex shoved the barrel of the gun in her neck. With his other hand, he reached over and grabbed Margaret's jaw, forcing her head toward his. He kissed her passionately on the lips.

Margaret hated him.

"What else, Mr. Davitt?" Alex raised his voice, turning the gun on Michael and clutching Margaret close to him. "What else were you going to do to my wife?"

"Stop it," Margaret cried. She could taste the bile in her throat. "Please, Alex. This is the first time I have seen him outside of the court proceedings. You must believe me," Margaret pleaded.

"I did not come to seduce your wife. This is an honorable visit. Trust me, I had only intended to put a note under her door requesting she meet Mr. Parnell and myself in the lobby to discuss the day's events at the trial," Michael replied.

"Trust you? I don't trust either of you."

"How could you question her loyalty?" Michael continued. "She has stood by you all these years. Her time has been with you, not me, an ocean away."

"Silence." Alex pointed the gun at Michael.

"It is obvious that you love Margaret," Michael said, watching Alex intently as he spoke.

"Would you not risk your life for hers if you found her in danger?" Michael took a step toward Alex.

Margaret prayed. God, please spare Michael.

Alex looked at Margaret.

"She wanted to stab me."

"Yes, but she must have been frightened. Did you intend for her to think of you as someone who would hurt her, rather than protect her?" Michael continued. "You vowed to protect her when you married her. Do you want her to cower every time she sees you? Is that what you want? A weak and frightened wife? I would have thought that you wanted her love in return."

"She doesn't love me." Alex put the revolver to Margaret's throat.

"Is her respect important to you? Don't you want her admiration? Her support? Her trust?" Michael asked.

Michael was now standing at the edge of the bed. Margaret's revolver lay within a couple of feet of his reach. She wondered if he dare try. If he moved to pick up her gun with his only hand, Alex would kill him. If Michael were to shoot Alex first he would spend the rest of his life in jail. She couldn't live with the guilt no matter what happened.

"I have always respected you, Alex," Michael continued, "especially when you rose to the occasion to accept the role of president of the Irish National Land League in America. Everyone admired your leadership skills in bringing together so many Irish-Americans. We are brothers in the Irish cause, you and I. Though we have chosen different ways, we both have the same aspiration."

"You would have been more helpful if you had led an army like we expected, instead of organizing a group of women," Alex replied.

"Too many Irish lives have been lost to violence. I didn't want to be the one leading them to another slaughter."

Alex looked down at the gun on the bed then up at Michael and smiled. "Pick up the gun."

"Alex, no," Margaret begged. It was against everything Michael stood for.

"Pick up the gun," he demanded.

Michael put his arm up. "If you want to shoot me, then do so, but let Margaret go."

Alex released Margaret and pushed her aside then stood closer to Michael. Alex cocked his gun.

"No, Alex. He is a good man. Michael doesn't deserve this. Please," Margaret begged.

"Be a man and pick up the gun," Alex demanded. "I'll count to five." Alex looked at Margaret. "If he doesn't pick it up, I'll shoot your cowardly hero."

"One." Alex smiled his wicked smile.

Margaret wasn't going to let Alex kill him. *Ava Maria gratia plena.* She rubbed the bead then moved the crucifix into her palm. She felt the hard sharp tip at the bottom of the cross then placed her thumb on top of end. The tiny feet of Jesus protruded from her palm. With a sense of calm, she took a step closer.

"Two."

Michael moved toward the bed. Margaret raised her hand behind Alex.

"Three."

"We all had such high hopes for you, Alex," Delia said, moving out from behind the chair. "I guess it is over now. It is so disappointing how things turned out."

Alex turned to Delia with a confused look on his face.

"And Michael, here you are playing the martyr again, taking all the blame for the Land League, and now trying to save poor Margaret without a weapon. Tsk, tsk."

While Alex continued to watch Delia, Michael inched over closer to him.

"Well, this is all very amusing, but I believe it is time for my tea. Should I order room service?" Delia reached over and rang the room service bell.

"What the hell?" Alex stepped forward toward Delia.

Margaret plunged the end of her long pointed cross into the back of Alex's neck, stabbing him over and over with it. "You bastard!" she shouted.

"Ahhhh!" Alex yelled. He spun around and hit Margaret with the side of his hand. Then he reached up and pulled the cross out.

Michael lunged for Alex's gun, but he lost his balance and fell.

Margaret's heart skipped a beat at the sound of shots being fired. Both Michael and Alex tumbled on to the floor. When Margaret looked up, she saw Delia with a gun in her hand. The door burst open and several police officers rushed in.

Margaret quickly went to Michael. There was a bullet hole in the fabric on the right side of his coat sleeve where normally an arm would have been, but since he didn't have one, he wasn't injured.

He looked up at her. "I guess I'm not much of a hero now," Michael said propping himself up with his left arm.

"You'll always be my hero." Margaret kissed him on the forehead. She smiled. Thank God he wasn't killed. She was relieved the whole ordeal was over.

Two officers dragged Alex to his feet. He winced with pain. His sleeve was wet with blood from a bullet hole in his upper arm.

Margaret looked over at Delia. The old woman's loyalties confused her. Had Delia planned to shoot Alex all along?

The officers put Alex in cuffs and led him to the door. He stopped and glanced back at Margaret. His eyes were wild looking. "Don't think you can hide from me. I'll always find you," he said, his tone part threat and part utter madness.

Margaret bit her lip. Not from jail, you won't, she thought.

"Gentlemen, what took you so long?" Delia looked around at the officers. "Men." Setting one hand on her hip, she said, "If you want something done, leave it to a woman." Delia placed her gun down on the table.

A couple of officers huddled around Delia as she gave a statement claiming she shot Mr. Sullivan in an attempt to rescue both Margaret and Michael from this notorious revolutionary leader of the American *Clan na Gael*. Margaret grinned. Delia seemed to have a knack for theatrical stories.

"You will have to come with us," one officer said to Michael.

"He's done nothing wrong. Please don't take him," Margaret begged. She couldn't stand the thought of him going back to jail.

"It is just a formality. There is nothing to worry about, mum."

"Do you want me to go with him?"

"No, your presence isn't necessary. It is just that Mr. Davitt here has a record."

"Don't worry, Margaret. I will be back later." Michael stood up. "I am so grateful you are safe. I can only guess at what you must have been going through with him. If I had known what kind of man he really was, perhaps things could have been different between us." He reached over and touched Margaret's cheek.

The officer motioned to Michael, and together they left.

"Well, dear, as now the room is empty of men, I think this calls for a glass of Madeira, don't you?" Delia suggested while walking to the door.

"Yes, I could use a drink," Margaret replied. "I will join you in your room shortly."

Alone, Margaret collapsed into a chair, numb as though the whole incident had not included her; but it had been her, not some stranger. She had found her strength. At last she would be free from Alex. Still, Delia's behavior toward Alex puzzled her. One minute they appeared to be friends and the next… It was hard to guess what their relationship had been.

<h1 style="text-align:center">Chapter 32</h1>

DELIA POURED THEM both a glass and handed one to Margaret.

Margaret gave out a sigh of relief as she sat down. "You surprised me when you shot Alex. I was so afraid," she said.

"Well, I couldn't let him kill poor Michael, could I? Besides, he was making me nervous with all his counting, as if this was some sort of cowboy showdown." Delia flicked her hand in the air. "And you, my dear, stabbing him like that. You could have gotten yourself killed."

"I know," Margaret replied.

She had expected to die. It had been part of her plan: she wanted to provide more time for Michael so that he could pick up her gun. But Alex hit her instead of shooting her. Maybe he hadn't wanted to kill her after all.

"I'm just so glad it is over."

"To the Love of Ireland," Delia held up her glass. "May someday she be free."

"To the Land League," Margaret raised her glass. Then she gulped it down. The liquid felt good on her throat.

"The Land League? Oh, darling, you have to admit that was doomed to be a failure from the beginning." Delia took a sip of her drink.

"I thought you supported the idea?" Margaret replied. "You participated in the fund-raising efforts."

"Yes, but the organization didn't turn out the way I expected. It lacked a certain, *Je ne sais quoi.*" Delia finished her drink, then went to the table and refilled her glass and poured some in Margaret's.

"How is Anna doing?" Margaret asked, taking a sip of her drink. "I expected to see her in the ladies box at the trial."

Delia stood next to the chair. "Poor girl, she was so upset with her brother Charles after the Land League fiasco that she took your example and got herself a new name. God knows where she's hiding now." Delia sat down, putting her drink onto the table next to Margaret's, then pouted. "She won't even write to me. My own daughter doesn't want to have anything to do with me. She thinks I'm… Well, never mind."

"What about your other daughter, Fanny? What became of her?" Margaret leaned forward.

"Oh, Fanny. My dear, dear sweet Fanny." Delia's eyes moistened. "She was in love with Michael. Had been since they were young." Delia looked over at the picture on the wall. "They would spend hours talking about Ireland. He was a Fenian back then and an officer in the IRB." Delia sniffed. "Fanny could hardly wait to show him her latest revolutionary poem. He encouraged her to write and she published several books of poetry and had many fans. They would have made a wonderful couple."

Margaret was stunned to hear this. She had no idea that Fanny was in love with Michael. Margaret had met her briefly once, at an Irish social gathering before Margaret ever went to Ireland. Fanny was a beautiful girl with raven hair and sparkling eyes. She was graceful and intelligent, too. Margaret could understand why Michael would be attracted to Fanny. How foolish of her to think there would be no other women in Michael's life. She was a married woman bound to Alex, whereas both Fanny and Michael were free to court if they desired.

"Michael was staying at my home in New Jersey the night Alex was elected president of the Irish National League of America. He wanted to attend the meeting. I told him, of course, that it was best not to."

Delia continued, "After the convention, I arrived home to find Fanny despondent. I thought it was because of the Land League. Both she and Michael had worked so rigorously setting things up in New York and I knew it was hard for her to give it all up." Delia sighed. "It was the day Michael left to sail back to Ireland that Fanny died."

Tears welled up in Delia's eyes. "She was crushed when Michael told her they couldn't marry; that he was in love with someone else." Delia cleared her throat. "I remember the look in her eyes. He was her hero. She took a sleeping dram that night and never woke up."

"Oh, Delia, I am truly sorry. I had no idea." Margaret reached out to touch her but Delia pulled her arm away.

"There was a grand funeral with white horses and many mourners." Charles paid for everything. Michael was riddled with guilt after that, and he traveled around Europe for a while to sort things out."

How did she not know this? All those years, it had never occurred to her that Michael might have other admirers, and how could she not suspect someone as beautiful as Delia's daughter Fanny might be amongst them?

"You see, my dear, why I didn't want you upsetting things." Delia set her hand on the chair arm.

Margaret brought her hand to her mouth as she listened.

"I suspected that Michael was in love with you the night he brought you to Avondale dripping in mud. But I wasn't sure how much you would risk for him until we came to Chicago."

"It was you who wrote the card inviting me to his room?" Margaret shifted in her chair.

"Michael would never do such a thing. He was too honorable and had too much respect for you to interfere with your marriage."

Margaret had let her desire for him cloud her better judgment that night. Who was in that room? Her stomach tightened at the thought. Thank God, she didn't go in.

"Once Alex knew about Michael, it was easy to manipulate him. He was such a jealous fool. If I hadn't intervened, he would have killed Michael years ago. I couldn't have that happen. Fanny loved him, and besides, he had been like another son to me."

Delia continued, "When you came to Ireland to help Anna I was worried that you and Michael would meet again. There were rumors that he was going to be released. I didn't want you destroying Fanny's hopes and so I let Alex know where to find you."

Had Delia arranged for her kidnapping, too, Margaret wondered, or had that been Alex's idea? Regardless of whoever was guilty of that event, other things were starting to make sense. "What about Ireland? I thought you wanted us to…"

"When Charles made the deal with Gladstone I knew our only hope for freedom lay in America with Alex."

"I don't understand." Margaret had no idea Delia believed so strongly in Alex's abilities. Yes, the old woman had said she admired him, but Margaret thought that was only to flatter him.

"I knew Alex was involved with the *Clan na Gael* before you came to Ireland the first time. He was the perfect choice: ambitious, clever, not afraid to use force… He even killed a man over a ridiculous accusation. I thought he would make the perfect leader for the Fenians in America. And you, foolishly thinking your articles and your book about Ireland could change things. I just needed to get you to give Alex a little push. You were both the perfect pawns."

"Pawns? You used us?" Margaret didn't like this one bit. "You knew all along that Alex was involved with the bombs?"

"Of course. Who do you think gave him the names of men to contact for nitroglycerin?"

"You manipulated Alex?" Margaret glared at Delia. Had she been deceived into thinking Alex was totally responsible when perhaps there was more to the situation than she realized?

"Please, Margaret. Don't be so naïve." Delia took a sip of her drink.

"How can you be so cavalier? Men died," Margaret replied.

"Darling, we could have accomplished so much more if Dr. Cronin and Devoy hadn't interfered. Not to mention that Beach fellow, letting the British know everything. If it hadn't been for him we might have carried out plans to assassinate the Queen."

"Assassinate the Queen? You and Alex had made arrangements to assassinate the Queen?" Margaret was astounded to hear such an outrageous thing.

"Oh, please, Margaret. You act as if you are an innocent schoolgirl living in a convent. You are a journalist. Alex hasn't done anything that other rebels haven't thought about or tried before. You are being too hard on the man. Alex would have made a much better King of Ireland than my son Charles."

"King? Alex a king? Of Ireland?" Margaret was horrified. Did Alex think he could bully Britain into giving him Ireland? He had always fancied himself to be an important man, but a king? The man was madder than a loon. And Delia? She was unquestionably a conniving old woman. "But you are an American," Margaret said. "What were you to gain from this?"

"So are you and Alex, and the twenty-seven men sitting in prison for bombing Great Britain. What difference does that make? We all had the same objective: to free Ireland."

Margaret gulped down her drink. "I am truly shocked." She had no idea to what extent this crazy idea had clouded everyone's mind, including hers. Michael was right. When she first asked him about Ireland, he told her that Ireland was like Venus. They had all been seduced into thinking they could free Ireland. Maybe someday, someone will.

"Well, dear, go ahead and write your article and print whatever you want. Just leave my name out of it."

"But, you were behind everything." Margaret couldn't help but shake her head. It all seemed like a myth.

"We both know no one would ever believe a woman was capable of such a thing. Blame it on Alex. Besides, you've never cared for him anyway."

Chapter 33

N A MATTER of hours Margaret's world had changed. She now was aware that she had been part of a conspiracy. Like puppets, she and Alex had been manipulated by Delia Parnell. The secrets of the *Clan na Gael* in America were no longer locked behind the door in her library, but instead, were headlines in every major newspaper in the world. Her husband had been arrested for murder and would hopefully spend many years behind bars.

Should she write about it? No. The burden was no longer on her shoulders. There would be plenty of stories written by others about the evil doings of those who claim to be fighting for Ireland's independence. Perhaps in the future, when things died down, new leaders would rise and reunite patriots to fight for Ireland's freedom again. Her battle was over, and she was now free from her bondage to Alex.

But what did freedom mean for a woman in 1889? Could she rebuild a life for herself that she could be proud of?

Margaret looked around at the mess in her hotel room. She knelt down on the floor and picked up her ribbon with the buttons.

She smiled as she touched each one. They had been holding her life together.

Her rosary lay on the floor, as well. Margaret scooped it up and brought it over to her wash bowl, rinsed off Alex's blood, then patted it dry and put it back in its velvet bag. She was grateful it had provided her the protection she prayed for when she most needed it.

Margaret carried a sheet of paper, a bottle of ink, and a pen to the table and sat down. She dipped the pen's nib into the black ink then tapped it on the side so the excess would fall back into the bottle, and she wrote:

Dear Delany,

Currently, I have no plans to return to Chicago. After the Parnell trial, I will be traveling on to France to cover the opening of the Paris Exposition. Let me know if Mr. White will be interested in articles from me in the future.

Margaret

There was a knock at the door. Margaret opened it to find Michael standing there smiling. His hair was ruffled and his eyes sparkled. He reached for her hand and brought it to his mouth. Margaret closed her eyes and inhaled deeply. His whiskers sent shivers down her. Then she opened her eyes and pulled him toward her. They had lot of catching up to do.

About the Author

Judy Leslie studied both Literary Fiction and Popular Fiction at the University of Washington. Her novel, *For the Love of Ireland,* is a historical fiction based on a true story about a woman journalist and a secret Irish American organization during the 1880s.

Judy is married and has two grown daughters, a granddaughter, and a cockapoo named Rosemary. She splits her time between living in Kirkland, Washington, and a cabin in the mountains of Leavenworth, Washington. Previously, she worked in Human Resources for a variety of businesses and as an entrepreneur. Both *For the Love of Ireland* and her *Cook's Cove* series were inspired by her earlier days as owner of an antique shop in Bellingham, Washington.

Other books by Judy Leslie include the Cook's Cove series.

Learn more about Judy Leslie's latest books on her website.
https://www.judy-leslie.com

Follow her on
https://www.facebook.com/judy.leslie.39
Instagram AuthorJudyLeslie
Twitter @judyleslie4

Acknowledgements

I would like to thank my husband Ralph, for without his support this book would have never been written. I would also like to thank my good friend Leslie Weldon for listening to me while I went through the writing process. Thanks to my fellow students in my fiction writing class at the University of Washington, and the members of Pacific N.W. Writers Association. Much thanks to my wonderful book cover designer at JS Cover Designs who captured the essences of the story in her design. Special thanks to my dog Rosemary, for reminding me several times a day that I needed to get away from the computer and go outside and play. Thank you.

Author Contact Information

http://www.judy-leslie.com

Other books by Judy Leslie

Cook's Cove

Author's Notes

According to the U.S. Census in 2007, approximately 40 million people of Irish descent live in the United States. Yet many of us who claim to be part Irish know nothing about our ancestors or Ireland's history. Yes, we have heard about the famine and the IRA, and Ireland's independence, but that is about the extent of it.

While doing research about the Irish in Chicago, I uncovered an interesting bit of history that connected a secret Irish-American organization called the *Clan na Gael* to events that took place in Great Britain during the 1880s. I discovered that a prominent Chicago attorney had been president of this secret organization and that his wife had been a journalist who wrote for the *Chicago Tribune*. I also learned that they had ties to an Irish member of the British Parliament and a famous Irish rebel. After doing more research, I decided to weave a fictional story around these characters and some historical events regarding the Land League that took place between 1879 and 1889.

Although many of my characters in this novel actually existed historically, they are fictional representations in my story. *For the Love of Ireland* is how I envisioned these characters might have behaved. I am guilty of bending the facts here and there, and shortening the timeline of events. I made Margaret a couple years younger, too. Regarding Henri's testimony, I did include some of the actual questions and answers from Charles Parnell's trial. Though the novel is based on a true story, it is a work of fiction.

Along with entertaining you, I hope I was able to provide you with a better understanding of the struggle for freedom, both for Ireland and Victorian women during the 1880s.

Here is some brief information about the real people my characters were based on.

Margaret Frances Buchanan Sullivan was born in Drumquinn, County Tyrone, Ireland in 1847. She grew up in Detroit, Michigan where she developed her skills to become a writer. After moving to Chicago to advance her career, Margaret became a highly respected journalist writing for the *Chicago Daily News* and later the *Chicago Tribune.* Many of her articles were printed in the *New York Times,* along with several other publications, often without a byline or under an assumed name. Margaret's book, *Ireland of Today; The Causes and Aims of Irish Agitation,* was published in 1881. In it she devoted many pages to Michael Davitt, whom she greatly admired. I doubt that a romance existed between them, however they remained friends for many years and Michael spoke highly of Margaret.

Michael Davitt was a member of the Irish Republican Brotherhood which was a precursor to the IRA. He spent more than nine years in prison and was known for being the founder of the Land League in Ireland. Though others started a similar organization, Michael Davitt was given credit for the Land League's success. Children across Ireland are taught about Michael Davitt in their history class in school. You can find out more about him by doing a search on his name on the internet or by going to my website: www.for-the-love-of-ireland.com or www.judy-leslie.com.

Alexander Sullivan married Margaret in 1874. He was an ambitious man and had a volatile personality. He managed to stay out of jail, though many knew he was guilty of the various crimes he was accused of, including murder. He was president of the *Clan na Gael* and the Irish National League of America. After his trial for embezzlement before the officers of the *Clan na Gael,* he was implicated in the murder of his accuser, Dr. Cronin. However, no evidence was produced that he actually committed the murder himself.

Charles Parnell was an Irish member of the British Parliament and President of the Land League. It was revealed at his trial that the letters implying his endorsement of the Phoenix Park murders were fraudulent. Like Michael Davitt, Charles Stewart Parnell is a historical figure. A statue of Parnell can be found in downtown Dublin today. He was responsible for introducing several bills that would change land rights for the people of Ireland. If you would like to know more about him you can search on his name on the internet or go to my website.

Delia and her daughters, Anna and Frances (Fanny) Parnell, were flamboyant rebel women. Unfortunately, they are only mentioned in passing in history books about the Land League. Anna Parnell wrote a book that is now out of print about her experience running the Land League while her brother Charles was in jail. It is true that after the folding of the Ladies Land League she changed her name and never spoke to Charles again. The reason for Fanny Parnell's sudden death after seeing Michael Davitt at Delia's home in America is up for debate, though heart failure is assumed to have been the cause. Delia Parnell was the daughter of the famous naval officer, Admiral Charles Stewart. She was born in Boston, Massachusetts in 1816 and died tragically in 1898 at Avondale from severe burns after leaning into the fireplace and catching her clothes on fire. She was known for her outspokenness and support of Irish rebels.

Many of the following books provided historical detail and inspiration for this book.

Sullivan, M. F. (1881) *Ireland of Today; The Causes and Aims of Irish Agitation.* Philadelphia: J.M. Stoddart & Co.

Cummings, K. (2009) *New Women of the Old Faith*. Chapel Hill: University of North Carolina Press.

King, C. (2009) *Michael Davitt*. Dublin: University College Dublin Press.

Galway, T. (1998) *Irish Rebel: John Devoy and America's Fight for Ireland's Freedom*. New York: St. Martin's Press.

Edwards, P. (2010) *The Infiltrator: Henri Le Caron, The British Spy Inside the Fenian Movement*. Dunboyne Co, Mead, Ireland: Maverick House Publishers.

Le Caron, H. (1892) *Twenty-Five Years in the Secret Service: The Recollections of a Spy*. London: William Heinemann.

Groves, P. (2009) *Petticoat Rebellion: The Anna Parnell Story*. Cork, Ireland: Mercier Press.

Molony, S. (2006) *The Phoenix Park Murders; Conspiracy, Betrayal and Retribution*. Cork, Ireland: Mercier Press.

McGee, O. (1979) *The IRB: The Irish Republican Brotherhood From The Land League to Sinn Fein*. New Jersey: Humanities Press.

O'Connor, T.P. (1889) *The Parnell Movement* (with additions containing a full account of the great trial instigated by the London Times). New York, Cincinnati, Chicago: Benziger Brothers.

Information was also gathered from numerous archived articles from the *New York Times*.